FOR EVELYN AND JANE—

BE FIERCE AND BRAVE AND STEADFAST

AND REMEMBER YOU ARE LOVED

—RLT

In the beginning, he was there.

A wispy form, but a form nonetheless. He hovered over the woods, and they curved around his presence, trees bowing as though in the company of royalty, wonders rising from the ground, enchantments crackling into being. The woods were his. But he would share.

They were too magical, too wondrous, too full of delightful fascinations to keep to himself.

The first to see the woods and its wonders was a child.

April 16, 1947

The most difficult thing to do in the face of great scientific discoveries (or those that defy science entirely) is to keep silent. But I know what happens when one does not—the way they look at you, the things they whisper, the titles they can strip and burn on an altar of "mad." If my brother were here, they might take note. But I am a man of science. A man of science cannot believe the things I believe. A man of science cannot have seen the things I have seen.

I am not mad; I have never been a victim of madness, only a keen observer and relentless detective uncovering the answers to mysterious questions and unexplainable phenomena. They will know this soon enough.

My army is nearly finished. I am in need of a few slight adjustments, perhaps a month more of tinkering, and my life's work will be complete.

And when it is complete, I will find my son. I will destroy the woods and whatever lies within them. And I will protect Stonewall Manor and its residents—my family—forever after, as I promised my mother.

—excerpt from Richard Cole's *Journal of Scientific Progress*

THE DAY THE
WORLD EXPLODED

1

April 16, 1947, was already shaping up to be the worst day in history, and Lenora had only just begun it.

Every now and again, Mother and Father would let Lenora or her sister, Rory, or her brothers, John or Charles, take a day off from school while the others attended as usual. They said it was good for the mind and heart to play, instead of working all the time. They said, too, that it was good for a child to spend one-on-one time with parents. They called these special occasions Fun Days—not all that creative, but efficient, as Mother and Father always were. Whoever was privileged enough to stay home for a Fun Day was often taken to the theater down the road for a noonday showing of whatever was playing, or to the ice-cream shop on the corner, or even, sometimes, out to the port of Texas City. The ships docking there came from all over the world, carrying all sorts of cargo, and watching them—touring them sometimes, if she was lucky—was one of Lenora's favorite things to do.

Today was Lenora's birthday. She was supposed to have a Fun Day.

Instead, John and Charles had woken up with a rattling cough, and Rory, never one to be left out, had begun coughing as well. Her cough sounded nothing like the one shaking from her brothers, but she'd cleverly convinced Mother that she was sick, too, and Mother had agreed to let them all stay home. All, that is, except for Lenora, who was not sick and would not pretend to be.

She did not like lies.

So even though it was Lenora's birthday, she was stuck in the old schoolhouse, Danforth Elementary, on the second floor, where the sixth graders gathered for instruction every weekday morning at eight.

She sulked.

Earlier, Mother had waved Lenora toward the candy apple–red Chevrolet waiting out front. Father sat behind the large brown steering wheel, staring out his window toward the dock, where a thin plume of yellow smoke puffed up from one of the ships.

Lenora had tried to argue with Mother about going to school—it was her birthday, after all—but Mother had said they would reschedule their Fun Day and quickly pushed her out the door with a "Father is waiting, dear."

When Lenora climbed in the car, she looked back toward the front window of their tidy white house. Rory was standing between the blue curtains, sticking out her tongue. Lenora had fumed all the way to school, and the fuming did not end when Father walked her to the red doors and kissed the top of her head and said, "I'm sorry you had to go to school on your birthday, angel, but try to have a good day. I love you." In fact, his words made it worse.

She hadn't said anything in response so that Father would know she was more than just a little upset. She deserved *two* Fun Days for this.

The warm, sticky air of their seaport town had made it hard for her to breathe. She hadn't looked back as she climbed the concrete stairs into her school.

She was still fuming in the hard wooden seat affixed to her desk. She drew random pencil lines across a piece of paper. Class had not yet started.

Most of her classmates, while waiting for Mrs. Easter to clap her hands and order them into their seats, as she did every morning so that lessons could begin, were clustered at the windows that lined the schoolroom wall. The light streaming in cast shadows on their backs, so Lenora could not tell who was who. They were exclaiming over the same plume of smoke Father had pointed out on the drive in. They were calling it beautiful. Lenora didn't know how anyone could call anything beautiful on this very disappointing day.

Her stomach knotted, and she rested her hands on her arms.

"Come look at the pretty smoke, Lenora!" said her best friend, Emma. Emma had not even wished her happy birthday. Lenora looked at her friend, who was dressed in a pretty white dress with tiny blue flowers on it. Her black hair spilled over the puffed sleeves. A blue bow was nestled in her hair, on the right side.

"I've already seen it." Lenora tried to make her voice

something more than a grumble, but disappointment chewed through her words.

"But it's even prettier than it was," Emma said, pulling Lenora up from her seat. And Lenora didn't have it in her to resist. She followed Emma to the windows.

Even Mrs. Easter was at the window now, pointing out the different colors, quizzing her students about what they thought might be the origin of the lovely shades. Lenora felt her stomach tighten again. Surely it was not a good thing to see smoke pouring from the dock. Her father had mentioned a few days ago that several of the ships at the port carried flammable materials. As the city's volunteer fire chief, he had been on high alert since the ships had docked.

But Lenora did have to admit that the smoke was beautiful. The thickening cloud had turned a deep yellow-orange color now. Lenora tilted her head. Someone jostled her, and she stepped back, but she could not tear her eyes from the smoke. She felt sick, worried. She couldn't say why.

The smoke was unlike anything she had ever seen before. It was beginning to turn the land around it hazy, like a fog had moved in. Maybe she felt uneasy because she had been the only one left out of her family's day off from school when it was *her* birthday. Rory would accompany Father to the dock when he went to explore the source of the smoke, since she was not really sick. She would be able to see the fire.

Lenora would like to see the fire.

Her classmates were still offering guesses as to the source of the smoke. Most of them agreed that it originated from one of the ships docked at the harbor. There were several: the SS *Grandcamp*, a large ship that came from France; the SS *High Flyer*, docked right next to the *Grandcamp*; and the SS *Wilson B. Keene*. Father had not told her what the ships were carrying.

One of Lenora's classmates suggested that perhaps the smoke originated from the railroad office, but Lenora didn't think this made the least bit of sense. Why would yellow-orange smoke pour from a railroad office that had been there since long before she was born? Nothing like this had ever happened in Texas City, though the town was what the local newspaper had recently called "the heart of the greatest industrial development of the South."

Lenora and all those who lived in Texas City were somewhat accustomed to hearing small explosions every now and then, because the city was home to two large chemical plants: Union Carbide and Monsanto. But never had there been anything like this—a cloud of smoke without an explosion announcing it. And never, ever had the smoke been so lovely.

The knot in her stomach tightened.

Lenora walked back to her desk and sat down, her chin propped on her fist. She would rather be at home. They were not even learning anything today. They were staring out the windows making educated guesses. Would it have been so terrible to let her stay home on her birthday?

Lenora smoothed her skirt around her. Mother had bought her a new dress for her birthday—a pretty green-blue and white-checkered one with a perfectly white collar lining the top. Lenora was not good at keeping her collars white, and Mother had warned her about this one when she'd pulled the dress from its elegant wrapping this morning. The dress was expensive, Mother had said. She had bought it because it was the same color as Lenora's eyes, and she'd thought it would look lovely on her. But Lenora had to promise to keep the collar clean this time.

The dress had been folded up over a brand-new pair of shoes of the same color as her green-blue dress, made of smooth suede. They even had a small heel on them, which had ignited Rory's jealousy. Mother did not permit heels on shoes until a girl turned twelve, which was Lenora's age today.

Lenora smiled a bit at the memory of Rory's envy. And then she frowned. Rory was at home.

"Lenora dear," Mrs. Easter said. "Are you all right?"

"I'm not feeling well," Lenora said, which was true. She wasn't sick, but the knot in her stomach was giving her some trouble.

Mrs. Easter crossed the classroom to Lenora's desk and put the back of her hand on Lenora's forehead. "Should I call your mother?"

And that was when the world exploded.

2

First it was the windows, shattering into millions of pieces that flew every which direction. Then it was her classmates, screaming in terror. And then it turned silent, while students toppled to the ground everywhere Lenora looked. She couldn't breathe. She watched Mrs. Easter fly in a forward trajectory as though something had pushed her from behind.

Lenora gripped her desk and felt the blast ripping her from her seat. She curled her foot around the chair leg—a hook of sorts. Mrs. Easter landed several feet away, on her back. She mouthed something, but Lenora could not hear her. Mrs. Easter scrambled to her feet, blood trickling from a wound on her cheek and another on her forehead. She frantically beckoned to the students, who all lay or stood stunned. No one heard her or no one was listening, because they all remained rooted in place, some on their backs, some on their stomachs, some still standing with their mouths and eyes wide.

A faraway pop sounded, and then another tremor shook the ground, and a boy pointed to a window that had not yet shattered but was spidering into cracks. Lenora followed the boy's finger.

The dock. The dock was concealed by a thick black curtain of smoke.

The dock had exploded.

Father.

Mother.

Rory.

John.

Charles.

A faint whistling sound penetrated the silence, and that seemed to be what set the world in motion again. A wave of students rushed toward the dark stairwell, pushing and shoving and trampling those who had fallen. It was chaos, but it was nothing compared to what Lenora feared was happening at the port, veiled by the black smoke. She moved, too, pressing against the other bodies, trying to slip through them, but she was stuck in the narrow passageway until the sea of students from every classroom in the school—kindergarten through sixth grade—began its descent. Lenora tried to find order in the madness, but she could not. The uneasiness in her stomach pulsed. She slid down the stairs more than she stepped, but she managed to hit the ground on her feet.

Father.

Mother.

Rory.

John.

Charles.

She had to find them. She had to make sure they were not hurt.

The school was a few miles from the town, but Lenora took off running anyway. Students bent all around her, emptying their stomachs. She had to stop and do the same. As soon as the heaving finished, she took off running again, straight toward the town and its gray cloak of invisibility.

Screams and shouts billowed behind her. The sound

in the world had returned full force, and Lenora almost wished it hadn't. Students yelled things she did not want to consider, like "Are they all dead?" "We're gonna die!" and "Are the explosions done?"

Lenora—and many others—ignored the shouts and questions and continued running. Her lungs ached, but she did not quit; she had never been a quitter. And now she had to find her family. She had to make sure they were not hurt in the blasts.

The scent of smoke and sulfur and singed wood, metal, and flesh trapped her breath so it came in halting gasps. She could smell the raging fires, but she could not yet see them.

Father would take care of the fires. He would save the day. He was a hero.

***

By the time she reached town, Lenora's body felt weak and winded. Her legs burned and her feet had numbed in the lengthy sprint, but she could not stop now. Another explosion shook the ground, and the whistling sound sharpened. She heard—even felt—large objects hit cement and grass with clangs and thumps. She took another step, but a bare foot lay in front of her, severed from its body. Her stomach churned.

Her heart lurched.

She could see now. She could see what awaited her in the town, and it made her knees buckle and her vision blacken. She put her hands on her thighs and hung her head and tried to remember how to breathe.

Bodies scattered the ground. Dead bodies. Pieces of bodies. A severed head, staring up at the sky. Two legs that did not belong to the same body, crisscrossed in an X. An arm with a ring on the third finger.

What about her family?

Father.

Mother.

Rory.

John.

Charles.

Where were they? Lenora fought to keep her eyes open, to keep her lungs grasping at air, to keep her legs moving forward, stepping gingerly over the bodies of people she did not recognize because of the thick film of soot covering their skin. She did not bend to wipe it away from their faces. She had no time to waste.

Her family must be alive. She would not find them here on the ground.

A popping and hissing sound drew her eyes to the left. Some electrical lines had fallen and were slapping the pavement and jetting fire in short blasts. The sulfuric smell snaked into her nose, unfolded in her throat, and swelled. She coughed. Some bits of wood rained down to her right, bouncing off the ground and then settling on a body bleeding from the ears and nose.

Lenora stood in the middle of the chaos and slowly turned around. She did not know what to do or where to go or how to find her family. She did not know how to process the wreckage that looked as though the entire town had been destroyed. She did not know how to keep breathing.

And so her knees folded again, and the world went dark.

3

Lenora woke inside city hall, its large glass windows punched all the way through so the outside smells leaked in freely. Sulfur, smoke, what she thought might be burning flesh. Lenora pinched her nose, but breathing through her mouth was not much better. Now she could imagine she tasted it.

Hushed voices hovered around the hall, and when Lenora propped herself on her elbow, she could see the bodies of the injured lying on the floor in various positions. Some had lost legs, some wore bandages on their heads, one man had dressings around his eyes. A woman with a twisted leg lay near him.

Lenora's head felt hazy.

"We'll transfer the most critical to John Sealy Hospital in Galveston," said a voice near her. Lenora glanced in its direction and saw a man with a shock of white hair on the top of his head bending over a woman with a bandage across her chest. A tall, slim woman with short, curly brown hair stood watching him. She had a clipboard and a pencil. "And the others we'll take in to Houston. The least critical we can keep here for a time."

"What about the children with no family left?" said the woman.

The man rocked back on his heels and sighed. "I don't know yet, Ingrid," he said. And then again, softer: "I don't know." His eyes looked weary. He stood up. "The injured are still trickling in." He looked toward the front doors, where a man was hobbling through. He moved to meet him.

Lenora scanned the hall. Mother and Father must be here. And Rory, John, and Charles. She stood up quickly, the world spinning for a moment before righting again, if a little tilted. She blinked. She did not see anyone in the immediate area who resembled Mother or Father, but this was a large room. She would search.

And she did, again and again and again, but she did not find any of her family. She saw some of her fellow

22

students, but she did not stop to talk, so heavy were her grief and fear.

The woman who had spoken with the white-haired man—Ingrid—stopped her on her fifth round through the hall. "Are you looking for someone?" she asked.

"My parents. They must be here." Lenora's voice shook.

"What is your last name?"

"Cole," Lenora said. "They are John and Agnes Cole."

"You are Lenora," Ingrid said. It was not a question. Ingrid eyed her before turning to the clipboard she held in her hands, which Lenora saw contained a handwritten list of names. Ingrid flipped through the pages, and then she looked at Lenora with sad earth-colored eyes. "There is no John or Agnes Cole on my list. But we have another makeshift infirmary inside the chamber of commerce. Perhaps they are there. Would you like to inquire?" Ingrid smiled, but it did not reach her eyes.

"I can go there myself," Lenora said, hope warming her chest. Yes. They would be there. Everyone she loved.

Ingrid placed a hand on Lenora's arm, which stopped Lenora from turning. "We cannot let our patients leave the building," she said. Ingrid's voice was so apologetic Lenora had to blink away her blurred vision. It was not that she was unaccustomed to kindness; it was that Ingrid's apology made her words so definitive. Lenora had always followed the rules. And now she knew that leaving the building was against the rules.

"But I am not injured." Still, she would try. Perhaps the rules could be bent, rather than broken.

Ingrid gave a half shrug and pointed to a line on the paper that Lenora could not read. "You were found unconscious," she said. Lenora shook her head. So? Ingrid bit her lip and said, "Dr. Sparks would like all patients to remain in one place. It's better for the record keeping." She smiled, her face brightening, if only a little. "Rescue workers are combing the area for all survivors. They bring them here and to the chamber of commerce, where their names are recorded and their family members are notified." She cleared her throat. "It's much too dangerous for anyone else to be out."

Lenora tried to swallow the knot in her throat. So the rules were in place for a reason, a reason that made sense. She said, "I just want to see my family. Make sure they're safe."

Ingrid's eyes softened. "I understand," she said. "It's well-known that we are running an infirmary here and at the chamber. That's why it's imperative that you remain in one place, in case your parents are looking for you, too." She nodded, as though agreeing with herself. "Do you understand?"

Lenora nodded.

"I will inquire right away," Ingrid said.

Lenora sat down in a corner to wait. Her parents would come. She just had to be patient.

4

The sky outside darkened as night fell over the town, and still Ingrid did not return. Lenora asked Dr. Sparks about her absence. He said Ingrid had likely gotten recruited to care for the patients inside the chamber, but she would return. She was needed here.

Lenora watched two students from Danforth Elementary reunite with their parents, and envy burned in her chest. She saw four students crumple when they were told their parents had died, and the fear frosted her throat.

Which would it be for her?

What happened to the students whose parents died? Lenora did not have any other family, except for her father's mad brother, who lived in Nacogdoches, too far away from Texas City. He had been estranged from the family for years. She didn't count him among her family. Father hadn't.

They had to be alive. She could not be alone—it would be unbearable. Mother and Father had teased her about her distaste for solitude and silence; they said it's why she was born third in a line of four children.

At last Ingrid returned. She had not found Lenora's family. "It might be time to contact other family members." Ingrid's voice was gentle, soothing. Lenora closed her eyes.

"I could try my house," she said, without looking at Ingrid.

Ingrid was silent for so long that Lenora opened her eyes again. "You think they would remain in their house while the town burned and their daughter was still missing?"

Lenora knew it was not a question that required an answer. She said, "I do not have any other family." It was difficult wedging the words around the blockage in her throat, but she did it.

A shadow crossed Ingrid's face.

"What happens to children like me?" Lenora said.

But Ingrid only pressed her lips together and patted Lenora's arm. She said nothing. She crossed the room to Dr. Sparks and whispered something in his ear. He looked in Lenora's direction and shuffled over with slumping shoulders. He looked so exhausted, but he had bright, kind sapphire eyes.

He knelt next to her. "Ingrid tells me you have been unable to locate your parents," he said.

"I'm sure they're coming. I could search my house, if you would permit me to leave." Lenora looked toward the entrance to city hall, felt the longing gnaw on her stomach.

"Rescue workers are searching every house that's still standing," Dr. Sparks said. "And even the rubble of those that aren't." He looked troubled.

"Have they searched mine?"

Dr. Sparks did not answer. Instead he said, "Your father was the fire chief." He seemed sure of his statement, but Lenora nodded anyway. He sighed, looked up at the ceiling, then back down at Lenora. "All members of the fire department were down at the docks when it exploded." He seemed to be saying more between the lines of his words.

Black spots grew and twirled in front of Lenora's eyes. A cry sounded from the back of her throat, wounded and raw.

Father.

"I'm sorry," Dr. Sparks said. "This is the worst trag-edy in Texas history."

"He'll come," Lenora said in a small voice. She did not believe it, and this made her angry. Her words gathered strength. "He's a hero."

Dr. Sparks didn't say anything. He only patted her shoulder.

She would know if they had died, wouldn't she? She would be able to feel it. Someone had to be alive. Someone had to be with her, keep her company. Someone had to fight with her and steal her favorite clothes and annoy her when she sat at the loud and riotous supper table.

"I'm sorry," Dr. Sparks said again. Lenora wiped her cheeks. "I will notify your uncle."

"My uncle?" Lenora said. She didn't know that

anyone in Texas City knew about Uncle Richard.

"I knew your uncle at the university. We were both science men. Had something in common." Dr. Sparks smiled. "He's a good man."

Lenora shook her head. No. She could not live with an uncle she didn't know. But what choice did she have?

"Please, let me go look for them." Her throat felt dry, but her will was intact. If he didn't permit it, she would search anyway. She would break the rules this time. They were ridiculous rules, and anger made her brave.

Dr. Sparks shook his head. "The streets are unstable," he said. "Buildings are still crumbling, electrical lines are still sparking, bodies are . . ." He didn't finish, perhaps remembering he was speaking to a child. She knew what he would have said. She had seen them. She would never forget them.

She closed her eyes, opened them again.

"We are doing everything we can," Dr. Sparks said.

"Let me stay here, then," Lenora said. "I'll wait for them."

"Your uncle's house is the best place you can be. We

don't have enough supplies to care for you here." He looked out toward the harbor. "And who knows if there will be another explosion."

Lenora swallowed hard. She said, "Will I see them again?"

Dr. Sparks did not meet her eyes. "If your family members are among the unconscious injured whose names we have not yet collected, they will find you more easily at your uncle's house."

And that was that. His knees cracked on his way up, and Lenora watched him walk away.

She examined her brand-new birthday dress. The hem was ripped in places. Dirt and grime ringed the collar. Black dust covered her beautiful shoes.

Lenora curled up into a tight ball and tried her best not to cry.

5

The next day, a tall, thin, strange-looking man walked through the doors of city hall. In fact, he looked so strange that Lenora could not help but stare. Silver streaks shot through the dark brown parts of his hair. It was cut somewhat short, but it stood out in every direction as though it had not seen a comb in many, many days. He wore a red velvet suit jacket with a crisp white shirt poking out from a vest that matched the color of his hair. Sticking out from the pocket of the strange, colorful jacket was a white kerchief, along with a golden chain. His mud-colored pants were pressed and perfect, and his golden-brown shoes had not a speck of dust or grime on them, nor were there any scratches. He looked like one of the wealthy business owners in town, but Lenora had never seen him before.

He dragged his left leg behind him slightly, and the

cane in his right hand tapped the ground in a steady rhythm. *Clunk, slide. Clunk, slide. Clunk, slide.* The cadence of his walk filled the hall, as people watched him make his way to nowhere in particular. It seemed he simply needed to keep moving.

Lenora's eyes caught on the cane, which was as strange-looking as the man. The end near the man's hand resembled Father's old rifle butt, a curved shining brown, but the other end was a long cylindrical silver barrel that widened into what looked like the broadest part of a funnel.

The man stopped in the center of the hall and pulled something out of his jacket pocket. It was a pocket watch, attached to the golden chain.

Dr. Sparks moved swiftly to his side and held out his hand, which the man did not take at first but studied, as though confused for a breath. When he shook Dr. Sparks's hand, he did not smile.

Lenora knew he was her uncle. She could see the resemblance now—in his face, but that was all.

Her stomach clenched tight.

Dr. Sparks and Uncle Richard—if her guess was

correct—moved in her direction. Uncle Richard did not look very happy. His dark eyebrows hung low over his dark eyes, which held an unreadable emotion—annoyance? Impatience? Surprise, maybe?

Dr. Sparks put a hand on her shoulder and said, "Lenora, your uncle has come to take you home."

"Home?" The word felt bitter in her mouth.

The light in Dr. Sparks's eyes flickered. "I am sorry," he said. "I only meant . . ." He looked at Uncle Richard for help, but Uncle Richard was staring at her.

"You look like your father," he said. He had a halting, abrupt way of speaking, and his voice was a touch too loud.

Lenora rubbed her chest. Dr. Sparks cleared his throat. "You will accompany your uncle to his home."

"Only until Mother and Father are well," Lenora said. Dr. Sparks tilted his head and studied her. He opened his mouth, but she would not let him say it. "They will come fetch me as soon as they're able." She leveled her gaze at Uncle Richard.

His lips turned down a little, but his expression was

otherwise unchanged. "Follow me, please," was all he said, and he spun on his heel.

"Goodbye, Lenora," Dr. Sparks said.

Lenora said nothing. She was still rather angry that they would not let her stay, at least until she knew that *someone* in her family was still alive. She knew Mother would say she was being rude, not answering, but in this moment, she didn't care.

She followed the sliding step of Uncle Richard toward the blasted-out doors of city hall.

"Mother and Father will come for me," she could not help saying to Uncle Richard's back. "I will only be with you for a short time."

Uncle Richard did not bother to reply, and this fueled her anger. It licked her throat, her eyes, her chest, and wandered back up into her mouth. "You'll see," she said.

Still, no reply.

The silence was excruciating.

6

Just outside city hall was an unusual car. It was not black or red or blue or any of the colors Lenora would see on the cars cruising the main streets of Texas City on Friday nights; it was, instead, a dull copper, as though all the paint had been stripped off. The wheels looked like a cross between those used on locomotives and those used on cars. There were eight of them on one side and, she assumed, eight on the other.

It was the oddest thing she had ever seen. Had she stepped back in time or forward into the future? Her head spun.

Perhaps she was dreaming.

Something on the ground beside the car caught her eye. It looked like a pearl necklace.

Her mother wore a pearl necklace.

Lenora did not think. She lunged for the string of

beads. It was covered in a black layer of dust, but when she wiped off one pearl, she could tell it was the same pale pink color as those on her mother's necklace. She looked around, searching for the familiar face. Her lungs blazed.

Uncle Richard cleared his throat, and Lenora met his eye. She stuffed the pearls in her pocket.

"It's my mother's necklace," she said, though Uncle Richard had not asked for an explanation.

Uncle Richard raised his chin and narrowed his eyes, the only acknowledgment that he had heard her at all. "Come along," was all he said.

He did not move toward the driver's seat, as Lenora expected, but instead headed for the seat behind the driver's. A stranger was suddenly at Lenora's side, opening her door. He was a large man, tall and muscular, outfitted in a perfect black suit with a pale yellow bow tie. His black hair was slicked back from his forehead, his brown cheeks shone, and his black mustache curled at the ends. He bowed slightly and said, "Welcome, miss. It has been some time since anyone has visited the manor."

"I'm not staying long," Lenora said. She felt she needed to say it; this man had a joyful energy crackling around him, and she didn't want him to think she would be at her uncle's house for good.

She would will her parents, her brothers and sister, alive if she must. She glanced toward her house, which was just down the street. She could see the roof from here.

It stood.

What if they were inside? What if they had forgotten about her or they thought she had died or they weren't able to get out?

The thoughts whirled in Lenora's mind until they became a whirling in her feet. But she didn't get far. The mysterious man with her uncle wrapped her in arms that were strong and sure. He smelled like the bergamot oil her mother had rubbed on her father's feet the nights he'd worked late inspecting newly docked ships.

The man dropped his eyes and nodded toward the car. He had opened her door.

"Wait," Uncle Richard said when Lenora was about

to slide inside. He gestured toward his side. "You sit there, behind Lloyd."

Lenora looked at her uncle for a brief moment before doing as she was told. Lloyd stared at her uncle, too, before walking to the other side and closing the door behind Lenora. He slipped into the driver's seat.

"I'd like to get home before dark," Uncle Richard said.

Lloyd gave one nod in the mirror.

The car started with a thundering rumble that Lenora had not noticed when it had rolled into town. She had been too intently focused on the new injured who had come to city hall that morning. Most of them were in critical condition and had been immediately transferred to neighboring hospitals. None of them were Mother or Father or Rory or John or Charles.

The car jerked forward. "I believe you will find Stonewall Manor to your liking, miss," Lloyd said.

Lenora did not want to be rude for the second time today, so she merely nodded. She had already told Lloyd that she would not be staying long; there was no sense in repeating this news.

Lloyd glanced behind him. "Lloyd," Uncle Richard said. It was a warning of some kind or another. Lenora stared at her uncle. Lloyd quickly faced forward again.

Uncle Richard sat rigid in the car. One of his hands gripped the door so tightly that his knuckles had turned white. She wondered if she would ever see anything about her uncle that was not strange.

As they drove out of the only town she had ever known, away from the ruin of the past few days and a lifetime shared with Rory and John and Charles and Mother and Father, Lenora closed her eyes. She had seen enough destruction. She did not want to see more buildings caved in on themselves, cars piled on top of roofs, mud everywhere. She rested her head against the window beside her, the vibration making her nose itch. She never got a chance to raise her hand and rub it, because she fell promptly to sleep.

His spirit was large and his influence was deep, as both had been in his life—the real life, the one where he could touch and converse with and swindle people out of their greatest possessions with little more than a conversation. That's how it always began: with a conversation, which bloomed into a false friendship, which then led to his greatest achievements, or, rather, their greatest losses. Some would say he was skilled in stealing life; he would say he was skilled in revealing the best parts of life, which could always be found once possessions and trappings were cleared away.

He had been hung for his crimes, in these very woods.

April 18, 1947

The progress I intended to make on my work today has been temporarily interrupted. I am on my way home from Texas City, where a terrible tragedy has necessitated my intervention. My niece is sleeping in the car. I am trying to distract my mind from the curves and ever-present dangers of the road with this journal, though I do not have much of the scientific kind to say.

Lenora is her name. This is the first time I have met her.

She is deeply troubled by her loss, as anyone can understand. She wants to believe, as most minds do, that her family is still alive. I saw the town, the bodies, the severed limbs. My brother's house is still standing, as though untouched by the devastation around it, but I lingered on its porch while Lloyd searched its interior. There were no bodies. The house was empty.

Little remained of the harbor, where the explosion originated (perhaps it is more accurate to say it originated in the ships docked there). Anyone who stood near the harbor—and there were many (Dr. Remus Sparks, an old colleague of mine, told me of the lovely smoke and the crowd it drew on the day of the explosion)—must have been destroyed, too.

I think my brother and his family—excepting Lenora (and why?)—must have been among them.

This knowledge feels too heavy to bear this afternoon. Why is life so full of agonizing loss? Why must we endure such misfortune? Why does the sun continue to shine?

If only my brother had remained at Stonewall Manor . . . if only I had believed him all those years ago . . . if only I hadn't waited so long to tell him of my discoveries, my change of heart, my plan to break the Stonewall Curse . . .

Well, there are a great many things that would have been different. We would have fought the darkness together. I would not have lost a son, perhaps. My brother would be alive.

Regret is a dangerous companion.

And now I have his daughter. He wouldn't like to know that; it's why he left in the first place. He couldn't raise children at Stonewall Manor, he'd said. Not with the woods so close. Not with the danger. Not with generations of children disappearing.

How I wish I had followed him, left this old manor to whatever lives in the woods. But who would have broken the curse?

I do not know what to do with a daughter. I am not equipped to be a father; the events of the past have proved that. I fear I will fail in a way that will destroy me and possibly Lenora, too.

And there is, as always, the business of the woods—the work that must be done and the hold it has on children. John felt it once; he knew its power, though he did not fully understand it then. He tried to tell me, begged me to use my scientific mind to find a solution, but I didn't listen. I didn't believe until my son . . .

I must accelerate my plans. There is no telling how long the woods will leave Lenora to me.

—excerpt from Richard Cole's *Journal of Scientific Progress*

STONEWALL MANOR, NACOGDOCHES

7

The car jerked to a stop.

"Here we are."

The voice reached her in a haze. Lenora opened her eyes, confused and disoriented. Lloyd spoke from the front seat. "I thought you might like the loveliest view of your new home." He waved a hand toward the passenger window.

"It's not my home," Lenora said, the words somewhat sharp and pointed.

Lloyd cleared his throat. She really had not meant to be rude again, but she needed them to understand. She would not be here long.

Uncle Richard grunted. She hoped she had not upset him with her impolite words; Father had always told her brothers and sister that good manners were essential in life. He would be disappointed.

Uncle Richard was asleep, however, and likely had not heard her retort. His hands loosely gripped a journal, a pencil balancing precariously on its edge.

Lenora turned her attention to the house outside the car window. It was the largest and most beautiful one she had ever seen. She could not see it fully, because trees lined both sides of the stone walk that stretched from the front door to the street, where the car idled, and hid the corners from view. The branches of the trees looked like arms reaching toward one another, arcing gracefully in a limb-and-leaf hollow. She counted eight white pillars on the front of the house, two towers (with pointed roofs and stacks of windows, just like out of a storybook!), and six steps leading to the front door. A rectangular balcony stretched the length of the second floor. Shutters painted a deep green framed eight long windows.

The house must be very grand inside; what had they called it? A manor?

"There are twenty-six bedrooms in Stonewall Manor," Lloyd said.

"Are they all filled?" Lenora could not help herself;

curiosity and questions had been a normal part of her life, from the time she could speak. Mother had found them trying at times, but Father loved them. Or so he'd said.

"Only two of them," Lloyd said.

Two people in this enormous house? It must be terribly boring to live here, and lonely, too. Lenora's throat dried out. Well. She would not be staying long.

"Do you live here?" Lenora said.

"No," Lloyd said. "I live in town. I only come around when your uncle needs me to drive him somewhere." He lowered his voice. "He is not fond of driving."

Lenora found this just as odd as everything else she'd learned about her uncle, but her curiosity was currently running in two different directions. So she said, "Who lives here, then?"

"Your uncle, of course," Lloyd said. "And Mrs. Jones."

"Mrs. Jones?"

"She is the cook."

"There is a cook at Stonewall Manor?" Lenora's eyes focused on Lloyd's face.

"Yes." His voice lowered. "She is a good one. She

makes the best cakes. You should request the strawberry one while you're here."

Lenora remembered that she had not celebrated her birthday with a cake. Mother would have baked a strawberry one, and they would have eaten it around their supper table the night of the explosion.

Her birthday. Her birthday would be forever linked with the explosion. Her vision blurred.

Lloyd said, "I believe Mrs. Jones has something prepared for you. Though it is past lunchtime."

Lenora had not eaten a proper meal in days. Her stomach felt vacant, just like this after-explosion life. Was it the pain of the disaster, or was it hunger? She could not tell the difference anymore.

"I have never lived in a place with a cook." Lenora's voice sounded very small.

"My wife would love it," Lloyd said. His eyes caught hers in the rearview mirror. His were shining.

"My uncle must be a wealthy man," Lenora said.

Lloyd coughed. "Yes, well." He stretched his neck, pulled at the collar. "He is a brilliant man. And this home has belonged to the Cole family for centuries."

"Stonewall Manor?" Lenora said.

"Surely your father told you as much." Lloyd looked at her in the mirror again. "He grew up here."

No. Father had never told her anything about Uncle Richard and Stonewall Manor. All she had known was that Father had once had a brother. He did not speak well of his brother—in fact, she recalled Father's eyes growing dark and cloudy—sometimes wet—the few times he'd mentioned Uncle Richard.

Lenora eyed her uncle. He did not look as bad as Father seemed to think. He looked like a sleeping man, like her father's brother. The wrinkles around his eyes had smoothed out, and she could see Father's face in his.

"Why did my father never tell me?" Lenora said. The question hung in the car. Uncle Richard opened his eyes.

"Time heals and hardens in equal measure," Uncle Richard said.

Lenora did not understand the words, but she gathered there were many things about her uncle—about her father, too—that she did not understand. Perhaps her stay at Stonewall Manor would reveal some of the answers.

Lloyd eased the car forward again. Lenora watched the manor from every angle. It really was beautiful. It was so different from the home she had shared with her family. She imagined wide-open hallways and secret passageways and large bedrooms that did not need to be shared. How John and Charles and Rory would have loved it here.

How Mother would have loved a cook, just like Lloyd's wife. And Father . . .

An ache elbowed its way into Lenora's chest. Her eyes dripped. She blinked hard. She did not want to cry, but sometimes it was impossible to control the tears.

Her family would be here before she knew it, and then she and John and Charles and Rory would run through these halls and the secret passageways and the large bedrooms and play hide-and-seek in the dark like they used to do in the old abandoned storefront near their home that Mother and Father had forbidden them to enter. (Lenora had always waited outside until the fun inside grew too jubilant. Rules were one thing;

missing out was another.)

Lloyd pulled around to the side of the house, where a circular drive curved out to the road. He parked the car beneath a covered patio. Lenora could not stop looking at the thick expanse of trees, which swallowed all the land behind and around the manor. Only the front of the manor was untouched by woods.

She climbed out of the car while Lloyd held the door open for her.

"Stonewall Woods," he said, nodding in the direction where her gaze settled.

"They are dangerous woods," Uncle Richard said. His voice was clipped, even, urgent. "Stay out of them."

Lloyd stiffened and tugged on the bottom of his vest, straightening what appeared to already be perfectly straight.

"Why are they dangerous?" Lenora said. They looked intriguing to her. The trees were not the same kind that lined the house. These trees were taller, thinner, with leaves that looked like needles. The sight of them, lined up in a regal wall of green, reminded her of home. The parts of Texas City that were not covered in homes and industrial plants looked very much like Stonewall Woods.

How far were they from Texas City? She had not even paid attention.

Lenora turned her eyes to Uncle Richard. He stared at the woods with such longing that she had to look away, or she would cry again.

"Stay out of them," was all Uncle Richard said before turning toward the entrance of Stonewall Manor.

8

Lenora's eyes were drawn back to the woods. Surely something so beautiful could not be dangerous. But then she remembered the smoke in Texas City and the explosion that destroyed everything she had ever known.

Beauty could deceive.

"Mrs. Jones." Uncle Richard's voice spun Lenora around. She saw a wispy woman with silver hair tied back at the nape of her neck and blue eyes that crinkled at the edges, as though she had known a lifetime of laughter. The woman's thin lips drew into a smile.

"Come along inside, love," Mrs. Jones said.

"This is Lenora," Lloyd said. He grinned at Mrs. Jones and slid past her through the door.

"I know who she is," Mrs. Jones replied while swatting his back. Lenora almost smiled at the easy way between them. Mrs. Jones held out a spotted hand. Lenora took it, and Mrs. Jones pulled her into a tight embrace and dropped a kiss on the top of her head. Lenora stiffened for a breath, then relaxed. It felt good to be held, if only for a moment. Even by someone she didn't know.

Did Mrs. Jones know her?

"I was here at Stonewall Manor when your father was a boy," Mrs. Jones said, as though she could hear Lenora's thoughts. "You look just like him."

Lenora beamed, but the smile quickly dissolved. Father. How she missed him.

Would she ever be done with this pain?

She would when they came back.

They had to come back.

Mrs. Jones seemed to sense Lenora's sorrow. Her eyes darkened, a hint of private grief gathering at the corners. She placed an arm around Lenora's shoulders. "Now, then," she said. "Let me show you inside."

They walked up the steps together, and when they were inside the manor, Mrs. Jones said, "Welcome to Stonewall Manor, Lenora." Lenora was glad she had not said, "Welcome home."

She gazed up at the sparkling chandelier hanging from the top of the hall, which was so tall her father would not have been able to jump and touch it, as he could do with the light at home. The table in the hall had not a speck of dust on it; Lenora ran her finger along it to check. (She had been tasked with the dusting at home, and she had never been much good at it.) The rug inviting Lenora deeper into the manor was brilliantly colored with red and green and blue and gold swirls. She walked very slowly; she wanted to observe every part of this spectacular place where her father had grown up. Why had he never said a word about it?

An assortment of brass clocks hung above the hall-way table, all turned to the same time, which was not the current time (2:49 p.m.) but 3:07 p.m. Their hands did not move. On the table was a golden telephone, the kind that had a bell for the mouthpiece and a tunnel-like apparatus for the earpiece. Lenora touched it with her fingers as she passed.

"It is lovely, isn't it?" Mrs. Jones said. Her eyes smiled for her.

"Very much so," Lenora said.

"And it will be your home," Mrs. Jones said. "We have a billiard room and a library—"

"I won't be staying long." Lenora hated to interrupt, but she had to make it clear to Mrs. Jones, who had not heard any of her earlier assertions. She softened her words with, "But in the meantime, a library will be nice."

Mrs. Jones looked at her for a long moment, her eyes turning soft and sad. Then she said, "You like to read?"

Lenora read every chance she had. She nodded.

"We have a lovely library," Mrs. Jones said. "I'll take you there first thing tomorrow." She turned, her shoulders slumping forward into a sadness Lenora did not understand. What was it Mrs. Jones carried?

"Would you like to eat first or change into some fresh clothes?" Mrs. Jones tossed the words behind her.

"Eat?" Lenora said. It came out like a question, as though she were asking permission. Her stomach was so empty it thundered.

Mrs. Jones nodded and bustled toward a swinging door with a small window cut in it. Lenora followed.

"You'll eat in the kitchen with me this afternoon,"

Mrs. Jones said. "But tonight and every other night you'll dine with Mr. Cole promptly at six o'clock." Mrs. Jones leveled her gaze at Lenora. "Your uncle is very punctual, and he does not like children to be late to the table."

Was that a warning? What would happen if she were late?

"Are there other children?" Lenora said. Her hope lifted its head. Perhaps Lloyd had miscounted the people living here. (She knew this hope was ridiculous—even as she felt it warming her chest. But hope is a ridiculous thing.)

Mrs. Jones pressed her lips together and shook her head. "No." She paused, rubbed a finger across one eyebrow. "No, love, there are no other children." Her voice held all the sadness in the world, Lenora thought.

No, not all of it. It did not contain Lenora's.

"Would you like a tuna sandwich and some grapes? I would offer more, but supper is in a couple of hours." Mrs. Jones reached for a plate.

"A sandwich would be wonderful," Lenora said. "Thank you."

Mother and Father would be proud that she was remembering her manners. The thought made her throat constrict. Would she ever be able to think of them without tears burning the back of her nose?

Mrs. Jones opened a small white icebox with a silver latch and pulled out a blue bowl, which Lenora assumed was the already-made tuna. She took bread out of a brass box sitting in a corner on the counter and slathered tuna onto two slices.

Lenora looked around the room. It appeared to be larger than her entire home. It had two sinks and two white stoves with black coils resting on top and a shining window that looked out on Stonewall Woods. It was expansive enough to fit a table inside it and still have room to do cartwheels—probably four of them. Lenora couldn't believe that this grand manor had existed without Rory even knowing. She would have loved it here. Rory always complained about their home—it was too small, she said. What she really meant was she hated sharing a room with Lenora, but the sharing had suited Lenora just fine; she'd never asked for a room of her own.

She would give anything to share all this with Rory.

They must be alive.

They must.

She touched the pearl necklace in her pocket.

What would she do if they weren't?

Who would she be?

9

The sandwich on Lenora's plate was cut into small triangles, and the green grapes rolled around it as she turned the plate in circles.

Her elbow brushed a newspaper. She saw the familiar plume of smoke and squinted at the day's date printed at the top of the paper. *April 18, 1947,* it said. Today's paper. Two days after the explosion, and they were still talking about it.

Of course they were still talking about it. It was the worst tragedy in Texas history, Dr. Sparks had said. How many had died?

Lenora picked up the paper, but Mrs. Jones snatched it out of her hands.

"I'm sorry, love," she said. "I didn't mean to leave the paper out." She hurried to the other side of the kitchen and stuffed the paper in the trash can.

But Lenora had already seen the headline: "Hundreds of Unidentified Bodies Found in Texas City, After Explosion." She could still picture them—the bodies, lined up on the ground, torn to pieces by the blast. She closed her eyes and shook her head, trying to dislodge the memory. She didn't feel so hungry anymore.

She felt something warm close over her hand and looked up to see Mrs. Jones's face hovering near hers. "Everything will work out in the end," she said. "You'll see." Lenora nodded, trying to swallow her tears. She didn't believe Mrs. Jones's words, not really, but she had to at least try.

It would work out. They had to be alive.

Lenora picked up her sandwich, willing herself to eat. It was a delightful mix of sour and sweet. Her mother had often packed this kind of sandwich in her lunch, for school, but something was different about this tuna.

"Apples," Mrs. Jones said, her eyes on Lenora's face. "That's what gives it a little bit of sweetness, along with the tart. I wasn't sure if you would like it, but I thought you might." She cleared her throat. "Your father did." She smiled, the skin around her eyes crinkling like bits of newsprint.

Lenora said nothing, though there were a thousand questions to ask. She simply didn't know where to start.

After a time, Mrs. Jones said, "No children live around Stonewall Manor. Not many guests anymore, either. It's not often that I get to cook a supper like I've planned for tonight."

"What is it?"

"Roast," Mrs. Jones said. She pointed to one of the ovens. "It's already cooking."

Roast. Mother made the most delicious roast. Lenora's chest tightened again. Would she ever be able to breathe?

"Your stay here will be good for Stonewall Manor," Mrs. Jones said. Her eyes glazed, then cleared. "It will be good for everyone."

Lenora watched Mrs. Jones, waited for her to say something more, to explain what she meant, but Mrs. Jones didn't. Lenora opened her mouth to inquire, but all that came out was, "I will not be staying here long."

Mrs. Jones dropped her eyes. "I know," she said.

But Lenora needed to say the words aloud, again, to believe them. "Mother and Father will come and take me home."

"Home," Mrs. Jones said. She patted the table with one spotted hand. "It is strange how home can mean different things to people." She stood. "If you are finished, I can show you to your rooms."

"Rooms?" Lenora nearly giggled, forgetting herself in the absurdity of Mrs. Jones's words. She sounded so formal, like a maid in one of her father's favorite old novels. Lenora pressed her hand to her mouth, and when she was quite sure there was not a giggle waiting, she continued. "Are there more than one?"

Mrs. Jones tilted her head, smiling with more than kindness—amusement, perhaps. "Well, love, every room in this house comes with its own private bathroom. So we call them rooms, you see."

"Stonewall Manor has twenty-six bathrooms?" Lenora said. She could feel her eyes widening. Her home only had one, and they'd all had to share it. It was the largest conflict of their day—mostly because Rory hogged it.

"Twenty-nine, actually," Mrs. Jones said. "There are others near the sitting room and the library and the ballroom. Some are only powder rooms, but . . ." Mrs. Jones stood. "Come along, love."

Lenora followed Mrs. Jones to a large, winding staircase that twisted out of sight. It seemed to go all the way up to the sky, but, of course, that was impossible. Magic wasn't real. Father had always made sure Lenora and her brothers and sister knew that. He said magic was deceptive and to never trust its illusion; it could bring great harm to the deceived. Lenora had found this a strange contradiction, since her father read books full of magic and enchantment and seemed to enjoy those the most.

The wall beside the stairs was covered with portraits of people Lenora did not know—perhaps family, but she could not be sure. She did not know much about this family. Her father had never mentioned them, never told stories about them, never said the words

"Stonewall Manor" at all. She stopped to look at the people—tight-lipped men and women with bright and intelligent eyes. She wanted to ask who they were, but Mrs. Jones walked too quickly for questions. Lenora ran her hand along the shining cherrywood of the stair rail. Not a speck of dust coated her fingers.

"See that she gets all she needs, please, Mrs. Jones." A man's voice hurtled toward them. Lenora stopped walking and looked down through the curled black iron of the stair rail. Uncle Richard stood in a dim hallway that shadowed most of his face. He had changed clothes, perhaps to get the smell and sight of Texas City off him. He now wore a suit that looked exactly like the other one, except in a rusted brown color. His left hand tapped his thigh. Lenora watched this so she did not have to look in his eyes, at the face that looked so much like Father's, except for the eyes. "And she will dine with me this evening."

"Yes, Mr. Cole," Mrs. Jones said.

Lenora looked down at her dress, grimy and wrinkled, and the shoes that were likely beyond repair. She had tried, at city hall, to scrub most of the dust from her hands and arms and face. But the clothes and shoes were another matter entirely.

She did not touch anything—not even the rail—as she climbed the rest of the way up. Mother would want her to be perfectly polite and well-behaved, a good-mannered young lady, and she could do this.

She *would* do it.

She would do anything to bring them back.

10

The second floor was sparsely decorated, with only a rug of curling gold and green and blue lining what seemed like an endless dark hallway. Lenora could see a few portraits peering at her from the walls before shadows swallowed them, and any bedrooms that were visible had their doors shut. She itched to see what waited behind each of the doors, but Mrs. Jones stopped at the first one on the right.

Lenora glanced toward the end of the passage, gaping at her like a black hole. At least she wouldn't have to walk into that darkness every day.

John and Charles and Rory would laugh at her cowardice. If they were here, choosing their own bedrooms, this is the one she would claim, simply because it was not wedged into a dark, endless corridor.

She wished they were here. They would explore with her. She wouldn't have to do it alone.

But maybe Mrs. Jones would show her the other rooms, if she asked. Mother had always said that if Lenora asked for help more, she would find life a little easier. Lenora liked doing things for herself—which meant when it came to things like dark corridors and closed doors, she would pretend she didn't want to know what hid in the bedrooms, rather than asking someone to accompany her in her exploration.

Perhaps it was time for a change.

Lenora cleared her throat.

"This is the west wing," Mrs. Jones said over her shoulder, before Lenora could say anything.

"Is there an east wing?" Lenora said.

"Yes. There is." Mrs. Jones fiddled with the door-knob. It was an old copper one, with a keyhole Lenora might be able to peek through. The door was painted a rich green, the color of a forest. It was Lenora's favorite color. It seemed a sign of sorts. She touched the door and smiled, but her lips did not quite stretch. Sorrow must do that—steal the smiles.

Mrs. Jones rattled the doorknob and jammed the key inside again. "It's stuck." She held up the key and examined it, then tried again.

"Here," Lenora said. She took the key, and the door opened perfectly for her.

Mrs. Jones smiled. "It's been some time since these doors have been regularly opened."

Lenora hovered in the doorway. "What's in the other bedrooms?" she said.

"Beds and armoires and fireplaces, same as yours." Mrs. Jones opened the door wider. It squealed in protest. Mrs. Jones laughed. "I'll have to get that oiled. This way, love."

But Lenora still lingered. Her eyes had caught on the door across the hall, the one with blue-green paint. It appeared to shimmer in places. She tilted her head.

"The bedrooms used to be reserved for guests," Mrs. Jones said. "But no one's come to stay in a while." She gently pushed Lenora through the door.

Her room smelled of dust and age. "It hasn't been aired in quite some time." Mrs. Jones seemed to know what she was thinking. "I opened all the windows as soon as I knew you were coming, but it doesn't seem to have rid the smell."

The room was large and every bit as grand as the other rooms of the house. The walls bore a golden-yellow color, with curling green accents painted along the top. But the bed was what commanded Lenora's attention. Never in her twelve years had she seen a bed so fine. Golden curtains hung around it but were pulled back so that she could see the burgundy blanket and pillows that shone from the top of the bed. The frame had four tall posts made of dark-colored wood, with golden leaves snaking around them. It was the bed of a queen, right out of a storybook. Lenora gasped.

"Do you like it?" Mrs. Jones said.

"I have never seen a bed so magnificent," Lenora said. She wondered what Mrs. Jones would say if she ran and jumped on the beautiful bed. But she was much too dirty, so, with great effort, she stilled the urge.

Rory would have done it.

Rory.

The ache nearly made her cry out.

Lenora turned to Mrs. Jones, who was pointing to

a large vertical chest that stood in the corner of the room. Its wood matched the bed—dark brown with golden leaves painted at its top. "You'll find a clean dress inside the armoire. I bought two dresses. I hope I estimated the correct size." Mrs. Jones turned back around and brushed errant strands of her silvery hair from her eyes. "We'll shop the day after tomorrow. Your uncle has some business in town, so he'll take you."

"But you'll come, too," Lenora said, her heart fluttering. She didn't know what she'd do or talk about if she were alone with her uncle. He seemed to prefer silence, while Lenora preferred sound. And how would he help her find dresses? He was a man.

"I have duties here," Mrs. Jones said, but she must have seen Lenora's face crumple, because she amended her words. "But if you would be more comfortable." She nodded. "Yes, it could be arranged." Her eyes remained on Lenora, which made Lenora drop her own.

"I'd like you to come," she said, in a small voice.

"Then I will."

Lenora considered it a promise.

11

Mrs. Jones gestured to a door off to the left of the bedroom. "The bathroom is this way," she said. Lenora followed her into a spacious room with a white claw-foot tub and what felt like marble for a floor. The walls were the same golden color as the bedroom, and there were two gilded mirrors, along with a sink and a toilet.

"A bath might do you some good," Mrs. Jones said.

Lenora agreed. Mrs. Jones moved back out into the bedroom, and Lenora followed her. Every time she looked around, she noticed something she hadn't seen before. Now she noticed some drawings on the walls, pictures of what looked like brass or gold machines. One was an elephant, knotted and layered. One was a snail with locomotive wheels. Another was a man made of brass and gears and armor.

"What are those?" She pointed to the pictures.

Mrs. Jones's eyes darkened with something Lenora could not read. "Art," Mrs. Jones said, after a moment's hesitation. She looked as though she had not even intended to say that. It was the strangest thing. But what about this place was *not* strange?

"I will leave you, then," Mrs. Jones said. "Supper will be served at six o'clock sharp, remember. Don't be late."

"Are all the rooms like this one?" Lenora said when Mrs. Jones was nearly out the door.

Mrs. Jones turned and leaned her bony hip against the doorframe. Her thin, arched eyebrows lifted.

"I mean . . ." Lenora did not quite know what she meant. "Have they all been lived in?"

"At one time or another," Mrs. Jones said. "This is a very old home. It has been in the family for centuries. Years ago multiple families lived here, not just the eldest in the line of succession."

What would that have been like, living here with Uncle Richard and her family?

"Did this room belong to someone?"

Mrs. Jones sighed. She crossed her arms over her chest, which made her brown dress pucker at the top.

"It belonged to a little girl," she said.

"What happened to the little girl?" Lenora said.

"You are a curious child," Mrs. Jones said, and Lenora could not tell if she was amused or annoyed.

"I know nothing about my family," Lenora said. Her voice wavered, and she tried to steady it.

But the wavering must have elicited Mrs. Jones's sympathy, because she said, "The master's little girl."

"My uncle had a daughter?" Lenora's heart pounded. What had happened to the little girl? She was not here now.

"It was a long time ago," Mrs. Jones said. "Eight years . . . or has it been nine?" Her eyes took on that faraway look again. "He lost them both on the same day."

"Who?" Curiosity was impossible sometimes.

Mrs. Jones lurched away from the doorway, as though it had burned her. "No one," she said. "I'm sorry. I shouldn't have spoken so freely. It's not my story to tell."

"But I should know about my family." Once again, Lenora's voice wavered on the word "family."

But this time Mrs. Jones did not talk out of sympathy. She only said, "I've washed and aired all the bedsheets.

We have plenty of time before supper, so if you would like to nap, I only ask that you listen for the supper bell. You'll know when it's time. You can't miss that bell." She chuckled.

And then she was gone, and Lenora was alone in the extravagant room. She stared out her doorway, at the door across the hall. She could see it now. A silver X shimmered in the dim light of the hall, spanning the full length of the blue-green door. It was pale, translucent, flickering in places, as though it had been drawn with a magical pencil.

Lenora drew closer. The mark disappeared.

Perhaps it had only been her imagination.

She returned to her room and opened the armoire in the corner to see two dresses of the same color blue but different in style. One had a white collar very much like the one she was wearing now—her birthday dress. The other had a layered frill along the front and puffed-up sleeves. That one she chose and laid out on her bed, along with the one pair of black shoes sitting at the bottom of the cabinet. They had no heel.

After her bath, Lenora considered throwing her

birthday dress into the fireplace and having it disintegrate the same way so much of her former life had disintegrated in the blaze that tore through Texas City. But if it could be washed, if it could be worn again . . . she had to keep it. It might be all she had left to remember her home, her family, the fullness of love she had known in her five favorite people.

No. It was not all. There were the pearls, too. She took them out, brought them to her lips, not caring whether they left a sooty stain.

She placed the dress outside her room, crumpled in a dirty heap, then stretched out on the royal bed that was even softer than it looked. The pearls were threaded between her fingers, their grime leaving black lines. She closed her eyes.

But images of Texas City kept skittering across her mind in a relentless reel. The plume of smoke. The explosion that shook her school and shattered its windows and made Mrs. Easter fly. The bodies, everywhere.

She stared up at the canopy above her bed, and, out of habit, reached beside her, where her sister had always been when they slept. The bed felt cold and empty—much too large. Lenora pulled back the covers and wriggled beneath them, drawing them up to her chin and then, on second thought, all the way over her eyes.

The pearls rested in Rory's place, shedding their black dust onto the blanket.

12

It was not a supper bell that woke her. It was a voice, thin and whispery.

Lenora, it said. *Come.*

She blinked her eyes in the stifling darkness beneath her covers and thrust them away from her face. She sat up on one elbow. The room had stilled, as though hanging in a suspension of both time and air. But then the supper bell clanged, breaking the spell of silence. The clanging climbed all the way up the stairs and under the crack of her door.

Lenora jumped from her bed and washed her hands, scrubbing away the black of the soot and whatever else clung to her fingers. She stuffed the pearl necklace in the front pocket of her dress and washed her hands again.

She was taking Mother with her.

The dining room was quiet when she entered. There were eight chairs at the table—one on each end and three on each long side. A golden candelabra decorated its honey-wood center. A brass chandelier hung down to meet it, sparkling its light around the room, giving it a shifting, shimmery look. A fireplace was nestled near a bright window. It was too warm for fires, but Lenora imagined that in the wintertime it must be quite lovely to sit in this room and eat.

Uncle Richard entered the room just as she was trying to decide in which seat to sit. For lack of anything better to say—and to fill the silence of the room, which she generally did by talking to herself—she said, "It's a lovely room." Uncle Richard did not answer, only nodded vaguely and took his seat in the single chair at one end.

"Is there somewhere I should sit?" Lenora said.

"Anywhere is fine, love," Mrs. Jones said, entering the room with four plates balanced on a tray. Two of the plates held towering salads, and the others were heaped with roast and asparagus, steam curling from their tops.

"Not at the other end," Uncle Richard said, his voice thick and raspy.

Lenora glanced at the empty chair on the other end of the table and wondered about her uncle's odd request. What would he do if she sat there?

Of course she didn't. She chose a different seat, close to the other end, and farthest from her uncle. He unsettled her. She didn't know how to read him, and she'd always been good at reading people. His moods were incomprehensible.

And she had a feeling he preferred that she sit as far away from him as possible.

At home, suppers had been a loud affair. John and Charles talked all over each other, while Rory tried to interject every now and then. Lenora had watched it all in blissful serenity and waited patiently for Mother and Father to ask her questions about her day.

This supper was much too quiet; only the ticking of a brass clock that hung above the fireplace imposed its cadence onto the stillness. Lenora, though she had never tasted food quite so delicious as what Mrs. Jones made, could do no more than pick at it. Her stomach was too knotted.

A clanking joined the ticking, then stopped. Lenora looked at her uncle. It seemed he couldn't stop moving. He bounced in his seat, as though powered by an invisible energy. She glanced under the table. It was his leg. Then it was his fork. Then it was his finger, tapping the side of his face.

It was an interesting dance.

He said not a word to her, though she tried a few times to ask questions about Stonewall Manor and the years when Father had lived there. Mrs. Jones had impeccable timing and seemed to be always present to redirect her curiosity, and after a while, Lenora gave up. She would not get her questions answered today.

But tomorrow was a new day.

Lenora ate her supper in silence, every now and then braving a glance in her uncle's direction. He kept a pen and a journal beside his plate. He would stare into space often, then scribble something in the journal, then look up, his eyes going glassy again, like he was lost in another world entirely.

What world was he lost in? Was it real or was it fantasy?

And why was it so hard for him to answer her questions? She wanted to know so much—what had happened between him and Father? How had her cousin—or cousins—died? Why had Lenora never known about this house and the people who lived in it?

Lenora studied her uncle again. He was scrawling something in the journal. His peppered hair moved in multiple directions, all over the top of his head. He raised his eyes and caught her gaze, but he did not seem to see her. His chair screeched against the floor. He said a terse "Excuse me, please" and gathered up his pen and journal and scrambled out the door. Lenora sat at the table for a few minutes, wondering what was next. She felt bewildered and slightly hurt.

Was this how it would be, then?

She stared at the chandelier and its warm light, which was not warm enough to melt the icy bits of sorrow settling into her heart, as though they intended to stay.

13

Mrs. Jones entered the dining room a few minutes later. "Did your uncle leave you?" she said. Her voice held a strong note of annoyance.

"Yes. Only a few moments ago." Lenora didn't know why she felt the need to defend Uncle Richard.

Mrs. Jones pressed her lips together. "I'll speak with him this evening," she said, her voice hard and definitive. "He must eat supper with his niece before getting back to his work."

Lenora wondered if anyone could tell Uncle Richard what to do, but she didn't ask this. Instead, she asked, "What does he do?"

Mrs. Jones's face folded, her eyebrows drawing low over her eyes. She busied herself with Uncle Richard's plates, saying only, "I'll clear the table."

Lenora knew Mrs. Jones had heard her, so she asked the question again. "What does he do?"

Mrs. Jones stopped in the doorway. "Do you really know nothing about your uncle?" Her eyes were so sad Lenora had to look away.

Lenora swallowed hard. "Father never talked about him at all." She felt terrible admitting this, but it was the truth.

A darkness seemed to fall over the room, and Lenora looked up to see that it was caused by the twisting of Mrs. Jones's face. She looked angry and sad, all at the same time. "Well," was all she said, punctuated by a vigorous shake of her head.

Lenora would not let it go at that. "Did they hate one another?" she said.

"Not always," Mrs. Jones said, setting Uncle Richard's plates back on the table and pulling out a chair. She sat heavily and leaned back. "Not when they were boys. They loved each other very much."

"What happened?"

"Time happened," Mrs. Jones said. She rose as quickly as she had sat, and before Lenora could ask anything else, she disappeared from the room.

Lenora waited for some minutes, hoping she would

return. Was she expected to clear her plates from the table, or did Mrs. Jones do that? She had just decided to clear them away herself, as she had always done at home, when Mrs. Jones returned.

"Are you finished, love?" Mrs. Jones said, as though they had not been talking about anything of importance.

Lenora nodded and said, "What is my uncle working on?" She would remind Mrs. Jones that the question was still unanswered. This is what she'd always done with Mother and Father. Mother called it inconvenient. Father called it delightful.

She rubbed her chest.

Mrs. Jones sighed as she leaned over to pick up Lenora's plate. "Your uncle is a scientist," she said. "He works on scientific things." She gave a low chuckle. "Things I could hardly understand. My specialty is food, not science."

"Food is science," Lenora said.

Mrs. Jones smiled at her. "Not your uncle's science."

"What kind of science does he do?"

Lenora had always loved science. Perhaps she could help him.

Mrs. Jones's gaze turned steely. "Perhaps he will tell you someday what he's working on."

"You can't?" Why were there so many secrets here?

"It is his business," Mrs. Jones said. "I don't claim to understand it."

"Do you think he would let me work with him? I've always enjoyed science. And I'm really good at it." Lenora tried to keep the desperation from her voice, but it crawled between the words anyway.

Mrs. Jones dropped Lenora's plate, and it shattered on the floor, a mess of jagged white pieces. "Oh dear," she said, staring at the floor. She cleared her throat and bent to gather the pieces of Lenora's plate into a pile. Lenora stooped to help her. "Thank you, love," Mrs. Jones said.

After a long moment, once Mrs. Jones had swept up the remains and returned to the dining room to make sure there were no more shards of glass, she said, "No, Lenora. I don't think your uncle would like a child in his lab."

Disappointment ballooned in Lenora's throat. "Oh," was all she said.

They lapsed into an uncomfortable silence until Mrs. Jones said, "Would you like some strawberry cake? I made it today, so it's fresh."

"Yes, please," Lenora said.

"You can eat with me in the kitchen."

Lenora followed Mrs. Jones, but before she walked through the doorway, she turned back to the dining room. It glowed in the light from the chandelier. It was so large and festive and extraordinary. It would have been a perfect place for her family. She wished they could have seen it. The room dimmed.

They *would* see it. They would come.

The room brightened again.

She turned away, thinking now of something else: how to break the eerie, secretive silence that hung over Stonewall Manor.

14

Strawberry cake was Lenora's favorite, but as she bit into this one, she tasted something bitter in her mouth. It was not the cake; Mrs. Jones was too proficient a cook to bake anything but a delicious cake.

It was the memories that did it.

Every year, her mother had baked her a strawberry cake for her birthday. She had not had one this year.

"My birthday . . ." Lenora let the words trail off. Mrs. Jones reached across the small dark-wood kitchen table and folded her hand over Lenora's.

"I made this cake to celebrate," Mrs. Jones said. Her eyes shone. Her silver hair shivered from the light breeze reaching through the window. "I knew you had a birthday a few days ago. I made your father's favorite cake."

She didn't say anything about the disaster. Lenora was glad.

But her throat was too thick to say thank you. She looked down at the cake, at its perfect pink frosting and its fluffy center. Her eyes burned. She swiped them with the back of her hand, the one Mrs. Jones wasn't holding.

She wasn't quite ready to let go yet.

"You can have two pieces if you'd like," Mrs. Jones said. Lenora knew she was trying to cheer her up. She thought perhaps it would be a good time to ask more questions—Mrs. Jones might answer them now.

So she said, "What happened to my cousin?"

Mrs. Jones patted her hand and then pulled her warm one away. "You'll have to ask your uncle about that, love," she said.

"But my uncle doesn't talk."

"Yes, well." A shadow bloomed in Mrs. Jones's eyes. "Your uncle is on the mend."

"From what?"

"Life." Mrs. Jones turned back to the cake on the counter. "Would you like another piece?"

Lenora had eaten every crumb on her plate, so she nodded. "Yes, please." Her manners, once again remembered. Mrs. Jones placed before her another large pink chunk.

"I'm afraid you may be somewhat lonely here," Mrs. Jones said, her words floating on a sigh. "It's a very quiet house. But there's a garden." Mrs. Jones bit her lip and looked at the floor. "It's overgrown, but perhaps we might convince your uncle to hire a gardener, as he did in the old days." She shook her head, as though clearing away an unwanted memory, before looking at Lenora with a smile that did not quite touch the corners of her eyes. "But you could explore the garden, as long as you remain in the yard." Mrs. Jones pointed to a third door that Lenora had not noticed in the kitchen. "That door leads straight to the garden."

The door had a small window cut out of it.

Mrs. Jones continued. "As your uncle said, the woods are forbidden. They are too dangerous and vast. Many children have been lost in the woods . . ." Her face took on a grayish tint, and she shook her head again. "We do not intend to send you to school, since the school year here is almost done, but you will go in September. I'm sure you'll make many friends there, and then it will not be quite so lonely here."

"Oh, I won't be here in September," Lenora said. It was almost a reflex now. "Mother and Father will come before then."

Mrs. Jones looked at her with eyes that seemed to weep without spilling any water. "We can always hope, love," she said. But her words lacked conviction, and Lenora felt her heart trip.

They lapsed into a heavy silence, where Lenora grasped desperately for words, for something to say that would fill the space. And finally she found them, the perfect ones: "My father is a hero."

"A hero?" Mrs. Jones smiled.

"A great hero." Lenora sat up a little straighter; she couldn't help it. She was proud of Father, all the lives he'd saved over the years. Surely that meant . . .

"Tell me," Mrs. Jones said.

"He saved people from fires. Many people. He would run into burning buildings and pull them out before they burned." Lenora found that once she started she could not stop.

"He sounds very much like a hero," Mrs. Jones said.

"He was never burned in a single fire. The mayor always said it was extraordinary." Lenora bit her lip and scraped the last bit of icing from her plate with her finger. "He survived this fire, too. I know it."

Mrs. Jones tilted her head, and, after a while, she said, "I see."

The words got caught in Lenora's chest. She couldn't breathe, and she certainly couldn't speak.

"I remember your father well," Mrs. Jones said.

Lenora found her voice. "You do?"

Mrs. Jones smiled, and this time it did reach all the way to the corners of her eyes. "I have been at Stonewall Manor for a long time."

"I would like to hear about my father's life here," Lenora said. "He never told us anything about it."

The shadow returned to Mrs. Jones's eyes, and Lenora was sorry for saying what she'd already mentioned—the truth that made Mrs. Jones angry and sad at the same time.

"No, I suppose he wouldn't have," Mrs. Jones said, which opened all kinds of additional questions in Lenora's mind, the loudest of which was: Why?

But Mrs. Jones said, "It is getting late. What time do you normally go to bed?"

"Eight thirty," Lenora said. She looked for a clock in the kitchen and found one hanging above the doorway leading to the dining room. It was a brass one full of gears crowding around the same white face of the other clocks she had seen in the entry. This clock, unlike those, worked. It was seven thirty.

"We have a little time, but not enough for stories," Mrs. Jones said. Lenora didn't believe her; she knew Mrs. Jones was merely avoiding the subject. "I could show you the library if you like. You could take a book to your room."

But Lenora felt so weary suddenly that she didn't know if she'd even be able to climb the stairs. If Father were here, he'd carry her. She yawned. "I'll explore tomorrow," she said. "I'm sure I'll find the library."

"As long as you steer clear of the east wing," Mrs. Jones said, without looking at her. "It's where your uncle works. He doesn't like to be disturbed." She cleared her throat. "And it is somewhat frightening in that wing." She raised her eyes to Lenora, amusement crackling in the blue pools. "All the ghost stories from Stonewall Manor have to do with the east wing."

"Ghosts?" Lenora said. She shivered. She had always hated ghost stories. And Stonewall Manor was so large and empty.

So was her room.

"Don't worry, love," Mrs. Jones said. "They're only stories. Now. Would you like me to walk you upstairs?"

Lenora almost said yes. But then she thought of the awkward good night that would happen at her door. Mother used to read to her and Rory and John and Charles. Father used to tuck them all in at night.

Her throat felt tight when she said, "I'll walk myself, as long as there are lights."

Mrs. Jones smiled. "There's a nightdress in the drawers by your bathroom. I hope it will be comfortable enough."

Lenora stood and began to move out the kitchen door that led to the hall. She had never seen a kitchen with three doors. Mother would have loved it.

"Don't forget to close your window before you go to bed," Mrs. Jones said before Lenora reached the door.

Lenora paused. "Why?"

"House rules," was all Mrs. Jones said, but Lenora knew there must be something more. There were so many secrets in this house. She hated secrets—all of them, good and bad. She would much rather know than be kept in the dark.

Lenora raced up the stairs, outrunning the monsters she imagined at the bottom. The voices of Rory, John, and Charles clambered up ahead and behind her.

But, of course, that was just her imagination.

She was all alone.

15

All through her first night at Stonewall Manor, Lenora tossed and turned. She saw visions of Mother and Father, of John, Charles, and Rory. She saw their happy, shining faces, lined up outside a house that looked very much like the one they had all lived in on Texas Avenue. John and Charles threw a baseball with Father out in the yard. Mother waved Rory inside so they could bake a pie together. She could see them through the window that looked out on the yard. The only one missing from the perfect family scene was Lenora. They did not appear to even notice her absence, and when she tried to reach them, she was barred by an invisible wall.

Somewhere around midnight, her dreams turned darker. She saw a shadow standing before her, beckoning her toward an expanse of black—endless and menacing. The shadow was shaped like Father—tall, thin, broad shoulders—but the shadow had no substantial form or face. All it said was, *Come, Lenora. Come find me.*

Father, she wanted to say, but in her dream she could not speak. Outside her dream, she could, however. And speak she did, without even knowing. "Father!" she cried, and her voice crumbled into jagged pieces as the sheets tangled around her legs.

Someone opened the door.

The family that finally caught him, after his travels all over the world and his mighty deceptions that made him decidedly richer and happier, lived in the house beyond these woods.

They strung him up like a criminal, the lowliest of death penalties, reserved for pirates and witches—neither of which described him—and left him to die.

April 19, 1947

I could hear the spirit calling. It disturbed me from my work last night, a whisper that slid in through the drafty doors of Stonewall Manor. I followed it upstairs and found it in her room. I could see it this time, a tendril of pearls snaking from the open window. We warned her to close the window, did we not? My niece did not heed our instructions; perhaps she did not believe it was necessary. And if she does not believe in such simple necessities, she will find herself endangered in a way that is even more tragic than the disaster in Texas City—because this tragedy, this disappearance of children, has lasted centuries.

My brother deserves better than that. I will not relinquish his child.

I reached Lenora's room before the voice could do its work. I slammed the window shut, cutting off its shimmering curl. It fell to the floor, a string of black ash, and then it disappeared before my eyes.

The things I have seen, what I have known, the experiences I have had with the woods and the evil within them—they would never believe me if I were to tell them everything. Sometimes I wonder if I am what they all think I am: mad with grief and sorrow that has never subsided in all these years. But everything I do has a purpose. I will prevail. I have nearly completed what I need to defeat the woods and what lives—lives? I do not know—inside.

If the power grows stronger, however . . . if it acquires another child, I fear I will not be able to overcome it. So I must keep Lenora safe, whatever the cost. I must keep her unmarked, untouched, unentangled by the woods. If I do not, it will destroy us all. I cannot explain how I know this; perhaps the knowing is passed down, generation to generation. Perhaps it is connected to the walls of Stonewall Manor. There were other Coles who knew many unexplainable things as well. It flows through our blood.

When I emerged from Lenora's room this evening, after hours of watching, waiting, ensuring the silver snake did not return, I opened the door across from it, the one that is kept for my son. I imagined him, asleep in the bed. I could hear him breathing.

He may never return.

But I must, at least, try.

—excerpt from Richard Cole's *Journal of Scientific Progress*

QUESTIONS AND
MORE QUESTIONS

16

The house was thick with shadows when Lenora rose and opened her door. The hallway did not have lights, or at least not any that were currently turned on. Lenora would have to say something to Mrs. Jones; she hated darkness—had always hated darkness because of the things that lived inside it: monsters and all manner of frightful things. And her dream still hung over her. A shadow man? She shivered.

Darkness would be bearable if Rory were here with her, or John and Charles in the room across the hall. She looked at the blue-green door. It was partially open, a dim light reaching out from inside it.

That was different. Yesterday it had been closed and locked, or so she'd assumed. Was someone inside? Had someone come to visit?

Lenora gripped her doorframe, took a deep breath,

glanced at the dark hallway (to make sure, one more time, there was no shadow man anywhere near her), and raced across it. She hesitated at the blue-green door. Mrs. Jones said no other children lived here. Why was the door open, then?

Her spine tingled. Was the shadow man inside? Was it better to know or not know?

She decided it was better to know. She pushed through the door (it whined the whole way, which made Lenora cringe) and stepped into the room.

It was empty.

Lenora looked around. The room was almost identical to hers, except that the walls were painted the color of a morning sky, and the bedcovers were a silken gold. But what pulled her deeper into the room was a tree painted in the corner, its branches filling the entire wall and curling onto the ceiling.

Hanging from the tree—from the ceiling, really—was a wooden swing.

Lenora had never seen a swing inside a house. She had never seen a room large enough to hold one. She ran her fingers along its smooth wooden seat. The rough rope pricked her fingers when she closed her hand around it. She sat on the rectangle of wood— could not really help it. It was a swing!

She applied her weight in slow doses, unsure this was a swing intended for actual use and not just decoration. Could one really trust a swing hanging from a ceiling? But when she braved lifting her feet, the swing held. She marveled.

The swing groaned when Lenora pumped her legs. She skittered to a stop. But she could not stay still for long. The swing groaned again, but she continued to pump. She did not go high, but she did close her eyes. The golden light of the morning, splashing through two windows with drapes pulled back and secured behind copper balls, warmed her face.

How wonderful it must have been to have a swing inside your room. Whose room was this?

Lenora's stockings slid against the floor as she tried to stop. It took her three tries and a bit of a jump, which made a thumping sound on the wooden floor. She had missed the rug. She smiled at herself and patted the seat of the swing.

She walked around the perimeter of the room, where drawings of different birds hung on the walls. They were very good. She touched each one in turn and then opened the chest of drawers beside the bed. Clothes were nestled inside. She peered into the standing chest. More clothes hung from wire hangers—pressed pants and vests that looked like the one her uncle had worn yesterday, only in brighter colors like periwinkle and scarlet and marigold. They smelled of dust and age but were still soft to the touch.

A boy had lived here. Where was he now?

Lenora ventured into the bathroom, where more drawings—these of strange animals and plants, unlike anything she had ever seen—hung on the walls, colored with perfect precision, as though someone had taken great care and detail with them.

She knew it would not do to stay in this room; if Mrs. Jones came looking, Lenora might get in trouble. Mrs. Jones might lock up the room again, and Lenora would not be able to come back.

She wanted to come back.

So Lenora stood in the doorway and examined the

darkness of the hall one more time. She peered into the black, checking for shadows. She looked at the winding stairs. There were so many.

But she could do it.

She ran, as fast as she possibly could, clutching the stair rail so her stockinged feet did not betray her and hand her to the shadow man of her dreams, whom she knew was right behind her.

Halfway down, she hoisted herself onto the rail and rode it to the bottom.

17

It seemed the house was still sleeping. All was silent when Lenora reached the bottom floor, her heart pounding, her breath coming in puffs. She composed herself and straightened. She had not changed from her dressing gown, which meant she'd have to brave the stairs and that dark hallway again.

She grimaced up at the top floor. She would make Mrs. Jones come with her this time. She would make sure there were lights, at the very least.

Downstairs the rooms were much brighter than the hallway upstairs, so Lenora's terror diminished but did not completely disappear. Stonewall Manor was not a bright and joyful place; it was made of stone and gloom. How could it be anything but a little frightful?

Since no one seemed to be around, Lenora began poking around. She opened the doors of rooms she had not been shown yesterday. There was a sitting room with yellowing furniture—perhaps it had once been white?—covered in some kind of plastic. There was another dining room, larger even than the one she and Uncle Richard had used last night. Lenora shook her head. Why had Father never brought them here? They could have had raucous family suppers around this table.

Was Uncle Richard really that bad? As far as she could tell, he was only slightly strange, but that could be forgiven, couldn't it?

What had happened in this house to drive Father away so completely?

Inside another sitting room, which was smaller than the first one she'd seen, Lenora moved toward a lamp, but it did not turn on when she pulled its chain. So she drew back the heavy curtains that covered one of the windows so she could better see the room. Light brown furniture occupied every corner, including a chair trimmed with gold—it looked almost like a throne. Lenora sat down on it, a puff of dust rising up and clinging to her nose. She coughed and stood.

So many unused rooms. It was a pity.

The next room she discovered was darker than all the rest. She switched on a light—this one worked—and gasped.

It was the library. The shelves reached all the way to the ceiling. A ladder with wheels was positioned at one end, as though someone had only just finished every book in the library or, perhaps, had just begun. Lenora gazed at the spectacular sight. She would never be able to read this many books in a lifetime.

John would have practically lived in this room—in fact, he might have claimed it for his bedroom. The thought made her stomach hurt.

She told herself it was hunger, not grief. John was alive. He would come soon. He would see this library, and he would disappear in it.

Lenora crossed the room to some heavy velvet drapes and tucked them behind a brass ball that jutted out from the wall. The morning light was soothing and soft. The furniture in the room was a deep red color that matched the drapes, and a carpet of dark brown with gold flourishes pressed in it unfolded in the center of the room. Lenora walked along the shelves, her hands touching titles she'd never even heard of. She was almost halfway around the room before she discovered one that sounded familiar, one that John would have spotted almost immediately.

The Origin of Species. He had always loved this book, though Mother and Father made sure to instill in him faith. Darwin, they had said, was known as a skeptic of God and all things spiritual. They didn't want John to become the same. Lenora smiled at the memory. John was the most zealous of them all. He hurried them into the car every Sunday morning, and when service finished he would play energetic hymns—which seemed a paradox but was never such in her family—on the family piano for at least an hour after lunch. He called it "The Gospel Hour, with John Cole."

What day was it? Had Sunday come and gone?

A piano was something Lenora had not yet seen inside Stonewall Manor. And surely a house this fine had a professional piano, maybe even one of those grand pianos. It would give her something to do. She had always hated practicing, but she would do it now—willingly and without complaint, which had never happened at home. By the time Mother and Father came to pick her up, she would have more songs memorized than Rory, who was the real musician in the family.

Lenora moved her fingers, as though playing a piano made of air. She closed her eyes and tilted her head back.

"I see you have found the library."

Lenora jumped, her eyes popping back open. Uncle Richard stood in the doorway. They were the first words he'd said directly to her since she'd entered Stonewall Manor as its guest.

"It is . . ." Lenora paused. "So grand."

Uncle Richard's lips twitched, and Lenora wondered if he might smile. But all he said was, "Help yourself."

He was about to turn away when Lenora said, "Uncle?"

He stared at the floor for a minute before tilting his face back to her. He straightened, his chin lifting. His eyes met hers, looked away, met hers again, and settled on the window. She almost turned around to see what had caught his attention, but instead she said,

"I wondered if you had a piano."

Uncle Richard's eyes slid back to hers. He looked at her for a very long time, and she wondered if he had gone into one of his Other World Fits, which was a name for his condition that she had come up with last night, while racing up the stairs to her room. She was not close enough to see if his eyes had glazed and were lost to what lived in front of him. It surprised her when he said, "A piano." His left hand tapped his thigh.

"I would like to play a little, if that is all right," Lenora said. "So I don't fall behind."

Uncle Richard nodded. "Yes." His voice was softer than she had ever heard it. He cleared his throat. "There is a piano in the ballroom."

A ballroom. Lenora could not believe this house.

Uncle Richard said, "Tell Mrs. Jones I said to show you the piano." He cleared his throat again—or was it a grunt?—and tapped his cane on the floor once. "It has not been played in too long. It might need tuning. I'll see to that." He turned to go, then paused. His head bowed, lifted, turned back to Lenora. "It will be good to hear music again."

Lenora had not heard her uncle speak so many words in the short time she had known him. She liked the sound of his voice. If she closed her eyes, she could imagine it was Father talking to her. But Uncle Richard did not speak again, and when she opened her eyes, he was gone.

18

Lenora took only one wrong turn on her way into the kitchen. She met a dead end and turned around to retrace her steps. She planned to explore more of the manor later today or tomorrow, but for now, she was much too hungry.

Mrs. Jones was moving about in the kitchen, her steps making a squishing sound on the floor tile. She scraped a pan and bent to retrieve something from the icebox. The kitchen smelled delightful—like sugar and cinnamon and other spices. Lenora's stomach rumbled loudly enough for Mrs. Jones to hear.

She turned to Lenora with a wide smile on her face. "Good morning, love," she said. "I hope you slept well."

Lenora nodded and crossed the kitchen to peer into the pan Mrs. Jones held. Cinnamon rolls. How did Mrs. Jones know this was her favorite breakfast in the entire world? Mother didn't cook them often; she said cinnamon rolls were not a sufficient breakfast. Lenora's chest squeezed.

Was it betrayal to eat cinnamon rolls when Mother had hated this kind of breakfast?

"Sit down, love," Mrs. Jones said. "I'll make you a plate. Would you like eggs and bacon as well?"

She thought Mother would be pleased with that, so Lenora nodded. She would have cinnamon rolls *and* eggs and bacon. A hearty breakfast with a side of treat.

The cinnamon roll took up half the plate. Lenora smiled.

"Have you seen your uncle this morning?" Mrs. Jones said. "He was up and about earlier."

"He found me in the library."

"You found the library, then?"

"It is . . ." She couldn't think of a word to describe it.

Mrs. Jones looked up from washing a pan. "It's a wonder, isn't it." It was not a question. "That library has been collecting books for centuries."

"I don't think my town library had so many books."

Mrs. Jones chuckled. "Yes, well, the Coles have always been readers."

After a few moments of silence, during which Mrs. Jones finished washing the pan and wiped the stove top and a place inside the icebox (she was very efficient at her cleaning; Lenora had always hated cleaning the kitchen the most), Lenora said, "Uncle Richard said there is a piano in the ballroom."

Mrs. Jones stiffened. She waited several seconds before turning around. When she did, her eyes were glassy. "It's a magnificent piano."

"He said you might show me where it is."

"After breakfast, I would be glad to," Mrs. Jones said, but Lenora caught a flash of something in her eyes that she couldn't decipher. Worry mixed with hope, perhaps. Or perhaps Lenora had simply imagined it. Mother always said she had an overactive imagination; it was how she explained Lenora's fear of the dark.

"I had a strange dream last night," Lenora said. She said it to fill the space, to fill the room, to fill the hollow in her chest. It was something she would have told Mother or Father, if they were here. It was something they would have discussed.

Mrs. Jones wiped her hands on her apron. "What kind of dream?"

She seemed interested, so Lenora continued. "A shadow man was calling to me," she said. "He looked a little like Father." Her voice cracked on his name. Did Father visiting her dreams mean that he had died?

No. It couldn't.

Mrs. Jones pressed her lips in a thin line and cleared her throat. Lenora wondered why her hands trembled as she folded them together. "Did you close your window last night?" Mrs. Jones said, her voice higher than it was before.

Lenora tilted her head. "I don't remember. It was closed when I woke up." She was sure of this, at least. The room had been much too stuffy for the window to have been open.

Mrs. Jones nodded. "Be sure to close your window every evening before you sleep."

"Why?" Though Lenora had already asked this question, Mrs. Jones had not answered it satisfactorily.

So she thought she'd try again; this tactic worked often with Father. Never with Mother.

Mrs. Jones's eyes narrowed briefly—so briefly Lenora might have missed it if she hadn't been already looking. The space between the cook—housekeeper? Lenora wasn't sure what to call her—and Lenora lengthened, a long silence swelling as Mrs. Jones appeared to consider whether to answer or hold back. She opened her mouth and closed it again, opened it, closed it. Finally she said, "It is your uncle's rule. You must ask him about it." She turned back to the sink and stared out the window toward the woods.

Lenora's insides burned.

19

Lenora scraped her entire plate clean.

"You eat like your cousin Bobby," Mrs. Jones said. She sat down in the chair opposite Lenora.

"The eggs were delicious." Lenora meant the words. They were so fluffy they were like greasy, salty clouds in her mouth. She wished there were more, but she wouldn't say so. She was a guest here; she didn't want to inconvenience her uncle.

After a minute, Lenora said, "I found Bobby's room this morning." She wasn't entirely sure it was Bobby's room, but it was her educated guess. How many other boys would have lived in that room, with suits that looked very much like Uncle Richard's?

"Did you?" Mrs. Jones's face took on a faraway look.

"It was the most wonderful room," Lenora said. "There were pictures of birds on the walls and a swing hanging from the ceiling."

"Oh yes," Mrs. Jones said. "I forgot about that swing. Bobby would use it when he was working out some problem. Science, math, even an English composition." Mrs. Jones gestured toward her head. "He said it got his brain working again."

Lenora could understand. Swinging inside a house felt exhilarating.

"I wish I had known him," she said.

"He was a good boy." Mrs. Jones blinked hard.

"What happened to him?" Lenora could not help the question. She needed to know. She could see by the look on Mrs. Jones's face that it was something dangerous, something tragic. Shouldn't she be warned?

Mrs. Jones shook her head. "We don't talk about Bobby in this home."

"But why not?" A chill skipped over her skin, slid down her throat, and dropped all the way to her belly. Was Bobby being hidden somewhere? Was he tortured? A scientific experiment?

Had Lenora stepped into one of those old terrifying stories about children who were born with problems and hidden away from the public, locked behind a door so they were not seen? Was Stonewall Manor a more dangerous place than she had at first thought? Is that why Father had stayed away?

But there was Mrs. Jones, sitting in front of her. Mrs. Jones, with her kind blue eyes and her gentle touch and her warm words. Stonewall Manor could not be a dangerous place with such a person living in it.

Could it?

Mrs. Jones leaned back in her chair and folded her arms across her chest. Her lips twitched, like words were piling up behind their wall. At last she said, "He is no longer here."

"You mean he died?" If Bobby had died, that meant Uncle Richard had lost two children. He had lost his entire family, like her.

No, not like her. She would not believe it.

"You ask so many questions," Mrs. Jones said. Her voice held amusement, though, not annoyance. "They are better answered by your uncle."

"But my uncle is never around."

"Then I suppose you will have to dig it up for

yourself." Mrs. Jones winked, and Lenora could see that her old humor had returned.

"And how would I do that?" Lenora said.

"I might try the library." Mrs. Jones stood up and took Lenora's plate from the table, rinsed it, and once again wiped her hands on her apron. "Ready to see the ballroom now?"

Lenora held up a finger. "One more question," she said.

Mrs. Jones raised an eyebrow. Lenora had always been impressed when people could do that. Rory could. Lenora had tried and tried and tried, but no matter how many times she practiced, her eyebrows were connected. One would not raise without the other.

"Why did my father leave Stonewall Manor?" If Mrs. Jones would just answer this one burning question, she wouldn't ask so many in the future.

Well, that was likely not true.

"Why, indeed." Mrs. Jones let out a long breath.

"He never told us," Lenora said. "He never told us anything."

"Hmm." Mrs. Jones shook her head.

"Stonewall Manor would have been large enough to hold us all." Lenora could not stop the flow of words. "We would have had more than enough space for everyone."

"You were not comfortable in Texas City?"

"Our house was very small. And there were six of us. Stonewall Manor would have been . . ." Lenora stopped, folded up the words she would have said, and unfolded the ones she needed to say instead. "Stonewall Manor would be a perfect place for all of us. Do you think . . ."

She could not finish the question, could not bear to see the look Mrs. Jones might cast upon her. Still hoping they were alive. Still hoping they would come. Still hoping she was not alone in the world.

When she looked back up at Mrs. Jones, the woman's eyes were a liquid blue. "Your father." She hesitated, as though choosing her words carefully. "Your father was a man of faith." Lenora sat up straighter. Would she tell her, then? "Your uncle is a man of science. Reason, he calls it."

"But why does that matter?" It didn't matter at all. John liked science, too.

Mrs. Jones chuckled. "You would be surprised how faith and science can alienate men."

"But they were brothers," Lenora said. "Didn't it mean something that they were brothers? They weren't just men, disagreeing. Family *means* something." Lenora had to force the words through her clogged throat. What had she done on the day of the disaster? Disagreed with Rory. Hated her? Perhaps. For a moment in time. A moment that meant everything, it turned out.

"Of course it meant something that they were brothers." Mrs. Jones was still speaking. Lenora leaned forward. "They tried very hard to work out their differences. But, in the end, they both decided they could not live under the same roof any longer. And your father left."

"But why not Uncle Richard?"

"Your uncle is the eldest. This home belongs to him."

"So Uncle Richard told my father he couldn't live here?" Heat flushed through Lenora's body. If they hadn't lived in Texas City, Father wouldn't have . . .

Lenora gave her head a violent shake. She gritted her teeth.

"It wasn't Richard who kept your father away," Mrs. Jones said. "Your father didn't want to live here. In fact, he tried to get your uncle to leave as well."

"Why?" It didn't make sense.

Mrs. Jones shrugged. "I don't know the kinds of conversations they had back then. I only know the one they had the day your father left. I'm surprised the town didn't hear it, to tell the truth."

"They were angry?"

Mrs. Jones's mouth turned up, then down, at the corners. "So angry."

"Because Uncle Richard wanted Father to stay?"

"Because Richard didn't want him to run away."

"Run away from what?"

Mrs. Jones shook her head. "I don't know. Something in the woods." Her eyebrows lowered and she pressed her hands together. "Something your father believed in but your uncle did not."

"Father never talked about Stonewall Manor or the woods or Uncle Richard." Lenora still could not understand this part. Even if Father had fought so passionately with Uncle Richard, they should have known about this place, about these people.

"Never underestimate fundamental differences of opinion between men," Mrs. Jones said. "It has torn many apart."

"But they were brothers," Lenora said.

"Yes, well . . ." Mrs. Jones shook her head but said nothing more until: "I always thought they'd find each other again."

Lenora looked at Mrs. Jones's face, saw the sorrow stretched across it, felt the stab in her chest. "They will," she said, but the words were flimsy and weak.

Mrs. Jones lifted her head and stared at Lenora, stared through Lenora, stared into a future that Lenora could not see.

"Mrs. Jones."

Lenora looked toward the doorway leading out into the entrance hall of Stonewall Manor. Uncle Richard stood with his cane, clad in a brown suit today that made him appear very distinguished and handsome. He held a leather satchel at his side. It had many buckles and strange bulges that looked like they might be hidden compartments. He was looking only at Lenora. "I trust you are keeping an eye on my niece?" The words seemed to hold a warning of some kind or another. Lenora felt a cold breath creep over her.

"Yes, sir," Mrs. Jones said. "We have just finished breakfast and I was about to take her to see the piano."

"Good, good." Uncle Richard grunted. He shifted, his cane tapping the ground three times. "I'm off to gather some samples." His dark eyebrows furrowed on his forehead, then smoothed again. He tilted his head, his eyes flashing a silent message to Mrs. Jones that Lenora wished for all the world she could understand. Was it about Father or Mother or her sister or brothers? Was it about his son?

Was it about imprisonment?

Lenora shuddered.

Mrs. Jones said, "Yes, sir," and Uncle Richard was gone.

"Where is he collecting samples?" Lenora said.

Mrs. Jones ignored the question. "I'll show you the piano, love. It will entertain you for a time."

Lenora wondered if that was an observation or an order.

20

The piano had some flat notes, and several of the keys stuck when she pushed them down. Lenora could tell it had not been used in some time. She tried her best to play every song she remembered Rory banging out on their small piano at home, but she was not nearly as talented as her sister—nor did she remember music all that well—and after a time, she let her hands fall into her lap and, instead, gazed around the spacious ballroom.

It was unlike any room she had ever seen. The only place she had seen anything close to something as grand as this was the old theater in Texas City, but even that did not compare. The ballroom sat near the east wing, where her uncle both lived and worked, Mrs. Jones had said on the way in. A maze of empty rooms—to be used for what? Lenora could not even imagine—led to it, so many that Lenora did not know if she would be able to find her way back out. The thought of getting lost in these spooky corridors—the ones Mrs. Jones had mentioned in the same sentence as "ghosts"—made her heart gallop and stumble.

The shiny black grand piano—it was a grand; Rory would have loved it—faced another stairway, this one straight and wide and carpeted in a deep bronze color. Lenora wondered if it led to Uncle Richard's wing. Mrs. Jones had not warned her away from it. Curiosity was much too persistent to ignore. She would explore it soon; she was not finished with this ballroom yet.

A large wooden rectangular balcony ringed the room. The ceiling was domed, with tall brown pillars reaching down from the sides, producing archways that would have made Mother smile. Mother loved the arches in the theater. She said they made a room seem like it was part of a castle, and Lenora had to agree.

A sparkling chandelier hung above the center of the room, casting the floor in diamond light. Lenora could imagine the men and women dancing merrily, music bouncing against the stone walls, laughter filling up the corners. Had there ever been a ball when her father lived here? Did Uncle Richard ever host one?

Perhaps they could plan one when her family returned. A celebratory evening of music and dance.

Lenora pushed away from the piano, the bench shrieking against the floor. She placed a hand on the wall. It was smooth and cold. It must be real stone, and perhaps it was why this home was called Stonewall Manor; that was a question Mrs. Jones would likely answer. It was safe.

If the walls were made of stone, the manor would stand forever. Even an explosion like the one that had destroyed Texas City would not level it.

They would all be safe here.

She would convince Father to let them stay.

There was only one window in the ballroom, and a moving shadow outside of it caught Lenora's eye. She crossed the room quickly and peered out. The pane was dusty, but she wiped the film away. Her uncle was walking out of the woods—the woods he had told her were forbidden. Dangerous.

Then why had he entered them?

She watched as he walked. He leaned heavily on his cane. He was dressed in peculiar gold and copper armor, buckled at his chest, along his right arm, and around his belly. He wore a dark top hat with what looked like thick glasses—one of the lenses was completely covered in a brass layer—perching on the brim of it.

He held something in his left hand, the one that was clad in a metallic armor, but from where she was standing, Lenora could not see what it was.

Uncle Richard turned his face toward the window, and without a moment's hesitation, Lenora flattened herself against the wall. She could not say why she didn't want Uncle Richard to see her staring at him; she simply didn't.

She bit her bottom lip and waited, and when the cold feeling left her chest, she peered out once more. Uncle Richard had stopped in front of a black iron gate. Lenora thought it might be an entrance to something—a garden, perhaps. The stone walls around it blocked her view.

Uncle Richard glanced toward the woods and placed his hand on the black iron gate in front of him. He dropped his head to his chest, lifted it, and turned back in her direction. Lenora flattened against the wall again, but not before she saw on his face the shine of tears.

Lenora breathed, but only barely.

21

Lenora heard Uncle Richard enter the house; there must be a door near the ballroom. Of course there was a door; how else would guests get inside?

She thought that he might like to hear some music, so she sat down at the piano and played a few notes, stopped, then started again. She felt his presence behind her, and her hands fluttered to a stop. She swiveled on the bench.

"The piano still plays," he said. He blinked his eyes rapidly. "How is it, then?"

"A little flat," Lenora said. "Some of the keys stick."

"I'll have the piano tuner come out. We'll get it fixed." He seemed to be about to leave again, as he always did when he had nothing more to say or no interest in what she was doing, but then he surprised her. He entered the room.

"You like to play piano?" he said.

"My sister was much better," Lenora said.

"Rory." Lenora was surprised that Uncle Richard knew her sister's name.

"Yes." Her voice was thick.

"Do you like to play piano?" He asked the question again; she had not answered it the first time.

Lenora thought about how to answer. What did she like to do? John was the gifted reader, although Lenora loved books, too. Rory was the pianist; Lenora played as well. Charles could figure out any math problem in the world; she had always been proficient at math, too.

Lenora tinkered—with science, with math, with music, with books.

Uncle Richard spoke again. "I could get you a teacher."

"I enjoy building things," Lenora said. "Science." She hoped that by saying this her uncle would consider letting her see his lab.

But all he did was grunt and turn away. His cane thumped against the floor.

So he was done talking, then.

"Uncle?"

At the door, Uncle Richard looked back.

"Does Stonewall Manor have a garden?" She already knew the answer, and she didn't care much one way or another. She simply wanted something more to say. She wanted to keep him here, for a moment or two. Forever, maybe.

He looked and sounded so much like Father.

"Yes," Uncle Richard said. "There is a large garden." He paused. "It's been some time since someone tended it." His voice bent but did not break.

"Am I allowed to tend it?"

Uncle Richard's hand reached out for the doorway, and his back hunched. His cane slid an inch or two, as though he were knocked off-balance.

Lenora's cheeks flamed. She hadn't meant to sadden him.

A long pause folded around her words, and then Uncle Richard said, "Yes, of course" and nothing more.

Lenora was left alone again.

22

After she had changed out of her dressing gown (Mrs. Jones walked her up to her room so Lenora didn't have to brave the darkness alone; the lights in the upstairs hallway had no bulbs in them, Mrs. Jones said), eaten her lunch of leftover tuna (it was just as good the second day), and penned a letter to Emma and Dr. Sparks (she would not give up on her family, and perhaps writing to someone directly would remind them that she was still waiting; she also wondered about Emma: Had she survived?), Lenora ventured outdoors. The gate where she had seen Uncle Richard pause was not locked, but it wailed mightily as she opened it. A bird mimicked the sound, and Lenora smiled. It was good to hear mockingbirds so far from home.

The day was bright and cheerful, with not a cloud in the vivid blue sky. The sun beamed down on her, burning through her new blue dress. She smoothed her skirt around her and stared at her shoes. Mother had never liked it when she dirtied her dresses, but Lenora had never seemed able to avoid it. She would, though. She would do it for Mother. Today. Now.

Lenora looked around the garden. It did not resemble a garden at all. There was no order to it, only large, tall weeds waving in the soft breeze that whispered around her. She pulled a few at her feet. They came out easily, as though someone had recently watered the ground, but they dropped dirt from their twisted roots onto her shoes. She sighed. She slipped off her shoes and placed them beneath the shade of one of four trees that stood in the garden, where every now and then she would rest after working her way through the rows, one by one, pulling weeds wherever she could find them.

Mother had kept a tidy flower garden around their home in Texas City. Lenora sat back on her heels, her dress puffed up around her, and plunged her hands into the dirt. She closed her eyes and imagined she could hear Mother's voice singing; she always sang when she worked in her garden.

How she missed Mother. She could see her thin back, curved and soft. She could see her golden-brown hair falling in short curls around her neck. She could see the straw hat Mother always wore when she went outdoors, to shade her shoulders and protect her face. But when Lenora tried to see her mother's face, it was smudged at the edges.

The breath left her lungs.

No. She could not forget. She could not forget them.

The sun now felt unbearably hot. Lenora stood and brushed the dirt from the bottom of her dress. She moved to the shade of the tree, where it was much cooler. She rested her back against the bark and slid down to the ground, one hand resting on the pearls she had cleaned and clasped around her neck today. Her other hand covered her mouth, trying to keep the sobs at bay.

"Mother," she whispered. "Please come home."

Would she ever know the safety and security—the love—of a family again?

23

After a time—minutes, hours, she could not be sure—
Lenora stood again. She felt exhausted, drained by
the heat or despair, or perhaps both. She turned back
toward Stonewall Manor and studied the windows that
faced the garden. She tried to find the ballroom, but
there were too many windows; she didn't know one
from the other.

Drapes covered all the windows—except for one side
of the house that she assumed was the east wing.

Her uncle's wing.

In that one window stood her uncle, staring out at
her with an unreadable look. He appeared evil in that
light, and it sent a cold bead of ice down Lenora's back.
But then his expression changed, and the sun caught
on the window, and she saw his face ignite with pain
and sorrow and hope and wonder, all that was both

terrible and exquisite about life. It was so unexpected that Lenora nearly cried out.

Her hand flinched into a wave, involuntarily. Uncle Richard did not wave back but continued to stare for a moment more, before turning from the window and loosening the drapes so they fell in front of the glass, concealing whatever he was doing inside.

Lenora felt her breakfast gathering in her throat and swallowed it back down. She looked at the garden, still overgrown but appearing, at least, to have some semblance of order now. She had done quite a bit of work. She thought of Charles, who would have loved running through a garden as spacious as this. She thought of John, who would know the scientific name of every plant the garden grew—even the weeds. She thought of Rory, who would have joined Mother in song. She thought of Father, who would have watched them all with a pleasure that painted a permanent smile in his eyes.

She rubbed her chest. Everywhere she looked, she could see them. It was so painful. They belonged here. They belonged with her.

"Please," she said to the wind. "Please come home."

And the wind whistled. She tilted her head, listening. Was it saying something? Did it have a message that she must hear? She held her breath, closed her eyes. But it was only wind without words. It cooled the sweat on her back. She drew in a deep breath, the rich smell of dirt and green clogging her nose in a way that was almost comforting. It smelled like home.

She stood there, breathing, listening, imagining, until Mrs. Jones's voice called to her. Lenora turned. Mrs. Jones stood at the iron gate, her chin resting on the top. "Oh my," she said. "You've done some work today, love."

Lenora tried to smile at her, but her cheeks felt too tight. "The garden could be lovely," she said, her voice flat and soft.

"It used to be," Mrs. Jones said. "Bobby was the gardener around here. He . . ." She looked stricken, as though she had not intended to say what she'd said.

"Bobby tended the garden?" Was that why Uncle Richard had looked the way he did?

"I'll fetch a bag to put all those weeds in," Mrs.

Jones said, hurrying away. She called over her shoulder. "Weeds are persistent things. They'll grow right where you lay them."

****

The two of them gathered all the weeds Lenora had pulled and stuffed them in a paper bag that Mrs. Jones carried behind the house, toward a circle of stones that formed a firepit. Lenora stared at the pit, black dust lining its bottom, and a surge of sadness barreled into her chest, her throat, her eyes. She choked. Mrs. Jones looked at her. "Are you all right, love?" And when Lenora could not answer, Mrs. Jones's eyes widened. "Oh," was all she said. Her voice came from a tunnel, and Lenora felt the woman's arms around her.

She could smell it, hear it, taste it. The black dust on her hands. The sizzling of electrical lines. The sulfur on her tongue. The people. Mother, Father, Rory, John, Charles.

Her legs would not move. She fell right where she was standing, and when she woke again, she was in

Uncle Richard's arms, her head bobbing against his chest. He smelled of peppermint and a faint hint of copper.

The voices were a blur.

"Get her a sleeping tonic."—*Uncle Richard's voice.*

"Yes, sir."—*Mrs. Jones.*

Someone stroking her hair. "There is nothing to be afraid of, darling. I'll protect you."—*her uncle.* Or was it her father?

"Here you go, love."—*Mrs. Jones.*

The gaps between the voices were jagged and confusing.

"Sleep, Lenora. I am here."—*her uncle.*

It was the loveliest dream.

He did not remain dead. He won in the end.

He had the woods.

And what wondrous woods they were.

April 20, 1947

It has been some time since I have spent a night away from my work. But it was necessary, as my niece has had a very harrowing experience—not with the woods, thankfully, but with my firepit. I imagine that when Texas City exploded, she saw many things a child should never see. Her face was very pale when Mrs. Jones summoned me last evening, an agony that felt much too familiar playing across her eyes and cheeks and mouth.

There is much I do not want her to know about the true magnitude of the disaster that took her family from her (from me, too?). I have carefully hidden the newspapers, sworn Mrs. Jones to secrecy, and avoided her when I could manage it.

Sorrow is a snare.

And yet she found her despair in a firepit. I can, I suppose, understand. I find my despair everywhere in this house. I find it in her room, where my daughter should be sleeping. I find it across the west wing hall, where my son should be sleeping. I find it in my own bedchambers, the mattress sagging on one side and perfectly rigid on the other, where my wife should be sleeping.

My work calls to me, and yet I cannot leave my niece's side.

Sometime around midnight, I saw the shimmering streak—much thicker than it was last night—slithering right toward my niece's window. But I had closed the window. I made sure of it, and when the silvery strand reached the pane, it did not penetrate it. It spread out into fingers, a palm, a hand belonging to someone or something unknown, from the bowels of the woods. The ghostly hand rested there, and when it finally peeled fingers from the glass, a message remained in its stead. A glittering message for Lenora. It said, <u>Come to your family, child.</u>

And now I believe the dark power in these woods is unlike any I have ever encountered in my studies—in my life. The stories I have found hidden in my library, the stories I could, myself, tell, the stories these townspeople know nothing about and would never believe, speak of the origins and the life of a man condemned and hung in these woods centuries ago. A man—dead and yet not quite—who remains.

There is no science that can explain this presence. There is no empirical formula that can distill it to its essence. There is no mathematical equation that can predict its makeup or its purpose or its strength. It is a dark and mysterious presence, preying on the sorrow in Stonewall Manor. And there is certainly enough sorrow to sustain it. There has always been enough sorrow.

Eliminating the sorrow of the hearts within these walls is not the answer.

My army is the answer. I itch to return to my work, to make the necessary adjustments, to see my vision fulfilled.

In the earliest light of the morning, I will return to my lab, to my life's greatest scientific work, gleaming like a promise, I imagine, in the rays that will pierce the window looking out on the woods.

The spirit will not have us.

—excerpt from Richard Cole's *Journal of Scientific Progress*

THE MADMAN
WALKS

24

Lenora was alone when she woke. The room was stuffy, but not unbearably so. She knew, without looking, that her window was closed. The curtains were open, though, and sunlight splashed into the room. She blinked.

A knock sounded on the door, and Mrs. Jones entered with a tray. She was smiling. "I thought you might like to eat breakfast in your room."

"How did you know I was awake?" Lenora's mouth felt thick. She was terribly thirsty.

"It's after ten in the morning. I thought I'd at least try." Mrs. Jones crossed the room and set the tray down on Lenora's lap.

"Where is Uncle Richard?" Lenora hoped she hadn't imagined him in her room last night; the loneliness was the most terrible thing about Stonewall Manor. She would never get used to it.

A shadow swept across Mrs. Jones's face. "He's in his laboratory," she said. She fiddled with the curtains. "Already at work."

"He didn't even come to see me."

Mrs. Jones turned, her eyebrows low. "He was here all night, love."

The words bloomed in Lenora's throat, and she looked down at her tray. It was blurry, but she could smell the muffin—blueberry, she thought. When her eyes cleared, she could see that she was right.

Mrs. Jones stared out the window. "It's a beautiful day," she said. "We were supposed to take a trip to town, but after yesterday . . ." Her voice trailed off, and her back bent, just a little.

"The firepit," Lenora said. She had trouble squeezing out the words around the large lump in her throat. She swallowed. It remained.

"Yes." Mrs. Jones turned from the window. "I'm sorry, love. I wasn't thinking—"

"I don't know why I . . ." Lenora felt her words shake and crumble. Mrs. Jones was at her side in a moment.

"You've had a terrible ordeal," she said, smoothing Lenora's hair. Lenora nodded. "I should have known better than to take you there."

"The ashes," Lenora said. "The dust."

Mrs. Jones kept smoothing her hair.

Lenora said, "It just surprised me."

"You'll never have to see it again," Mrs. Jones said. "Your uncle is moving it off the grounds. Someone else will take care of burning waste from now on."

Lenora shook her head. "That's not necessary." Getting rid of the firepit? For her?

Mrs. Jones waved a hand. "Your uncle was very distraught about your reaction."

"I'm sorry." The words were automatic. "I didn't mean to cause any trouble."

"It wasn't your fault, love." Mrs. Jones stroked her cheek, let her hand fall, pushed the tray forward. "I know you're hungry. See if you can eat." She moved toward the door.

"Will you stay with me?" Lenora said. "It is very lonely up here."

Mrs. Jones turned and looked at Lenora, her mouth slightly open. She glanced around the room, at the bed, at Lenora. She nodded. "Yes, of course."

She sat in the wing chair Lenora thought her uncle had sat in last night.

Lenora ate mostly in silence, with Mrs. Jones commenting every now and again about the weather ("It's been a very sunny spring this year.") and the heat ("Sometimes it can feel like you're in an oven out here in Nacogdoches.") and what Lenora planned to do today ("Perhaps you'd like to rest up in the library. A good book does wonders for the mind and body.").

What she really wanted to do was visit her uncle's laboratory. But she dared not ask.

The blueberry muffin was sweet and moist. She was glad there were two on her tray.

Maybe, while she was here, she should learn how to cook. But that didn't appeal to her at all; she'd never liked cooking, even when Mother made her stand in the kitchen and watch. This year—her twelfth year—would have been the year Lenora had to plan a whole supper and execute it herself. She had been dreading it.

She would give anything for the responsibility now, if it meant she could be home, with her family.

But what good did wishing do?

25

Mrs. Jones carried the breakfast tray downstairs, and Lenora followed her on silent feet. The library was dark when they entered, and Mrs. Jones moved toward the windows to let in some light.

"The lamps don't work," Lenora said.

"Yes, I know," Mrs. Jones said. Her voice held a touch of annoyance. "Your uncle has used all the light bulbs this house could spare." She pressed her hand against her mouth, as though she was willing it to stop speaking without her permission. Her eyes clouded. Under her breath, she added, "At least the ones he can reach."

"Why does he need so many light bulbs?" Lenora said.

Mrs. Jones shrugged. "I don't even ask anymore." But Lenora could tell she was avoiding the question. She knew why Uncle Richard needed light bulbs. And now Lenora wanted to know.

She glanced toward the doorway. The library was close to the hallway that led down the east wing, at least the lower part, where she had seen Uncle Richard disappear. His laboratory must be behind the closed door she could see from the library entrance.

She'd go look. As soon as Mrs. Jones was gone.

She pretended interest in the books, so as not to raise any suspicion. She was a rule follower, yes, but when the rules didn't make sense, what did you do? Follow them anyway?

No. That's not what Lenora did. She challenged them.

Lenora ran her hands along the spines of books as she walked past the shelves, just as she had done yesterday.

"The children's books are over here," Mrs. Jones said, pointing to a corner near the window. Lenora hadn't realized there was order to this library. It was like a real library, then.

"Bobby loved to read." Mrs. Jones's voice had grown

soft. Lenora looked at her, observed her eyes full of memories, her lips curved down, her hands wiping something from her cheeks. Mrs. Jones must have loved Bobby.

The longing pulled at Lenora. Where were the people who loved her?

"What kinds of books did he read?" Lenora needed to say something, to dismiss the sob welling up in her.

"He loved *Moby-Dick* and *Treasure Island* and anything that had gardens or animals in it." Mrs. Jones gazed up at the bookshelf and took down a few titles. "Here's one you may enjoy, if you haven't already read it."

Lenora took the book from her. She traced the gold title: *The Secret Garden*. She had never read it, but it was Mother's childhood favorite, so of course she would read it now. Why hadn't she read it when Mother was alive?

Lenora caught herself. Mother *was* still alive. Mother was coming. She was likely on her way even now; it had only been four days.

"Does Uncle Richard ever use this library?" Lenora

was curious about the kind of books Uncle Richard read; she would like to read those, too. You could tell a lot about a person by the books they read.

Mrs. Jones pulled her lips tight. "He has his own library in his lab," she said. "For easier access, I suppose." Her eyes roamed the expanse of books and she shook her head. "He never had much patience for fantastical stories, anyway. So he does not need this library."

"But Darwin is here," Lenora said. She held up the book, and it almost slipped from her hands. It was a heavy one.

Mrs. Jones smiled. "That belonged to your uncle when he was a child. He was a great reader, but only of the scientific." A soft laugh escaped her lips. "Your father and Richard used to fight about what I would read to them when they were boys."

"You read to them?"

Mrs. Jones's eyes fixed on Lenora. "I have not always been Stonewall Manor's cook."

Lenora had so many more questions. But the one that climbed from her lips was, "Will you read to me?"

She missed reading together the most. It was the

time when she could put her head on Mother's shoulder and feel the words vibrate through her.

Mrs. Jones stared at Lenora. It took her a very long time to nod. "Yes. I suppose I could."

"Now?"

"Not now, love. Later, perhaps."

Lenora wondered if later meant never. And then she remembered her plans: to find her uncle's laboratory. It was okay for Mrs. Jones to leave; she would occupy herself with exploration.

"I would like to see the books in my uncle's library," Lenora said. It was a hint, but Mrs. Jones did not appear to take it as such.

"They are scientific tomes," Mrs. Jones said. "Long and boring, I suspect."

"That's all he keeps?"

"And some spiritual ones, I suppose."

"Spiritual?" Lenora tilted her head. "I thought my uncle was a man of science." That was what Father and Uncle Richard had fought about, after all.

"Science and faith can coexist. And men can change." Mrs. Jones put a few more titles on a table beside what looked like the most uncomfortable chair in the whole room.

The words flipped around inside Lenora's head. Uncle Richard had changed. Had Father changed, too? Why had they never reconciled?

Lenora looked at the book in her hands when she asked her next question. "Did Uncle Richard and Father ever talk after Father left Stonewall Manor?"

Mrs. Jones traced the title of one of the books in her hand, her eyes downcast. "I am not aware of any communication between them," she said. She lifted her eyes. They were blue lagoons of sadness.

"Why not?" None of it made sense to Lenora. "Father always said the most important thing we could ever do was forgive one another. What was so terrible that Father could not forgive?"

Mrs. Jones shook her head. "Your father left Stonewall Manor because of a family tragedy. Tragedy often twists hearts in unrecognizable ways."

"Enough to keep brothers apart?" Lenora felt anger tangling around her words. And what was the tragedy? Why would no one tell her?

Mrs. Jones said nothing.

"Is my uncle a criminal?" Something fluttered in Lenora's chest, like a piece of paper whirling in the wind.

Mrs. Jones laughed. "No," she said, and she laughed harder.

"Then what is it?" The words came out much louder than Lenora intended. They clanged against the walls and thudded to the floor.

Mrs. Jones dropped her eyes again.

"I would like to know," Lenora said, in a much smaller voice now.

Mrs. Jones still did not look at her. "Yes, well," she said. She took one more book off the shelf and placed it on top of the others. "One who goes digging for secrets does not always find good news."

Lenora didn't know what to say to that.

What was there to say to something that sounded so true?

26

Lenora was disturbed from her reading—or, more precisely, her dozing—by the voice of Mrs. Jones. She had not intended to fall asleep, but after Mrs. Jones left her, she'd collapsed into a chair, to think.

Now she'd wasted precious time, and there were voices outside the library.

Mrs. Jones stood just outside the door that Lenora thought led to Uncle Richard's east wing laboratory. (Lenora supposed it might be good to make a map, so she could keep all these rooms straight, instead of letting them float around in her mind like random pieces of a puzzle.) She was talking to someone. It must be Uncle Richard; no one else lived here.

Lenora crossed the room as silently as she could manage. She peered into the shadows. Her eyes had trouble seeing the two figures at first. When they adjusted to the dimness, she could make out her uncle leaning against a doorway that opened, yes, into the east wing of Stonewall Manor. He was staring at Mrs. Jones, and his eyes shone like stars.

"Did you find something, then?" Mrs. Jones said.

"I found a curious tree," Uncle Richard said. "Otherworldly, you could call it. And the soil around it . . ." His voice was low, but excitement clung to the edges. His left hand tapped his leg in a steady rhythm, and every few seconds he lifted his cane and clunked it to the floor, punctuating words he did not speak.

"Otherworldly," Mrs. Jones said. Her voice held a whole pile of skepticism; Lenora could hear it clearly.

Uncle Richard narrowed his starlight eyes. "You do not believe me."

Mrs. Jones said nothing.

"Would you have believed John?"

Lenora almost sucked in a breath. Was he talking about Father? She worked hard to keep her eyes focused on Mrs. Jones, whose back stiffened.

"Because John believed it. He saw it himself. He

knew." Uncle Richard's voice cracked and broke.

Lenora swallowed hard. What did her father know?

"He loved those woods." Mrs. Jones's voice was thick and indignant. "He would never—"

"He tried to warn me," Uncle Richard interrupted. "I didn't listen."

The silence was heavy with unspoken words, a history that Lenora could not even guess.

"This is my life's work," Uncle Richard said. "And it will work. I will break the curse. I will bring him home."

Mrs. Jones lifted her chin, and Lenora could see the quiver in it, even with all the shadows. Mrs. Jones stared at Uncle Richard for a moment, then cast her eyes to the ground. "Yes, sir," she said.

Mrs. Jones was turning away. Lenora thrust herself from the doorway and bounded across the room on whispering feet. She sank into the chair in which she had been reading before she'd heard the voices. She pulled out the book she had forgotten to mark with one of the lace bookmarks Mrs. Jones had laid out for her. She hated when she forgot to mark a book. There was nothing worse than trying to find your place again.

She opened the book, however, and pretended to read.

Mrs. Jones entered the library and gasped. When Lenora lifted her eyes, Mrs. Jones had a hand pressed to her chest.

"Mrs. Jones?" she said. "What's the matter?"

Had she done something wrong?

Mrs. Jones let out a violent, whooshing breath. She moved deeper into the room. She pointed at Lenora, and Lenora's heart leaped. What had she done?

"Tell me why you chose that chair out of all the others," Mrs. Jones finally said.

Lenora looked down at the rich green fabric of the wing chair. "Because . . ." She did not want to say the wrong thing. "Because it looked comfortable. Because it's green." Her hands tightened on the arms of the chair. "I'm sorry."

"No," Mrs. Jones said. She shook her head, her silver hair shaking with it. "You've done nothing wrong, love. It's just . . ." She seemed lost for words. She scratched her cheek, or maybe she was wiping away a tear that hadn't yet fallen. Lenora could smell the freshly baked bread in her clothes. "It's just that Bobby always chose that one as his reading seat, too. Every day he sat there and read until lunchtime." Her voice sounded fragile, as though it would break any moment. She smiled thinly. "I walked in and thought I was seeing a ghost."

Lenora looked down at the book in her hands.

"I thought he had walked right back out of the woods and . . ." Mrs. Jones drew in another sharp breath. Lenora's eyes snapped to her face. The woman looked horrified, and Lenora knew why. She couldn't let it go; it was not in her nature.

"Bobby went into the woods?"

"I should not have said anything," Mrs. Jones said. Her shoulders slumped forward. "I only complicate things."

"Is that why Uncle Richard doesn't want me to go into the woods? Because something happened to Bobby?"

Mrs. Jones held Lenora's gaze for a long time before she said, "Bobby walked into the woods and never came home."

The weight on Lenora's chest grew heavier.

"Your uncle fears the same will happen to you." These words, though they were frightening, spread a warmth all the way through Lenora. Uncle Richard wanted to protect her.

"He thinks Bobby is still alive?" Lenora said. "Is that why he is searching the woods?"

Mrs. Jones sighed. "Your uncle has some strange ideas about the woods."

"That my father believed?" Lenora pressed her hand to her mouth. She hadn't intended to suggest that she'd heard their conversation. And now it was too late. Mrs. Jones was looking at her with narrowed eyes.

"I don't know what your father believed."

"What do you believe?"

Lenora didn't think Mrs. Jones would answer, so long was the wait. But finally Mrs. Jones said, "I think your cousin is dead. I think your uncle hasn't been able to come to terms—"

"Maybe he is still alive. Maybe he just needs to be found. Maybe he's lying somewhere hurt or injured and he can't find his way to help because of the injury."

Lenora didn't realize she was crying until Mrs. Jones wrapped her long arms around Lenora's shoulders. She shuddered. She didn't know when the conversation had turned to her family, but somehow it had.

It had been four days. Why was there no word?

"Hush now, love," Mrs. Jones said. She rubbed her hand along Lenora's back. "Perhaps a nap after some lunch would do you good."

Lenora pulled away from Mrs. Jones. She sniffled.

"Your uncle is on his way out," Mrs. Jones said. "You and I can dine in the kitchen again."

"Where is he going?"

Mrs. Jones waved her hand in the air, as though dismissing the question entirely. But she answered it. "Not far. He likes to walk."

Lenora thought that she would like to walk with Uncle Richard, and she almost asked permission—but something about the way Mrs. Jones said the words, the way her mouth pulled down at the edges, the way her eyes flashed with something angry and fierce, told her it would not be wise.

Besides, if he were out, that would give her the

perfect opportunity to peek inside his lab.

So she put on her brightest smile and said, "I would like to finish this one chapter, and then I will eat."

Mrs. Jones smiled back at her and nodded. "Very well," she said. "I'll prepare your plate and wait for you in the kitchen."

Mrs. Jones lingered in the doorway for a moment, and Lenora opened the book on her lap so Mrs. Jones would think she was really reading. When next she looked up, Mrs. Jones was gone.

Lenora rose from her chair.

27

At the doorway of the library, Lenora checked every direction, to make sure her uncle had not returned—to make sure, too, that no ghosts awaited her. She needed to stop thinking about ghosts; they were not productive for her current quest.

Were they ever productive?

A definitive no.

The closed door leading into the east wing was not far. Lenora raced through the shadows (she was getting faster, with all this practice) and reached it having hardly touched the ground at all, it seemed.

The door was a dark cherry color, and the knob turned when she tried it out. Good. It wasn't locked.

It opened with a *click*.

She wasn't sure what she expected, but when she stepped into the hallway, she saw that it was much different from the one in the west wing. For one thing, all the portraits that lined this hallway were turned on their face, only the brown cardboard backing of frames showing. Names were scrawled on the backing. *Stephen Cole, 1874*; *Gladys Cole, 1912*; *Benedict Cole, 1839*. She took them down, one by one. In each picture was a child with a shock of white hair and a thin black X drawn over his or her face.

Strange. But what wasn't in this house?

She returned the pictures to their places, her mind snagging on the X. What could it mean?

She found one that said *Cole Family, 1937*. Lenora flipped it over. She recognized her uncle immediately. He was handsome in a black top hat and a deep green suit coat, and he smiled. Lenora had not seen her uncle smile since she had come to Stonewall Manor. It lit his whole face with mirth.

The woman beside him must have been his wife. She had beautiful black curls that flowed down her shoulders and eyes like the sky at dusk. Her belly was round and full, and one of her hands, pale and elegant, rested on the side of it. And in the middle of them was a boy who looked to be about Rory's age, nine or ten. He resembled his mother, mostly, with black curls piled on the top of his head and shining blue eyes. They looked like a happy family. A lump wedged itself in Lenora's throat. She put the picture back as it was. She had come into this wing to look for a lab, not pictures.

She glanced back at the portraits as she moved on. It was odd that they were turned on their faces. She wondered what that meant, too.

What she noticed next was even odder.

Along the deeper length of the hall were white sheets draped over tall, bulky forms. They looked like ghosts standing at attention. Lenora lifted the bottom of one of the sheets and saw an iron boot, with silver and gold gears attached to both sides of the ankle. She lifted the sheet higher and saw gears attached to the sides of copper knees, which were ever-so-slightly bent. A torso, two arms, and a head. She let the sheet fall and stood up.

There were hundreds of these forms lining the

hallway. They were taller than she was. Wider, too.

Was this what her uncle was creating? An army of robots? Why?

She wouldn't find any answers standing in the hall, so Lenora moved on.

A light at the end of the hall beckoned her. She moved silently past the white figures, glancing at them out of the corners of her eyes to make sure they didn't move; she could imagine her uncle setting some kind of trap, and she didn't want to be caught in it.

She stopped at another dark cherry door. Her heart hammered inside her chest. It was only slightly cracked. She nudged it the rest of the way open and stepped in quickly before she could talk herself out of it.

She crept around the room, which was larger than her family's sitting room at home and had a ceiling so tall she had to squint to see its grainy texture. She picked up an instrument here and set down another there. She saw beakers and tweezers and forceps and copper tubes and clock gears of every size and pieces of old metal and what looked like miniature furnaces. She had no idea how to make sense of the mess in this room.

A door on the far side of the room was propped halfway open, as though Uncle Richard had slipped through it in haste and forgotten to close it behind him. Lenora pushed on it, but it did not budge any farther. Something on the other side obstructed it. She tried to slip through, but there was nowhere to go. How did Uncle Richard get inside?

Lenora turned back to look at the room. In the far corner, the one that shared a wall with the door but was farthest away from it, something massive and tall—it almost touched the ceiling!—was concealed beneath another white sheet. A sheet that enormous did not exist. Uncle Richard, or someone, must have sewn several sheets together to make it. Lenora walked closer to examine the mysterious shape, and she had only just reached the corner and bent down when she heard a noise behind her. She froze.

She did not even have time to duck beneath the desk that stood to the right of the enormous white blob before her uncle entered the room. He didn't notice her at first, so she stood as still as she could manage, holding her breath. Her eyes searched for an escape, but it was too late.

"What are you doing here?" He had seen her. His face was so full of rage that Lenora cringed.

"I'm sorry," she whispered. She should not have come here; she knew it now.

"You are not permitted in the east wing." Uncle Richard's voice rose, clanged against the walls, and drilled into Lenora's chest.

"I know." She sidled toward the door, feeling small and exposed. "I was only curious."

"Curious?" Uncle Richard threw up his hands. She had never seen him so angry. There was no hint of sadness; it had been swallowed by fury. "You could have ruined my life's work. This is no place for a child!" Spit flew from his mouth. Lenora slid along the wall, trying to find the door.

Another voice entered the room. "Sir."

Lenora could have hugged Mrs. Jones, so relieved was she to see someone else in the doorway. "She is only a child."

"A child doesn't belong here," Uncle Richard said, and Lenora felt the words like they were a rope tied around her neck, tightening, cutting off her breath. If she did not belong here, in a place that had been her family's home for centuries, where, then, did she belong?

"I'm sorry," Lenora said again. She felt tears prickling her nose. "I won't come again."

"See that she doesn't." Uncle Richard's voice was an iron wall, hurled at Mrs. Jones. No one could argue with a voice like that.

"Yes, sir," Mrs. Jones said. She reached for Lenora's shoulders and pulled her gently but firmly out of the room. She shut the door behind her.

Outside the room, Mrs. Jones held Lenora, and when Lenora closed her eyes she could almost imagine that it was her mother, soothing away a nightmare.

She could almost believe.

28

Uncle Richard did not join Lenora for supper. Lenora stared at his place all through the meal, wishing she could take back her intrusion.

Mrs. Jones accompanied Lenora up the stairs to the west wing so that Lenora did not have to climb into the darkness alone. When they reached her doorway, Lenora said, "Must he always be this way?"

Mrs. Jones tilted her head and studied Lenora. "What way, love?"

"He works all the time." Lenora looked at her feet. There was more, but this was the safest explanation.

"Your uncle is a very busy man." Mrs. Jones put an arm around Lenora's shoulders. "He's doing important work."

Lenora thought of the robots. "What is he working on?" She didn't know if Mrs. Jones knew the answer, but the question was always worth asking.

"Heaven knows." Mrs. Jones let out a long breath and dropped her arm. "Something scientific is all I know."

"An invention?"

"That was his specialty."

"Robots?"

Mrs. Jones's head swiveled in her direction. "Your uncle always had a fascination with robots. He tried to build them when he was young."

There were so many stories Lenora wanted to hear—about her uncle, about her father, about what went on in the east wing. "Is he working on something for himself? Or someone else?"

Mrs. Jones pressed her lips together and looked toward Lenora's window. She had left it open this morning, and Mrs. Jones crossed the room to close it. When she turned back around, she said, "Your uncle used to work for the government, but that was many years ago. He works for himself now."

"You know what he's working on, don't you." Lenora could feel her eyes narrowing. "And you won't tell me."

Mrs. Jones sighed. "It's not my place, love. Those

questions are for your uncle."

"He won't tell me."

"Perhaps he won't. But I can't."

"Because he forbids you to speak?"

Mrs. Jones looked surprised. "No, love. Your uncle does not forbid me anything."

That was worse. It meant Mrs. Jones didn't *want* to tell her. Lenora folded her arms across her chest and stared at her bed. She felt angry, but there was more than that. She was losing hope.

"I've seen the robots."

"I figured you had," Mrs. Jones said. "You went exploring."

"They were covered in sheets."

"It is how your uncle hides them."

"No one goes into the east wing. Why does he need to hide them?" Her eyes moved to Mrs. Jones's face, so she saw the pained look slice across it.

"Your uncle . . ." Mrs. Jones folded her hands in front of her, threading her fingers, pulling them apart, threading them again. Lenora watched her. "He is obsessed with building these . . ." She shook her head and did not finish her thought but started another. "He has been working on robots for many, many years. Decades, maybe."

"What does he plan to do with them?" Lenora said.

"That I do not know."

"But you do." It was there, on Mrs. Jones's face. She couldn't hide that she was lying. Lenora had always preferred faces like that; it made things simpler.

Mrs. Jones shook her head and started toward the door. Lenora felt like shouting, she was so irritated and bothered by all these secrets and mysteries. She had never liked mysteries; she preferred the whole truth.

And even Father was not able to give her that.

29

Mrs. Jones hovered in the doorway, as though she did not want to leave Lenora alone. She said, "You must not venture into the east wing again. It is forbidden. Your uncle would not be pleased at all, and then . . ."

Mrs. Jones pressed her lips tight, and Lenora felt the unspoken words, like freezing fingers, settle on her spine. And then what? He would send her away? He would do worse? What was Mrs. Jones hiding?

"Why?" Lenora said. "Why doesn't he want me there?" And what she meant was, *Why doesn't he want me here?*

"Because it's dangerous."

"The robots are dangerous?"

Mrs. Jones leveled her gaze at Lenora, her eyes sharp and clear. Lenora felt electrified by them, shocked into obedience. "Your uncle works with tools and elements that could burn the skin off your hands or set you on fire or kill you in a matter of minutes. He only wants to protect you."

Was it true? Was that all?

Or did he want her gone completely?

"The east wing is off-limits. Do you understand?" The words were short, clipped, matter-of-fact, but Lenora could sense that there was something more behind them. Fear?

Why?

Lenora nodded her head and tried to shake the unease out of her chest by moving. She paced, her mind flipping through the things she knew. The robots. Her uncle's trips into the woods. Mrs. Jones's fear.

Her uncle wanted to protect his secret more than he wanted to protect her. She was sure of it.

"Promise me you won't go looking again," Mrs. Jones said. She tapped her fingers against the doorframe.

Lenora could not promise. So she simply said, "I will not put myself in any danger." It would have to be good enough.

Mrs. Jones looked at her for a long moment. Lenora

held her breath and arranged her face into the most innocent expression she could manage. Lenora knew that Mrs. Jones could see through her thin and inadequate words, but a smile played at the edges of Mrs. Jones's mouth. "All right, then," she said. "You've been properly warned. You know the danger. You know the expectations."

Lenora nodded.

Mrs. Jones continued. "Your uncle locks the door when he is in the east wing and when he is not. Don't expect to find it unlocked again." She smoothed her skirt across her belly. Her face had a satisfied look about it, as though the thought that Lenora would not have another chance to intrude brought her significant pleasure. Or perhaps it was relief.

Well, Lenora would find a way. She did not have John or Charles or Rory here to convince her to disobey, but she would do it for them. Their voices were always in her head; she could imagine their chanting even now. *Do it, Lenora. Do it. Break the rules. Be a rebel.*

"Good night, Lenora." Mrs. Jones turned to go but stopped again. She looked back. "Tomorrow we'll go into town and buy you some new things."

Lenora nodded.

After Mrs. Jones had gone and she had taken a warm bath and changed into her dressing gown, Lenora lay awake in her bed, her thoughts folding and unfolding in her head. She wondered about the robots. She wondered about Uncle Richard's oddities. She wondered about the enormous white sheet she had found in his lab and what might possibly be hiding beneath it.

She would gather all the pieces and put them together as soon as she could.

She would show Uncle Richard what she could do.

30

Mrs. Jones had biscuits and gravy already prepared on a plate when Lenora entered the kitchen the following morning. She had first visited the dining room, to see if Uncle Richard was there. She assumed he'd be going into town with her and Mrs. Jones, since that was the original plan. She couldn't imagine what she would say to him after yesterday.

"As soon as you're finished with your breakfast, we'll leave for town," Mrs. Jones said as she slid Lenora's plate across the table and sat down.

"What about Uncle Richard?" Lenora said. "Is he already awake? Did he already eat?"

The smile vanished from Mrs. Jones's face. "Your uncle is busy this morning," she said, in a crisp, even tone that curved around annoyance. Lenora did not know if Mrs. Jones was annoyed with her or Uncle

Richard. "He will not be coming today."

Lenora knew it had something to do with what she had done yesterday. She said, "I'm sorry I angered him." And the tears sprang up so quickly she could not blink them away.

"No, love," Mrs. Jones said. "It has nothing to do with you."

Didn't it?

"Your uncle rarely leaves the house," Mrs. Jones said. She touched Lenora's cheek and looked down at her hands. "That's all."

"Doesn't he have friends?"

Mrs. Jones's eyes turned glassy. "Not anymore."

Lenora wiped her cheek. She was about to ask another question when Mrs. Jones said, "He was a different man once."

"What do you mean?"

"He was a brilliant man. Highly sought out for his scientific ideas."

"And he isn't now?"

Mrs. Jones let out a long, ragged breath. "Not many people listen to what your uncle has to say now."

"Why not?"

Mrs. Jones laughed, but it did not sound amused at all. "His oddities . . ." She paused. "They leave many questioning whether he has something genuinely valuable to say."

Lenora's body warmed. "That's ridiculous." She didn't know why she felt the sudden need to defend Uncle Richard; he had shown no love to her. And he was so different from Father, who was warm and affectionate and bright. But he was family. He was Father's brother. He was all she had.

"It's the way of the world," Mrs. Jones said.

It was not the way the world *should* be. Lenora gritted her teeth and said, "Being odd doesn't mean a person has nothing valuable to say."

"Yes, well." Mrs. Jones grimaced. "The scientific world is very critical, and reputations can be delicate. One can become famous for his ideas one day and be cast out another."

"Is Uncle Richard an outcast?"

Mrs. Jones fiddled with an invisible speck of dust on the table. She said, "Lloyd will drive us to town."

"He should come," Lenora said. She felt fierce, justified. "Just because."

"Your uncle has nothing to prove," Mrs. Jones said.

It didn't matter. Lenora flung herself away from the table, and before Mrs. Jones could say another word, she bolted from the room, right toward the east wing. She heard Mrs. Jones call for her, but she did not stop, only sailed past the stairs, through the door that was, fortuitously again, unlocked, and down the hallway. Her feet did not make a sound, padded by the long maroon carpet that ran the length of the floor. So when she burst into Uncle Richard's lab, he cried out and dropped what was in his hands. It clattered to the floor, which made Lenora flinch.

"You," he said. He looked furious—might even appear dangerously so, if not for his eyes, which were magnified comically behind thick goggles. That, coupled with the state of his hair, which could only be described as unruly, gave him the look of a true madman. Lenora backed away but kept her hand on the doorframe, to ensure that she stayed right here until she said what she came to say.

A ray of sunlight lunged through the window, grabbed the copper tube in Uncle Richard's hand, and hurled its orange light into Lenora's eyes. She blinked and shifted.

"I'm sorry to disturb you," she said. She hated the way her voice quivered. She was not afraid of him. He was family.

"I told you not to come here!" Uncle Richard's voice had a suffocating effect, clamping around Lenora's chest and squeezing.

"I know," Lenora said. She held up her hands. "I'm sorry. I only wanted—"

"I am doing important work! I cannot be disturbed!" His voice had not softened one bit; in fact, it was harsher than she'd ever heard it.

Perhaps it had been a mistake to come here. She had not considered her uncle's anger as carefully as she should have. She knew nothing about him; what if he was dangerous? What if this was the reason for all the secrets?

She was not usually so given to impulsive action without careful consideration. She was the voice of reason among her brothers and sister.

But who was she anymore? Without her family? Without John and Charles and Rory canceling out her caution?

The words tumbled out of their own accord. "I only wanted you to come with us to town. I thought it might do you good to get out and away from all this"—here she gestured to his lab and all the strange supplies—"and I miss my mother and father and sister and brothers so much and you are family and knowing you is like being with my family, and they would have loved it here and . . ." Her voice faltered, curved, snapped in two with a crackling hiss.

Uncle Richard stared at her. What was it he saw? He tilted his head and squinted, his eyes still magnified behind the lenses.

She had almost turned away when he said, "I am busy today. Perhaps another time."

Lenora shook her head. "You are afraid."

Uncle Richard finally took off the lenses. "I am afraid of nothing."

"You are afraid of the people. You are afraid of what

they will say, because of your . . ." She pressed her lips together and glanced around the room. "Your ideas and your inventions."

Uncle Richard's mouth dropped open, and Lenora knew she was correct.

"You are afraid of me." The words were soft, almost a whisper.

Uncle Richard kept staring at her.

"Why?" Again, a whisper.

Again, no answer from Uncle Richard.

Lenora swallowed her fear and said, "Are you afraid because you lost some people you loved? Is that it?"

Uncle Richard's eyes sharpened like two points.

"Get out." He dragged the words between his teeth.

"I have lost people, too," Lenora said, and then she stopped. No. She wasn't ready to leave them for lost. They were alive. They were.

But if they were, they would have come for her by now. Wouldn't they? They would have sent word. *Someone* would have sent word. She would know.

Perhaps they were dead. Lenora's chest ached.

A sound whirled around her and Uncle Richard. It

was loud, alarming, full of such profound pain that Lenora sank to her knees. She could not bear the sound that spilled out from her depths.

Uncle Richard fell to his knees right beside her. He did not touch her, but Lenora felt him there, hovering, enfolding her with a presence so warm she could almost imagine that she was held safely in the arms of someone who loved her. And then Mrs. Jones burst into the room and wrapped her arms around Lenora, and the three of them remained, a small coil of sorrow.

The pearl necklace, tucked beneath the collar of Lenora's dress, pressed into her skin and warmed away the cold.

After a time, Uncle Richard said, "I will fetch my coat."

31

They rode in silence to the town, which was twenty miles away. Lenora had been asleep the last time they had traveled this road, which wound through the trees that surrounded Stonewall Manor. Lenora's gaze was drawn to those trees, tall and thin and so numerous that the space inside them was almost completely black. The tops of the trees curved toward the expanse of forest, as though protecting what lay within it.

"I have never seen woods like these," Lenora said, to no one in particular. "They are strange."

Uncle Richard stared out his own window. Mrs. Jones glanced back from the front seat, and Lenora caught Lloyd's eye in the rearview mirror. He looked pained. Lenora wondered if she had said something wrong. Uncle Richard said, "There are many dangers in these woods. That's why you must never enter them."

Lenora looked at Lloyd again. He raised his eyebrows, like he didn't believe her uncle. She wondered why.

"I have been in woods before," Lenora said. "I have seen bears and snakes, and once I even saw a mountain lion." She remembered that day, with Father. John had run ahead and missed the mountain lion, and he was so upset they had not called him back to see it—as if it would not have disappeared the moment one of them spoke.

John didn't bother with technicalities when they didn't suit him.

Lenora looked again at the woods outside her window. "What is so dangerous about these woods?" The air in the car seemed to vanish the moment the words were out. She was sorry she had spoken at all. No one was breathing. Lenora looked from one of them to the other, but Lloyd did not meet her gaze, Mrs. Jones kept her face to the front window, and Uncle Richard had closed his eyes.

So she was startled when Uncle Richard said, "They

are no place for children. That's all."

"Because of the wild animals, or . . ." Lenora let her words trail off.

"Because of the spirit," Uncle Richard said. "Because of the curse."

Mrs. Jones sucked in a breath.

Spirit? Curse? Uncle Richard was supposed to be a scientific man.

The air in the car felt heavier. Lenora decided it was best not to ask any more questions. Perhaps her uncle was as mad as they all thought he was. When next she glanced at him, she saw that he gripped the side of his door so hard his knuckles were white—like they had been on the drive from Texas City. It disturbed her to see his terror.

***

Lloyd parked the car in front of a small boutique. People turned to look as they climbed out. Lenora thought they were looking at the strange car, but then she saw people whisper to one another and point to her uncle. What were they saying behind their cupped hands? Was it rumor or truth?

Uncle Richard and Lloyd headed toward a pipe shop, while Mrs. Jones guided Lenora toward the boutique. Lenora would rather be going with her uncle. She'd always hated shopping, especially for dresses.

She tried on far too many for her liking. Her favorite color, before the explosion, as she had taken to calling it (though she tried not to name it too often; it was still too painful), had been green, but she could not look at it now without thinking of her family, without thinking of her birthday and the beautiful blue-green dress. So she stuck to safer colors that she would never have worn in her previous life. Purple. Red. Black. She found herself drawn to black, and she hated this even more than she hated the shopping. Black was such a drab color. A color that meant death and mourning and ends that should not be ends. She put all the black dresses away and picked up a few pink ones—the kinds of dresses Rory would have loved.

"The green one was lovely," Mrs. Jones said. She was

trying to be helpful, as a mother would be in this situation. She held up another dress for Lenora to try on.

Lenora sighed. She would like to be done as soon as possible.

Finally, finally, finally they had assembled the number of dresses Mrs. Jones wanted her to buy. Seven dresses, two pairs of brand-new shoes. Mrs. Jones carried them to the counter. Lenora couldn't believe that her uncle could afford anything so fine, but she didn't argue. When Mother and Father returned, they wouldn't need to buy her new dresses or shoes for school. She would take good care of them.

Uncle Richard and Lloyd were waiting outside the boutique, and when Uncle Richard saw Mrs. Jones at the counter, he entered and paid for the dresses and shoes without so much as a word. He had a new hat—a brown top hat that looked exactly like his black one. It made his eyes seem darker somehow.

"Are you hungry?" Uncle Richard said on the way out, and at first Lenora didn't know he was speaking to her until he said it again. "Are you hungry, Lenora?"

"A bit," she said, because she wasn't ready for the day

to end, not without spending some time at the same table as Uncle Richard, in a place where they could talk or she could listen in on the kind of conversation he would have with Mrs. Jones and Lloyd. She simply wanted to be with people.

"I know just the place," Uncle Richard said. "Mrs. Jones, do you remember Ripkin Deli?"

"I sure do," Mrs. Jones said. A ghost of a smile danced across her lips, and her eyes were bright and shining. Lloyd caught her eye and grinned. A feather of hope fluttered in Lenora's chest. Hope, it seemed, was contagious.

"It's just down the way," Uncle Richard said. "We'll walk, I think." He looked up at the sky, and Lenora did, too. It was so blue it nearly took her breath away. There were no clouds, and the sun was high and dazzling.

"It's been a while since you've been out in the open," Lloyd said. His eyes flickered with amusement. "You could do with some sunlight, old man."

Uncle Richard could not suppress his barely there smile.

Lenora pressed her hand into his.

32

As they walked down the street, Lenora's hand still in Uncle Richard's, she noticed that people stopped whatever they were doing to stare and point surreptitiously at them. She heard a man they passed say, "Well, look at that. The madman walks again." Someone else laughed.

Lenora glanced up at her uncle. His face was pale and drawn. He must have heard the man. But he did not address the speaker, not even with his eyes. He stared straight ahead. Perhaps he was in his own world again. Perhaps that was his armor, how he kept himself safe. Anger blazed in her throat. How dare they make him cower.

After that, Lenora met the gazes of the people boldly, challenging them to disrespect him again, while she was around. She felt proud to be his niece. She couldn't explain why.

While Uncle Richard stood in line at the counter to order their sandwiches, Mrs. Jones waved Lenora over to a booth with red padded seats. The tables were chrome and shone enough to reflect back a distorted image of faces and figures. Lenora slid into a booth of her own, while Mrs. Jones and Lloyd shared the one across from her.

"It's been some time since the people here have seen your uncle," Mrs. Jones said, as though trying to explain the reaction Lenora had observed in the town.

"They're not very nice," she said.

"Not everyone understands the scientific mind," Lloyd said. "It doesn't matter. He knows who he is."

Did he? Lenora glanced at her uncle. She knew the words of the people, the gazes, had bothered him.

"How long has it been since he came to town?" Lenora said.

Lloyd and Mrs. Jones exchanged a look. Mrs. Jones shook her head. "Years," she said, at the same time Lloyd said, "Almost a decade."

"A decade?" Lenora said.

"Your uncle prefers to stay at home," Lloyd said.

"After the accident—"

"Lloyd." Mrs. Jones's voice was sharp and barbed.

Lloyd looked at Mrs. Jones. They seemed to be saying something without words. Lenora hated it when adults did that. As though she couldn't tell.

She said, "What accident?" just to show her annoyance. But she was also curious. She looked back at Uncle Richard, who was bouncing up on his toes and resting on his heels in an erratic rocking motion.

"Your uncle has never been all that good with people," Mrs. Jones said. Lenora sighed. She wanted to know about the accident.

"She deserves to know," Lloyd said. "It was her family."

"It is not our place to tell it," Mrs. Jones said. "If Mr. Cole wanted her to know, he would tell her."

"Because he talks so much?" Lloyd said.

Lenora almost smiled, but the anger was too hot in her chest. More secrets? When would they be done with secrets? They were heavy, suffocating things. And the more there were, the more she worried that the fate of her family was a secret, too. Would they keep it from her forever?

"Why are there so many secrets at Stonewall Manor?" Lenora asked. She couldn't help it. "I've never liked secrets. And the people who keep them are selfish."

She hoped that hit its mark. Lloyd covered his mouth with his hand, but not before Lenora saw his smile. Mrs. Jones stared at her, her mouth open a smidge.

"What do you think I'll do with your secrets?" Lenora said. "I'm family."

Mrs. Jones shrugged her thin shoulders. "Ask your uncle."

"I will, then," Lenora said.

They waited. Lenora didn't intend to say anything else, so her anger and annoyance would sink into Mrs. Jones, perhaps make her feel bad for her silence. But her curiosity, as was often the case, got the better of her. "If my uncle never comes to town, how do we have food at Stonewall Manor?"

"He orders it," Mrs. Jones said. "Someone delivers it every Wednesday or I pick it up for him."

"But you don't drive."

"Lloyd drives me," Mrs. Jones said.

"What about fresh vegetables and fruit?" Lenora said. "We always had a garden in Texas City." Mother had tended that one, too, though Lenora and Rory were supposed to weed it. Neither of them ever did. "But the only garden I have seen at Stonewall Manor is a flower one."

"Your uncle doesn't have time for a garden," Mrs. Jones said. "Your cousin used to tend the one his mother planted, but . . ." Mrs. Jones stopped abruptly.

Uncle Richard dropped into the booth a second later, and all conversation ceased. "It'll be a few minutes," he said, and he folded his hands together and rested them on his nose, closing his eyes, as though he was praying. Lenora watched him, unsure what exactly he was doing. She glanced at Lloyd, who also stared at her uncle, and Mrs. Jones, who stared at her own hands.

After a moment, Uncle Richard opened his eyes, excused himself from the table, and disappeared into the men's bathroom. By the time he came back out, the food was waiting on their table. Lenora wondered if he had hidden in the bathroom on purpose and watched for the delivery. Perhaps he didn't want to engage in conversation at all.

But he could not avoid it while they were eating. And Lenora only waited a few minutes to ask, "Can you tell me about the accident, Uncle?"

The sandwich Uncle Richard was holding slipped right out of his hands. He stopped mid-chew and flung a fierce glare at Mrs. Jones and Lloyd, his eyes blazing.

"Hush, love," Mrs. Jones said sharply. "Let us enjoy this meal today."

"But no one will tell me anything," Lenora said. "My father didn't tell me about his brother or my cousins or my aunt. Why didn't he?"

Uncle Richard said nothing. He merely pushed his plate away. It screeched into the middle of the table.

Lenora shook her head. The question had soured the whole meal, and she wondered, not for the first time, why it was so hard for her to tame her curiosity, to keep her questions inside.

They were quiet all the way back to the car, all the way back to the house, all the way into the front door.

Uncle Richard played the gentleman and held the door for Lenora and Mrs. Jones, waving to Lloyd as he pulled out of the drive in a shiny black car. As she crossed the threshold of Stonewall Manor, Lenora hugged her uncle around the waist with a teary "thank you," after which he let the front door slam, extracted himself from her arms, and hurried away toward the east wing, offering no words in return. Lenora stared after him. The light in the hallway dimmed with his retreat.

Would she ever have a family again?

The woods, it turned out, were not enough. He wanted something new, something that lived beyond the woods. He craved it, the ache so enormous at times he thought it might swallow him completely.

All he needed was patience and time. Patience had always been a weak spot, but time—he had plenty of that. He had waited two centuries already, or very nearly so. Two centuries was all the time required; he could feel it in the flex of his fingers, in the stretching of his solidifying spine, in the heart that had begun to pulse once more, if erratically.

Almost there. Soon he would become flesh and bone and blood again.

He only needed one more.

April 22, 1947

The town was just as I remembered—nosy, peculiar, judgmental. I should not have visited. But Lenora . . . she needed me. I have never been good at recognizing these things, but I could see it for once. Perhaps it is the deep pain we share. Or perhaps I simply do not want to make the same mistake with her that I made with Bobby, and that has catalyzed my vigilance.

I have not visited the deli since Edith and Mary died. It was difficult walking through the doors and ordering as I had always done when they were alive and well. It was more difficult sitting at a booth, eating the same sandwich I would eat all those times we sat there as a family. Lenora made it somewhat bearable; she appeared, for a time, almost happy. And then she began digging into the past. She said the last words I heard my son say: "No one will tell me anything." Lenora and Bobby were right. I have always been hesitant to share the troubling details of life. It is a flaw I have never quite overcome.

Bobby didn't know the details of the accident. He

didn't know the real danger of the woods.

One day I will have to tell Lenora. One day I will have to tell her a great many things. But for today, I must focus on my work. I must clear my mind of its distractions and finish what is demanded of me. I must vindicate the memory of my son, break the tie these woods have on our lives, and restore Stonewall Manor to a fraction of its former glory.

Time, I fear, is running out.

So sorrow—and those it plagues—must be set aside, boxed up, kept from the spirit in the woods.

There is a great deal of work to be done.

—excerpt from Richard Cole's *Journal of Scientific Progress*

INTO THE WOODS

33

Lenora walked the grounds of Stonewall Manor. It was late afternoon, the hottest part of the day, but she found herself drawn to the garden. There was still much work to do, but she thought that if Mother saw what it had been and what it was now, she would be proud of Lenora's labor. She stood with her chin resting against the iron gate and imagined what the garden could possibly become—perhaps close to what it had been—if her mother were here to coax beauty from the disarray. She shoved herself away from the metal bars, which curled in graceful arcs like bowing branches of a tree, and moved on.

It was strangely quiet on the grounds. The birds had silenced their songs. Lenora looked up at the sky, but it was still perfectly blue and clear. No cloud on the horizon, no storm waiting to drench her with its fury.

She tilted her head and listened. Not a creature stirred. It was the strangest thing. She whistled, but nothing whistled in answer. The mockingbirds had vanished.

Lenora looked back at Stonewall Manor. A shadow clung to this side of it, making it appear mysterious—even sinister—in the bright sunlight that touched everything else. It looked like an old Gothic mansion, something from the pages of Sherlock Holmes—a place where secrets were kept and crimes were hidden in stone crypts.

Lenora shook off a chill.

She was letting her imagination get the better of her. Perhaps it was the heat.

The thing that bothered her most, what haunted her so relentlessly, was the quiet in the halls of the house. She scowled at her feet. What was life without voices and noise and laughter? How could one live in a silent place on a silent hill with a silent existence—and call it pleasant? When would they—Uncle Richard and Mrs. Jones—realize that Lenora could not carry on without people when the only life she had ever known had been filled with people?

She could not.

Lenora lifted her face to the burning sun. The silence was louder than anything she had ever known. It was as though the entire world had been drained of all its animation here on the grounds and inside the walls of Stonewall Manor. Lenora was completely and utterly alone. Everywhere. Even in nature.

The chasm in her heart quaked.

A resounding crack startled Lenora. She squinted toward the woods, which were much closer than she had thought. Darkness was all that met her. She turned her back on it, unwilling to see what might be hiding within. Was something watching her? The hairs on her neck seemed to think so.

Lenora walked quickly toward the tower on the east wing. The west wing had a tower exactly like this one, though Lenora had not been able to locate the stairs that led up to it—another mystery of the house. Would she ever uncover them all? She thought it likely impossible. There were too many secret passageways, too many mazes that called themselves halls, too many closed and locked rooms. If someone else were here, if . . .

Lenora closed her eyes, trying to breathe, trying not to cry, trying to drown out the thoughts that twirled through her mind by listening to her breath. But the thoughts were too loud.

They should be here. They're not coming. You'll always be alone.

Her legs exploded into motion, as though trying to outrun the words. She would never be able to run fast enough, but she would try. Her steps filled the quiet path with a storm of sound. She burst through the iron gate and fell to her knees just inside the garden, where she plunged her hands into the loose earth and pressed her cheek to the ground.

"I miss you, Mother," she said, her voice thick and wet. "And you, Father. And Charles and John and Rory. I miss you all so much."

Something shifted deep inside her. She felt sickened, choked, emptied out of everything she had been. The tears came in shaking waves. She closed her eyes. She wanted to disappear. She wanted to return to Texas City, to the day of the explosion. She wanted to begin the morning anew, pretend she was sick like Rory had, so at least they would all be together, dead or alive.

"Please come get me," she said. "Please be alive."

What was the last thing she had said to her father? Nothing. She had ignored him on her way in to school. She had been so angry with her sister. She had been angry with Mother. She had not said goodbye to any of them. And now she might not ever get the chance.

She struggled to breathe. The missing swept over her. She missed hearing her mother talk about the swamp hibiscus and the parasol flower she was growing in the garden and how the ridiculous heat had withered them. She missed seeing John stretched out on the entire expanse of their couch while he was reading. She missed hearing Father's stories about the fires he'd put out and the lives his men had saved over the years. She missed feeling angry with Rory. She missed Mother's and Father's hugs before bed and the way they would dance in the kitchen when they thought no one was looking.

She missed being scolded for not acting like a proper lady, for always coming home with a dirty dress, for the notes—her scientific observations—she left all over the house. She didn't write those notes anymore. She was not the same person without her family.

Her mother's pearl necklace slipped out from beneath her collar and rested against her lips. It felt right, even if it didn't quite feel like hope.

"Please come home."

She could not bear it if they didn't.

She said the words again and again and again, as though these ones she loved could hear her somehow, as though her whispers might pull them from the rim of death and construct a wedge of protection around them, as though it weren't already too late.

And then her ears heard a magical sound. A voice. It was only a whisper, but it was the loudest thing in her world.

Lenora.

34

"Father?"

Lenora sat up, pulled her feet beneath her, rocked back on her heels. It was not the proper way for a lady to kneel, but Lenora was not concerned with dainty etiquette when she had heard her father's voice, calling her name.

Was it possible?

Lenora. I am here.

Lenora's head twisted toward the woods. "Where?" she called. "Where are you, Father?"

Was her father inside the woods, waiting for her? Had he come for Lenora after all? Had he been trapped in the woods all along, because of exhaustion or an injury?

She had to find him.

Lenora's more practical side introduced another

question: Why would Father be in the woods?

But Lenora did not care about the practical side of things, not when her father might be alive. She had lived too much in the world of practicality; Rory had always teased her about that. Perhaps there was magic and miracle after all.

Besides, hadn't she overheard Mrs. Jones say that Father loved the woods?

And Uncle Richard said Father had tried to warn him—about what?

She could find out *and* find Father.

Lenora stood, turning in the direction from which the voice had reached her. She squinted her eyes, trying to see into the line of trees that stretched out across the grounds. They bent slightly in a breeze she could not feel. Were they beckoning?

No. Of course not.

Lenora. I am here.

Where? She squinted.

She waited for some minutes, expecting a form— her father—to emerge, but when nothing did, she took matters into her own hands and moved toward the trees. At the edge of the woods, she stopped. The trees were still, as though holding their breath. They remained as dark as ever. She glanced back toward the house, checking every window for movement, but there was nothing. She hesitated, listening.

What waited for her within these woods? Her uncle had called them dangerous. Were they? And, if so, did that mean Father was in danger?

Was Father really inside? What if he wasn't?

But what if he was?

"Father!" Lenora said. Her mind was made up. "I'm coming!"

She held on to her mother's pearl necklace and stepped inside.

The world exhaled. The trees bent majestically, as though bowing to Lenora, but surely that was only a trick of her imagination. The air brightened with a golden glow. Lenora blinked. The trees had straightened again. And then, before her very eyes, they shifted, each one of them bending the bottom of their trunks in such a way that turned them into flattened seats, inviting her to sit and stay awhile. She touched the smooth bark of one and moved along to another. She stopped at the third. Its leaves hung around her, hissing. It sounded musical, not threatening.

"Where are you, Father?" Lenora said, but her father did not answer.

She sat on the platform provided by the tree, resting her chin on her fist. She looked toward the entrance of the woods, but the manor seemed very far away. She could just make it out. How had she traveled so far, when it didn't feel as though she had gone more than a few steps?

A dark cloud hung behind the manor now, transforming the stone walls and gabled roof and wraparound porch from a home into a menacing, frightening fortress. Lenora drew in a sharp breath and tore her gaze from it.

Perhaps the danger was in Stonewall Manor, not in these woods.

Lenora. I am here.

Lenora stood abruptly. Where was the voice coming from? How would she ever locate her father in these vast woods? She was not a hero like him.

The despair crashed into her, and Lenora could do nothing more than cover her face with her hands and weep.

"Lenora," said a voice, off to her left. It was the voice of a boy, the voice of her brother Charles, soft and gentle and curious.

"Charles," she said, searching the trees. She could see nothing. "Where are you?" Her words came out hushed, a piece of panic clinging to them.

"Lenora." This time the voice was not soft, it was loud, a voice that shook the trees so they sizzled. It vibrated through her chest.

"Charles!" Lenora said, and then again: "Where are you? Please. Tell me how I can find you." She turned around and around and around, but as far as she looked, she only saw trees. Emptiness. Despair.

Her vision blurred, and she tripped over something on the ground. She did not even look to see what it was.

She needed to get back to the grounds of Stonewall Manor. Something was wrong.

But there was no break in the trees now. There was only the dark woods.

35

"Lenora." The voice called her again, and this time it was so unlike Charles's voice that she ceased her running and stood, rooted, unable to move. Her eyes widened. Someone was here with her. What had she done?

She had put herself in danger—and for what? A mirage of the people she loved. They were not here.

Her head felt cloudy.

"Who are you?" Lenora said. "Why have you brought me here? What do you want? Where is my family?"

"So many questions," the voice said. It was not unkind; it was merely strange. A purring kind of voice. "And they will be answered, in time. But first we must find out if you can see me. So look."

Lenora looked. She saw nothing.

"Down at your feet," the voice said.

She dropped her eyes. There was no person, not even

a little one—which would have made Lenora think she was dreaming—but there was what looked like an unusually colored salamander—which made her think even more certainly that she was dreaming. Its skin was an opaque pink color, its eyes like beads of gold with a black circle pressed into the middle, and it wore a crown of pink fur around its neck, similar to a lion's mane.

Lenora felt a laugh bubble into her throat, and it was so unexpected she could not stop it.

The creature frowned, its tiny pale eyebrows drawing low over its golden eyes. The golden light in the woods dimmed. "Now, that's no way to greet a Scorlaman," it said.

"A Scorlaman?" Lenora said. She had never heard of such a thing. She didn't think she could conjure up a creature like this, not even in her dreams. Charles was the imagination in the Cole family, not Lenora.

The creature rose up on its hind legs and gestured with its spindly arms. "I bet you have never seen anything like me before." He seemed proud of this.

Lenora pressed a hand to her lips, to keep another

giggle trapped inside. He was only as tall as her ankle, and she had been afraid of him! "No," Lenora said, when she was certain the laugh would not escape along with words. "I haven't."

That's when the Scorlaman did something astonishing. He grew before Lenora's eyes, becoming as tall—no, somewhat taller—than she was. She gasped, terror rippling through her chest. "That's because I am native to these woods," the Scorlaman said. And when he saw that Lenora was about to run, he said, "Don't worry. I am no danger to you. You don't have to be afraid of me."

And for some reason, Lenora believed him. "You live here, in Stonewall Woods?"

The Scorlaman tilted his head. "Is that what you call them?"

"It is their name," Lenora said. That's what Uncle Richard had called them, at least, and this land had never belonged to anyone but the Cole family.

"No," the Scorlaman said. "They have a different name." His eyes flashed, and Lenora wondered what it meant. Was he angry with her for some reason? "These woods do not belong to the Cole family. They belong to the earth."

"My uncle calls them Stonewall Woods," Lenora said.

"He would, wouldn't he?" the Scorlaman said. "He is a Cole."

Lenora said nothing.

"Your uncle is mistaken about a great many things," the Scorlaman said.

Lenora folded her arms across her chest, feeling the urge, again, to defend her uncle. "Like what?" Her voice was sharp, challenging.

The Scorlaman also folded his arms across his chest. "Tell me," he said. His voice was smooth and calm. "Has your uncle told you these woods are dangerous?"

Lenora jolted. "Yes." She paused. "Are they?"

"No." The Scorlaman's gaze glowed. "And I will show you, as I did his son."

"Bobby? You knew him? He came here?"

"Yes," the Scorlaman said.

"He was lost in these woods," Lenora said.

"Not lost," the Scorlaman said. "He was found."

"But he has been missing for many years."

"He had no desire to return."

Lenora pressed a hand to her forehead. Her other hand fluttered to her mother's necklace.

"What is that?" the Scorlaman said.

Lenora's hand stuffed the necklace under her dress. "Nothing." Her head was spinning. "If Bobby is here, I must take him home."

"He is content to remain here," the Scorlaman said.

Lenora looked at the strange creature for a long time. She said, "I would like to see him."

"That could be arranged," the Scorlaman said. "But first I must know that I can trust you."

Lenora frowned. "Of course you can."

"But I do not know you."

"I am Lenora," she said.

The trees rustled.

The Scorlaman smiled, his golden eyes brightening. "And I am Bela the Scorlaman, keeper of Gilgevnah Woods." The creature held out one hand. Lenora noticed he had only four fingers on it.

"Gilgevnah Woods," Lenora said as she took the warm, reptilian hand in hers. She tilted her head. "It is all so strange." She gestured to Bela. "You, these woods, what my uncle has said about them." She tried to make sense of what she remembered Uncle Richard saying, but her mind felt foggy and unfocused. Was it the woods, or was it simply a coincidence?

"Your uncle has lost his mind," Bela said. "It happened when he lost his family."

"No," Lenora said. No. She wouldn't believe it.

"His son ran away from him," Bela said. "Because of his madness."

Lenora looked at Bela. She could not tell for sure if what he said was true. So she said, "I would like to talk to Bobby myself."

"In time," Bela said. "First we must see to a few things."

"And my father?" Lenora said. The words scraped across her chest. Her father's voice had brought her here. Where was he?

"Your father?" Bela said, a look of confusion—or so Lenora thought—on his face.

"I heard my father's voice," Lenora said. "He is here, I think."

Bela said nothing.

"Will you help me find him?"

Bela turned away. "There are many oddities that exist in the world that people never notice," he said, as though he had not heard her at all. "The creatures and wonders in Gilgevnah Woods are only seen by those we choose to reveal ourselves to." He looked back with something that could be called a smile, his flat teeth the same color as everything else on his body: pale pink. And perhaps it was the loneliness, or perhaps it was the overwhelming sorrow that had burdened her these last several days, but Lenora found that she smiled back at him.

"These woods are not as dark as my uncle said they were," Lenora found herself saying. The woods had, indeed, brightened considerably. She could see grass glistening on the ground as though each blade carried a small diamond.

"They are only dark if you cannot truly see," Bela said.

"See what?"

"The magic." Bela turned his back on her and began

walking deeper into the woods.

"I do see," Lenora said, following him slowly. "It is . . ." She had no words for it.

Bela's skin glowed a brighter pink.

Then Lenora heard her uncle's warning in her mind—it was unexpected, and somewhat unwelcome now. *Stay away from the woods.*

Why? she wanted to yell back.

"Why would my uncle warn me to stay away from something as wondrous as these woods?" Lenora wondered aloud. She hardly felt herself saying the words at all. They felt flimsy in her mind, as though they were not hers but someone else's.

It was strange and intoxicating.

"You will know in due time," Bela said. "And I fear you will not like the answer." He stopped and turned, his golden eyes glinting. Lenora's heart squeezed, lurched, then thudded. "You must not tell your uncle you have been here."

"Why not?"

Bela's face twisted into an expression that was difficult for Lenora to decode. She had never seen a creature like this one—a creature that could talk and walk and express emotion. "He does not wish us well." Bela spun on his heel again. "But that is a story for another day. Today is for showing you wonders."

Though her heart pounded and her skin prickled, Lenora followed.

36

Doubts began soon after Lenora lost her sense of direction. It was easy in the woods, with the trees everywhere. She should have brought bread crumbs or something. She should have turned around immediately. She should turn around now.

The minutes passed, and the doubts grew louder.

How would she emerge from the woods without being seen? What would Uncle Richard say or do if he found out where she'd been? Would he send her away? Would she be confined to her room, to more loneliness?

That would be an agonizing consequence—not just because of the solitude, but because now she had seen the diamond grass and the swaybacked trees and the friendly Scorlaman.

And there was more—so much more. She saw waist-high flowers with blooms that looked like brilliantly colored pillows and made her feel as though she were walking in a fairy forest. She asked Bela if fairies existed in these woods, because she'd always been intrigued by the little creatures (they defied her scientific mind, but that didn't matter; they were lovely), but Bela said that Gilgevnah Woods was not home to any creatures like fairies. They were too common, and this was an uncommon wood.

Bela must have noticed the troubled look on her face at his confession; he quickly amended it with, "Have no fear, Lenora. I will remain by your side to protect you from whatever might wish to do you harm. There is not much in these woods that would harm you, but if you do not know their danger, you might mistakenly touch something that you should not touch." He pointed to a grove of mushrooms that glowed in bioluminescent colors when he and Lenora entered the small clearing. "Take these mushrooms, for example," he said. "You must not touch them. They are poisonous to your kind." He tore off a piece of one, and the mushroom shrieked before immediately growing another appendage. He smiled. "For me, however, they are quite tasty." He stuffed the piece in his mouth and chewed.

Lenora felt the joy bubbling up inside her. It was so good to have company, to take her mind off her family, to know that she was not alone.

Bela took her to another, larger clearing, where what appeared to be the wispy petals of dandelions hung and swayed in the air, suspended by strings she could not see. "What is this?" she asked.

"These are the thistle creatures," Bela said. "They will not harm you."

"They are alive?"

"Look closely," Bela said. Lenora squinted. She could see their faces. She could hear their voices.

"Hello, Lenora," they said in a whisper-like hum.

Lenora once again wondered how her uncle, a man of science, could not love this place. In these woods were creatures both ancient and altogether new. How could he not see the potential for new scientific species? She wished she had a jar so she could take something home with her, show it to him, convince him the woods were simply magical woods.

Bela must have known what she was thinking. He said, "The creatures of this forest die as soon as they are taken outside the woods."

"Why?"

"They are sustained by these woods. It provides everything they need."

Lenora looked at the white creatures all around her. The scene could be mistaken for a still photograph of a snowy day in a shadowed wood. But the strangeness of it caught in her throat. She felt such an unexpected— and unexplainable—sense of alarm that she spoke in a shaky voice, the words spilling all over one another. "I must return to Stonewall Manor."

Bela folded his arms across his chest and frowned. "So soon?" he said.

"Yes." Lenora's voice was barely a whisper. She did not want to return. She wanted to stay here, with these people—creatures—who made her feel like she was less alone in the world. But she could not make her uncle worry. She said, "It will be supper soon. I must not keep my uncle waiting or he will wonder where I've been." She tried to think of what might sway Bela to make him release her.

Was she a prisoner here? The idea frightened her. Yes, the woods were lovely, but she did not want to stay if she could not freely go.

She said, "He will come looking for me."

Bela's face shifted into a smile. "Ah," he said. "I see you have come to understand the importance of keeping what you find in these woods a secret."

Lenora did not answer.

"I will take you back," Bela said.

"And will I be able to come again?"

"The woods will always welcome you, Lenora," Bela said. The trees punctuated his words with a gush that crackled the leaves. "Provided you say nothing about it." Bela gestured around him. "This would all go away if the world knew about it."

"Why?"

"It is the way of a magical wood. It is the way of anything in the world. You find something exquisitely marvelous. You get used to it, take it for granted. You forget that it is exquisitely marvelous. And it disappears."

Is that what Lenora had done with her family? Become too used to them, taken them for granted? Was it Lenora's failure to see them as exquisitely marvelous that had taken them away? Her throat burned, and her vision smudged at the edges.

"You have much sorrow, Lenora," Bela said.

"I miss my family," Lenora said. She swallowed the thickness in her throat. "But they will be here soon." Her voice cracked around the words, and she looked down at her feet.

"These woods could heal your sorrow," Bela said. "It is part of their magic."

Lenora looked up into his gleaming golden eyes. "How?"

Bela studied her for a moment before saying, "You must come deeper into the woods." His golden eyes glowed like tiny suns.

They were already in the grove of sitting trees. A bell clanged. Lenora's head cleared, and the woods looked darker. She felt a heavy sense of dread, though she could not explain it.

"I must go," she said.

"We will see you again," Bela said. He returned to his four legs. Lenora turned away. "Remember, Lenora." Lenora turned back. Bela was shrinking. "These woods are made to provide companionship and happiness. But for that, we will have to venture deeper."

Without another word, he vanished completely.

"Bela?" Lenora said, but there was no answer. The woods darkened to black, as though its golden light was extinguished with the disappearance of its keeper. Lenora ran toward Stonewall Manor as fast as her legs could carry her.

37

As the stone walls loomed closer, Lenora slowed. The day was much drearier than it had been before she entered the woods. She stood outside the elaborate entrance, marked by six steps and a wooden porch along the length of the house, and stared, trying to find some sign of life. Not even fireflies glowed around the mansion. It was as devoid of life as any abandoned home would be.

As her home back in Texas City might be.

No. She would not think about that.

Lenora lifted her chin. If the people inside Stonewall Manor did not wish to engage with her, then she would find her companionship in the woods. They could not deny her that.

"What's keeping you, love?" Mrs. Jones stood at the entrance, one hand on the door. Her face held questions. "And where have you been?"

"In the garden." Lenora had never liked lying, but sometimes it served a purpose. She couldn't tell Mrs. Jones about the woods. She wouldn't risk her only chance at happiness.

She knew she could not find happiness within these walls.

Mrs. Jones pulled Lenora into the kitchen. "You'll eat with me tonight," she said. Her eyes were shadowed, secretive.

"Where is Uncle Richard?"

Mrs. Jones busied herself with the food, dishing a heap of mashed potatoes onto Lenora's plate. "Gravy, love?" Lenora nodded. When Mrs. Jones had finished with the crispy chicken and steamed carrots, she sat with her hands folded and her head bowed. Her lips moved, but she didn't say words aloud. Lenora stared at her. When Mrs. Jones finished, she said, "Your uncle had to take an unexpected trip."

"Where?" Lenora's heart fluttered. Had her parents finally contacted Uncle Richard? Would she be going home now?

And then she felt a blast of anger. Why had he not taken her with him?

Mrs. Jones waved at the food. "Eat, before it gets cold." And then: "It is none of our concern where your uncle goes. He will return in a few days." Her voice wavered.

"But you said Uncle Richard never goes anywhere," Lenora said.

Mrs. Jones scowled at her plate.

"Did he find my parents?" Lenora said. "Will they be coming back with him?"

Mrs. Jones's head snapped up, and her eyes grew soft and moist. She shook her head, and Lenora's heart thumped. Mrs. Jones opened her mouth, but nothing came out, and Lenora was glad. She inserted into the empty space a question that would keep Mrs. Jones from telling her what she feared, which was that her parents would never be found and Texas City was not at all where Uncle Richard had gone. "Did he drive his car?"

"Your uncle doesn't drive," Mrs. Jones said matter-of-factly. "Not anymore."

"He used to?"

Mrs. Jones didn't answer.

The clock above them chimed. They were late for supper by fifteen minutes.

Lenora almost asked why Uncle Richard didn't drive anymore when Mrs. Jones said, "You should be glad your uncle isn't here. He would not have liked your tardiness to supper." Mrs. Jones tried to arrange her face into a stern mask, but she was much too gentle. Lenora could see through the act. She almost smiled. Mrs. Jones would make a lovely grandmother.

"The garden needs quite a bit of work," Lenora said. "I wanted to make some progress."

"Yes, well." Mrs. Jones turned her attention to her food, though she only picked at it. Lenora could tell something was bothering Mrs. Jones. Had she seen Lenora come out of the woods?

The woods. With Uncle Richard gone, she would be free to roam the woods for the next several days.

"When will Uncle Richard return?" Lenora tried as well as she could to wrap innocence around the words.

"The day after tomorrow," Mrs. Jones said. She

narrowed her eyes at Lenora, seeing right through the innocence. "Why?"

Lenora shrugged and looked down at her plate. "I'd like to have the garden cleaned up by then. I think he would like to see it as it used to be."

Mrs. Jones's face softened at that, and Lenora knew she had chosen the exact right words. She felt somewhat guilty for the lie, and to atone for it, she would make sure she *did* clean up the garden. She could not spend all her time in the woods, after all. There were many hours in a day.

After supper was done she helped Mrs. Jones with washing up and then retreated to her room to consider all she had seen.

It was much too wonderful to forget.

38

The next day, Lenora woke early, eager to slip away, unnoticed, into the woods. With Uncle Richard gone, she didn't have to fear discovery. Mrs. Jones was much too busy with the dusting and cooking at Stonewall Manor to be concerned with what Lenora was doing all day. Lenora planned her grand escape with a cover: She would sit in the library for a time. She would bang on the piano. She would let Mrs. Jones see her in the garden. And then she would disappear into the woods.

Breakfast was much too quiet. Mrs. Jones was already somewhere else in the manor. Lenora missed friendly conversation; her thoughts turned, naturally, to Bela.

Perhaps she didn't need the cover plan and could, instead, return immediately to the woods.

Lenora washed her plate and set it to dry on a towel beside the sink. She turned toward the icebox. She had an idea. She would pack a lunch and leave a note for Mrs. Jones (saying something like "I'll eat my lunch in the garden" or "I wasn't hungry and I've gone to take a long nap"—yes, that one might work better so Mrs. Jones didn't come looking). With a note and no expectation for lunch, she could spend more time in the woods without raising suspicion. Lenora shoved a sandwich wrapped in a towel and a small red apple into a satchel she found in one of the cupboards, scrawled a quick note, and ran out to the garden. She watched the windows of Stonewall Manor to see if any drapes moved, but they were all still. She raced toward the woods.

Bela was waiting for her just inside, looking remarkably humanlike—that is, if humans were pink and glowed and had a lion's mane around the head and . . . well, maybe not so humanlike after all, she supposed. She smiled at him, genuinely pleased to see him. "Hello again," she said.

"Lenora. I was hoping you would come back early so I didn't have to wait here all day."

"You would wait all day for me?" She could almost

taste her giddiness. Waiting all day is what a friend would do.

"Of course," Bela said. "We are friends, aren't we?"

It had been so long since Lenora had called anyone a friend. She had sent a letter—how many days ago?—to Emma but had not received a reply. What had happened to all her friends and classmates? Were they safe, or . . .

"Lenora." Bela's tail flicked in front of her face. "Are you here with me or somewhere else entirely?"

"I am here," Lenora said, and she was struck by the way the words resembled those that had drawn her into the woods yesterday. She looked around, into the golden light that glowed between the trees. What was the voice that had called to her yesterday? Why had it sounded like her father's?

She almost asked Bela, but before she could, he said, "Did you tell your uncle you came here?" He glanced behind him, toward Stonewall Manor, then back at her.

"No," she said. "I didn't tell anyone."

Bela smiled, his pink mouth widening on his pink face. "Good. Then we will have some fun today. But first sit." He gestured toward one of the sitting trees. He said, "I want to hear your story." He sat down on a tree.

"My story?" Lenora was confused.

"Your story of sorrow," Bela said. "Sorrow is what draws people inside these woods." Lenora felt the words tangle in her head. "It is a powerful thing." The pink fluff around Bela's neck bristled. "These woods exist to heal sorrow." His golden eyes beamed into hers. "Your sorrow."

"How?"

"In the telling of your story." He folded his hands with the four fingers. "And more."

Lenora felt the words tumbling from her lips. It had been so long since she had talked about the disaster— had she ever talked about it? She couldn't remember. The details of the days after were hazy. But the details of the day—her birthday—were still clear.

The story was halting, tearful. She began with her disappointing birthday and how angry she had been that Mother and Father had made her go to school, when she was the only one who should have been allowed to remain home. She ended with the explosion that shook the world and the uncertainty of where her family might be.

Silence wrapped around them for a time. And when Bela broke it, it was to say, "So if you had remained at home with your family, you would have died."

"No. They are not dead." The words were habit now.

"Would you have rather died?" Bela said. "Bobby told me something similar."

"What was his sorrow?" Lenora said. She thought it might be the same sorrow her uncle carried.

"Sorrow stories are private things," Bela said.

"But you said you would take me to him."

"In time, perhaps," Bela said. "But you must see the forest first. You must decide to remain."

"Remain?" Lenora said. A small ball of alarm wedged into her chest. "What do you mean?"

"Remain in these woods. Like Bobby."

"How could I do that? What if my parents return for me?" What if they weren't here in these woods? What if they were on their way to Stonewall Manor even now?

She would rather live in both worlds—that of

Stonewall Manor and that of Gilgevnah Woods—than be chained to one.

Bela nodded. "Perhaps we should see what the woods have to tell you."

"They can tell me about my parents?" Lenora felt hope bloom in her chest, warming all the coldest places.

"If they wish," Bela said. "But you'll have to venture deeper than you did before." Lenora shuddered. Bela tilted his head. "You are afraid of what you might find."

Lenora did not argue.

"Your uncle has planted plenty of fear in your heart, just like he did in his son." Bela's golden eyes flashed, but he did not look threatening. His face turned sad. "He is a dreadful man."

"Perhaps the woods could heal him, too," Lenora said.

"The woods cannot do for him what it can do for you," Bela said. "He has carried his pain much longer than you have. It has so distorted his vision and heart that he seeks to destroy us." Bela's eyes lifted to Lenora's. "Did you know this?"

"No." But she could certainly imagine it; she had

seen the army of robots. Is that what he planned to use? "What would happen if he succeeded?"

"He will not succeed," Bela said. "We have been around since the beginning of time, since the advent of sorrow. In different places, around the world."

"So you haven't always been here, near Stonewall Manor?"

Bela did not answer.

"How old is Gilgevnah Woods?" Lenora said.

"Nearly two centuries old."

"You said if I told someone about Gilgevnah Woods, this would all go away," Lenora said. "But my uncle cannot destroy it?"

"Our fate rests with a child," Bela said. His pale pink skin darkened. Lenora thought this might be a show of emotion, but she could not read which.

"And if I told, you would die?"

"I do not know. Perhaps we would simply go elsewhere." Bela turned away. "Come along. We have many sights to see today."

39

When they had been walking for only a few minutes, Bela said, "Would you like to play a game of hide-and-seek?"

It had been Lenora's favorite game to play with her brothers and sister. She did not even have to think about the question. She nodded eagerly.

They played twelve games of it, Bela beating her every time. She did not know the woods as well as he did, and, besides, he was smaller in his original size, which he used for the game, and could fit into the most unlikely of places. Once, he'd even twisted into a small hole in one of the trees and somehow dimmed his golden glow. She thought this advantage somewhat unfair, but she didn't complain; she was playing hide-and-seek, and it had been so long since she'd played.

After that, Bela and Lenora played chase. She was

always "it"; Bela was much faster than she was. He would wriggle out of sight, and Lenora would follow in the direction she thought she'd last seen him. But directions were useless this deep in the woods; she could not tell north from south or east from west.

She lost him frequently.

Lenora stepped onto some flattened grass, and it started singing. She placed a hand on her chest and listened. It was beautiful singing. The melody twirled on the wind, leaving iridescent purple swirls in the air, and Lenora turned around and around, trying to see from where the music came, but the purple flourishes were everywhere. They encompassed her. The sound domed around her.

Bela appeared. "It is the grass." He bent to touch a blade, and it sang louder. "It enjoys the presence of creatures and people."

"It is lovely," Lenora breathed. Everything about this place was lovely.

Bela beckoned her to follow him. "You must see this as well," he said.

He took her to another grove where the trees were

not like the others but were smaller in stature. They did not bend to welcome her but seemed, instead, to come alive. Their branches became arms, gesturing in a manner that appeared very humanlike. And when Lenora looked closer, she saw that etched onto the bark were faces wearing eyes and noses and smiles. Lenora cried out.

Bela touched her arm.

"We are the Pinales People," the trees hummed, as though they were all one voice and presence.

Lenora could only stare. "I have never seen anything like this," she said, and she meant it about the whole entire woods. It was the most magnificent place she had ever known—a wonderland.

"And you will never see anything like it again," Bela said. "Watch."

The trees lifted from the ground onto roots that looked like octopus tentacles—not frightening ones but beautiful, glittering ones—and began to dance around Lenora. After a time, Lenora could not help but join them. She felt wild and free and uninhibited, moving to a music she could not hear but could feel, deep inside her. She laughed so hard, tears ran from her eyes. It had been so very long since she had felt this kind of joy.

The woods were magical indeed. Her sorrow was set aside, for the briefest of moments.

The trees soon shifted back into their original places. Their eyes blinked, as though they waited for something. "Thank you very much for an enchanting time," Lenora said.

"We must be on our way," Bela said, and he bowed to the trees. They closed their eyes, and as Lenora watched, their faces faded back into the bark.

"Come," Bela said, and Lenora followed as quickly as she could. She arrived at a field that was full of flowers, she thought, but when she entered, the flowers erupted. They fluttered all around her, every color of the rainbow, and she saw that they were not flowers at all but butterflies perched on stems. They wore tiny humanlike faces. Some rested on her shoulders, some on her head, some in the palm of the hand she held out to them. They began to sing in a voice so melodic that Lenora had to close her eyes. Her heart swelled, filled, nearly burst with pleasure. She began to sing, too, though she had never heard the song before.

When the last note had faded, Lenora asked the butterflies, "How did I know your song?"

In one voice, they said, "Because we all have the same song inside us that longs to be free. It is the song of your being. If you forget your song, we sing it for you."

It was all so remarkable that Lenora wished she could remain there forever, hear them sing again, join them in a voice that did not sound like her own, which had never been melodious.

But she must find Bela.

"Thank you," she called to the butterflies as she passed through their field.

The woods still glowed with a golden light, but Lenora could no longer see the sky; the crowns of the trees were too thick. She felt a sting of panic in her chest. "Bela!" she called. He did not answer. She looked to her right and her left. Which way had he gone? These woods were immense. How would she find him?

How would she escape?

Would she?

Her apprehension rose with every step. She could not tell if she was walking deeper or walking out, but all she could do was continue walking.

40

Water glistened up ahead in a small pool. Lenora moved to the edge and peered into the silvery glass. She could not see through the water, could only see her reflection, which, as she watched, changed subtly. Staring back at her now was a girl who looked very much like her except she was more beautiful, with perfectly curled hair and bright blue eyes and a clean dress and a glowing face. Lenora squinted her eyes, and the person looking back at her squinted her eyes, too. It was Lenora, all cleaned up. Lenora looked down at her dress, streaked with dirt in places. The image changed again, and she saw her sister, springy red curls touching her shoulders, bright green eyes challenging.

It was so real.

"Rory!" Lenora reached for the image in the water.

But before she could touch it, Bela's voice shook her in an echoing bellow. "Careful!"

She ripped her hand back as though something had burned her. She looked over her shoulder, and there he was, his pale pink body glowing in the shadows. "I found you," she said, for lack of anything better to say.

"I found *you*," Bela said, smiling.

"I thought you had left me."

"I'll never leave you, Lenora."

It was a warm promise.

She looked back at the water.

"Come away from the water, Lenora," Bela said.

"Why?"

"It is dangerous."

"But I saw my sister."

"The water shows you what you most desire. It cannot deliver it."

"But I saw my sister!" The words were wrapped in a wail. Lenora did not move. "She is there." She pointed.

"Lenora." Bela's voice had grown sharper. "Come away from the water."

A tendril of black silvery glass poked up from the

surface of the water, curling at one end. Lenora stared at it, mesmerized.

"It is time to go home," Bela said.

"Home," Lenora said. "Home is Texas City. And it no longer exists."

The tendril of water thickened, became a swirling snake. It moved toward her in slow and measured coils. She reached out a hand. The surface of the water flickered. Mother's face, smiling. Father's face, stoic. John's face, searching. Charles's face, mischievous.

And just when Lenora closed her eyes and waited for the water to take her to her family, she heard a cry so fierce she scrambled away from the edge. She opened her eyes. Bela lay on the ground at the bank.

"Bela!" She moved toward him.

"Stay back," he said, his voice weak and strangled. "Give me a moment." He closed his eyes, and when he opened them again, his skin was the darkest pink she had seen yet. He struggled to his feet. "You must stay away from this pool," was all he said.

Lenora nodded, her breath hitching.

"You've been here too long." Bela moved away from

the pool. "I will take you back." Lenora hesitated, but Bela swung back around. "You must come with me."

"Why is the pool dangerous?" Lenora said. She was afraid to look at the silvery waters, afraid they would pull her closer. "I thought nothing intended to hurt me. I thought . . ."

"There are many wonders in Gilgevnah Woods," Bela said. "But there are also dangers for those who do not understand its ways." He glared in the direction of the pool.

"What would have happened?" Lenora wasn't sure she really wanted to know, but she asked the question anyway.

Bela only said, "Come along."

Lenora felt a cold wind moving through the woods. The golden light had all but disappeared.

It took a very long time to reach the border of the woods, but, at last, Lenora saw the sitting trees. Her heart slowed.

Just before she passed the border, Bela said, "You will come back? The pool has not scared you?"

"I will come back," Lenora said. She wouldn't let a

silvery pool keep her from this magical place where she didn't have to be alone. "As soon as I can."

She would return as long as she had a friend to return to.

Bela lifted his hand and waved.

41

It was later than she thought when she reached the grounds of Stonewall Manor. The sun was nearly gone. She had forgotten all about the lunch she had packed; it was soggy in her dress pocket. Her stomach rumbled.

Lenora hurried into the house. Mrs. Jones was pacing in the kitchen.

"You are late for supper again," Mrs. Jones said. She held up an iron bell. "I rang it and rang it and rang it." Her face was a mask of fear, but Lenora watched as she smoothed it, took a deep breath, and said, "I expect you to follow the rules when your uncle is gone, just like you do when he is here."

Lenora looked at her shoes. Mud and dirt browned their sides. She lifted her eyes again, hoping Mrs. Jones wouldn't notice. "I'm sorry," she said. "I got carried away in the garden."

"You weren't in the garden," Mrs. Jones said. Her blue eyes flashed, and Lenora's stomach twisted. "I looked. I did not see you there."

Lenora's heart turned flips, one after another. What could she say? What would Mrs. Jones believe?

She searched for something that would not be too far from the truth. "I fell asleep," she said. It almost felt true. All the wonders she had seen in the woods, they could not be real, could they? "I remember lying down in some tall weeds, for the shade they could give me." This was a complete and utter lie, and her heart bent into a painful ball. Father would be disappointed in her. He always said the truth was the most important thing to tell.

I'm sorry, her heart said. Would he understand, if he were here?

He had gone into the woods once. He had come back out. What was so dangerous about that?

"You did not hear me calling?" Mrs. Jones raised her eyebrows. She did not look like she believed Lenora.

Lenora shrugged. "I haven't been sleeping well," she said.

"You've been closing your window at night?" Mrs. Jones's voice was gentler now.

"Yes, of course. It's what Uncle Richard wishes."

"Your uncle also wishes a prompt supper," Mrs. Jones said. "And for his niece to stay out of the woods."

So she knew, then.

"How—"

"Your hair." Mrs. Jones fingered a strand and showed it to Lenora. It was completely white.

Lenora gasped. She took a handful of hair and twisted it toward her. Not all of it was white. Not even most of it was. Only a few errant strands.

What did it mean? Was it a mark of some kind? For good or for evil?

The questions swarmed, but Lenora swallowed them.

Mrs. Jones placed a bowl of chicken soup in front of Lenora. It smelled delightful, and Lenora's stomach vibrated with hunger and throbbed with guilt at the same time.

What kind of girl was she turning into, now that Mother and Father were gone?

They were not gone. They were not.

"Have you heard anything from Uncle Richard?" Lenora said.

"I didn't expect to," Mrs. Jones said, without looking at Lenora. She took a bite of her soup and promptly dropped her spoon. It clanged against the table, providing a cadence to Mrs. Jones's groan. "I burned my tongue." She took a long drink of water. Lenora blew on her own spoonful for quite some time before taking a bite. It was the best chicken soup she had ever tasted.

This thought was a betrayal. Her mother had been a good cook, too. But she had not been Mrs. Jones.

"I only thought he might have checked in to see how I . . . to see how we were doing." A sadness wrapped around Lenora's words, and she could not hide it. Mrs. Jones's head lifted. She looked at Lenora, but Lenora stared at the table.

She didn't want to see more sadness, more pity.

"I didn't know where you had gone," Mrs. Jones said. "I worried that . . ." She didn't finish her thought but moved on to another. "Your uncle would be distraught if you disappeared."

"Would he?" Lenora's cheeks burned.

Mrs. Jones narrowed her eyes. "Yes." There was not a doubt in her tone. "And so would I. So take care."

For the rest of supper, Lenora was so intently focused on her soup that she hardly noticed when Mrs. Jones stood from the table and began clearing the dishes. She did not think about soup, of course. She thought about Mrs. Jones and her warm words that tugged her heart in two different, opposing directions. She thought about Uncle Richard and his absence and what it could possibly mean. She thought about the woods.

Her spirits lifted. She had a companion in Bela and entertainment in the wonders of Gilgevnah Woods. She did not have to be lonely or miserable anymore. She would find everything she needed within the woods— even, she hoped, her family. If the woods could not bring them to her, they could, at least, tell her how to find them.

She could hardly wait to return.

42

Over the next several days Lenora continued to explore the woods with Bela. The two of them raced together, played games together, talked together. She'd never thought she could live without her family. The robe of sorrow she wore had grown heavy and cumbersome, but in the woods she was able to cast it aside. She could live, and she could live joyfully. It was unexpected. It was exhilarating.

What existed within the woods did not exist anywhere else in all the world—she was quite sure of that. She met rabbits that poked their white heads from large holes in the ground and invited her to underground tea parties, which she attended by entering a hidden grass door that opened on a tunnel system tall and wide enough for her to walk upright with her hands straight out at her sides. She watched birds burst into flame and then reappear on another branch of another tree in such a way that reminded Lenora of the fireworks her father used to supervise every Independence Day. She stepped on toadstools that transported her from one side of a swamp to another, each one emitting a ringing note like that of a piano, so she could play a song as she crossed.

Little by little, Lenora began to slip away from life at Stonewall Manor. She spent more and more time in the woods—every moment she could spare. She felt the presence of her family inside it; she couldn't explain why. But she could not feel the presence of family in the cold, ancient manor, and that made all the difference.

And though Lenora ached when she thought about her brothers and sister and how much they would have liked exploring Gilgevnah Woods with her, she began to feel less alone.

She grew accustomed to lying. When Mrs. Jones asked where she had been all day, she came up with a host of excuses. She fell asleep and didn't hear Mrs. Jones, she was hiding in the library, she found a secret passageway and almost couldn't find her way back out, she didn't feel well and had lain down, she was exploring. Some of them were more obviously lies than others, but the more she used them, the less guilty she felt.

It all got easier with time and practice.

Mrs. Jones never said anything about her lies, but Lenora noticed she often looked at her with a grave face of concern. But Lenora went to sleep and woke up thinking only of the woods. Nothing could keep her away from them.

Her uncle was absent longer than Mrs. Jones had expected, but Lenora didn't care. She didn't even worry about why he hadn't yet returned. She was glad to have the freedom to enter and exit the woods without fear that Uncle Richard would find her.

***

On the fifth day that Uncle Richard was gone, Bela told Lenora about another body of water that existed in the woods. He said it was not nearly as dangerous as the first one she had encountered. This one could tell the future. It was, however, much deeper inside the woods than they had been yet, and she would have to trust him to get to it.

She did not have to go; it was her choice.

"What if we get lost?" Lenora said. She knew she would never be able to find her way out.

"I have lived in these woods for centuries," Bela said. "I could never get lost." His pink skin practically glowed in the golden light that came from—where? Lenora still had not figured it out. Bela took her hand. "Stay with me and all will be well. You do not have to fear, Lenora. You are loved."

The words scattered their seeds inside her chest, lodged into her most vulnerable places, and opened their petals. She smiled.

She was loved, here in these woods. She would like to stay here forever.

So Lenora followed Bela.

The deeper they went, the darker and colder the woods became. But Bela placed a hand on her arm. She could feel his warmth seep from his fingers, into her skin. She did not shiver, even though the air turned chilly enough to warrant a jacket. The woods breathed around them. Trees bowed in their direction, creatures watched as they passed, light blinked in a sparkling rhythm before vanishing completely.

Though it was dark, Lenora did not feel afraid. These were her friends. This was her home.

"We are nearly there," Bela said. He pushed aside some low-hanging branches.

Lenora heard a voice calling her name. She looked around. "What was that?" she said. She stopped, and Bela did as well. He turned to her, his golden eyes like luminous stars in the darkness. Lenora swallowed hard.

"Did you hear something, Lenora?" When Bela said her name like that, she felt like she belonged nowhere else but here, inside Gilgevnah Woods. Bela's voice changed and became the voice of her father. "You belong here," he said.

"I know." Her mind felt cloudy and unreliable. Father's voice could not be coming from Bela's mouth. She heard her name again. She shook her head, trying to clear it. "Someone is calling me," she said.

"I hear nothing," Bela said. His voice was no longer Father's. He tilted his head. His face flickered into the face of her father. Lenora cried out.

"Father?"

"He is here, waiting for you," Bela said. "But you must continue on with me. We only have a short way to go, and then you will be able to gaze into the Waters of Aevum and see the future. You will see your family."

Yes. She needed to see her family.

Lenora took another step forward, holding tightly to Bela's hand. The darkness was infinite now, but Bela's eyes guided them on.

A bell clanged from somewhere, startling Lenora. Her name hovered on the air again. The entire woods had stilled, as though everything in it held its breath.

"Come, Lenora," Bela said. "You must come with me."

"I can't," Lenora said. "Someone needs me."

She could feel it, in her chest.

"Your cousin would like to meet you."

Lenora hesitated. "Bobby?" Her mind was so knotted. She wished she could untangle it.

If she saw Bobby, she might be able to convince him to return to Stonewall Manor. She could make her uncle happy again. She could remain here in Bobby's stead, until her family returned, since she was not needed or wanted anywhere else. She was loved here. She was not loved at Stonewall Manor.

But first she must say goodbye. She could not leave Uncle Richard without saying goodbye. Mrs. Jones said her uncle would be distraught if she disappeared.

Was it true? It didn't matter. She had to make sure he knew it wasn't his fault.

"Lenora," Bela said.

"I must go back." Lenora's voice wavered. She cleared her throat and tried again. "I will return tomorrow and look into the Waters of Aevum."

"You do not want to know your future?"

She did. Very much. She wanted to know if her parents were still alive. She wanted to know if she would see them again. She wanted to know if Bobby would return to Uncle Richard and if Uncle Richard would finally be happy and if they would all live happily ever after.

The voice called again, louder this time. It seemed to be right behind them.

"Please take me back," Lenora said.

Bela stared at her for a moment, and Lenora was

overcome by the kind of terror she could taste. It was sour, thick, and icy. What if Bela did not show her the way back out? What if her uncle had been right? What if Bela had drawn her so deep into the woods for a specific purpose—a malevolent purpose? Her eyes flicked around the woods. It was so dark she could see nothing except Bela's eyes. The trees seemed taller, thicker, much more ominous than she remembered.

"Please," Lenora said, her throat so tight she could hardly speak.

Bela's face folded into what Lenora assumed was a smile, though it looked ghastly in the golden light glowing from . . . So that's where it came from: his eyes. It was not a comforting truth; if he decided to leave her, the light would be gone. "Very well," Bela said at last. "This way."

Bela did not keep his hand on her arm this time, and the cold bled into her bones and rattled them. By the time she reached the entrance of the woods, where she could clearly hear now the voice of Uncle Richard calling, she was shivering so violently she could not say a word.

"You will come tomorrow," Bela said. It was not a question.

Lenora could only nod.

Bela bowed and backed away from the entrance. "The woods will miss you, Lenora," he said, and then he vanished.

Lenora's legs buckled. She put her hand against one of the sitting trees, to steady herself, and a vision of her mother and father and Rory and John and Charles played across her mind—her family running from the fire, her family scattering, her family falling. She tried to breathe. She tried to walk. But she did not make it out of the woods before her head hit the earth.

43

Lenora woke, if it could be called waking, when someone picked her up from the ground. Her vision was hazy, dreamlike. The sky was dark. Stars winked at her from a black expanse, like smudges of bright white pinpoints in a smoke cloud. The man who carried her was warm and strong, and she buried her face into his shoulder. He smelled of sweat and spice and a hint of metal. "Father," she murmured. "You came."

She was so tired. She could hardly think. So she closed her eyes.

"Sleep, my darling," the man said. It was a voice very like her father's but not exactly his. Lenora tried to peel her eyes open to see him, but she could not. "We will talk in the morning. I have returned, and I will not leave you again." The tender words held her as gently as his arms.

"Uncle." The word was hardly a whisper. She relaxed against him, but she did not sleep. Her eyes felt too heavy to open, but her ears were awake and listening. Her uncle carried her up the stairs with soft steps and heavy breaths. He laid her on the bed and drew the covers up around her. Lenora almost protested, because she was dirty; she knew she was. She had spent all day in the woods, exploring. Playing. Breaking the rules. As if that were not enough, the dirt would mess up her beautiful bed.

But when she tried to speak, Uncle Richard cupped a hand to her cheek and said, "Rest, Lenora. Please," and the words pulled her eyes open. Uncle Richard stared down at her with such love and longing that it nearly broke her heart. He looked so like Father right now. His angles were sharp and jagged, his cheeks flushed. He had not shaved in many days. His eyes were tortured and yet contained within them a wide gulf of relief. His cheeks glistened with tears. He released a shuddering breath and drew one hand to his mouth. He turned away, his back bent, his shoulders shaking.

Lenora felt emotion rise and contract within her. She

was too exhausted to cry. She closed her eyes.

She felt her uncle's presence with her until sleep wrapped her in black. Her last thought was a wondering: Was her uncle crying for her?

44

Lenora woke to muffled voices arguing outside her door. Then the door opened and Mrs. Jones entered, carrying a tray.

"Oh," she said, upon seeing Lenora. Lenora sat up and leaned against the headboard. The room spun only slightly. "You are awake."

"Of course," Lenora said. "Isn't it morning?"

Mrs. Jones cleared her throat and set down the tray. "It has been several mornings, love."

"What?" How was that possible?

Mrs. Jones's eyes darkened. She cleared her throat again and said, "You were very tired."

From the woods?

"How could I have slept for days?"

Mrs. Jones touched Lenora's hair, and her eyes turned sad. "Well," she said. "Your uncle says it's what happens when one ventures into the woods."

"You sleep?"

"You are drained. Of your . . ." Mrs. Jones gestured to her body. She shook her head. "He would tell you best."

Lenora reached for her mother's necklace, but it was not around her neck. "Where is my necklace?" She looked around.

Mrs. Jones stood and crossed the room to the dresser. She held up the pale pink pearls. "Your uncle didn't want you to sleep in it." She motioned toward her neck.

Mother had warned them not to sleep in necklaces, too.

Mrs. Jones handed Lenora the necklace, but Lenora did not put it on. Instead, she held it.

Mrs. Jones cleared her throat again. "We were not sure if you would make it," she said. "Your uncle was very worried."

"What happened?" Lenora searched her memory to see if she could put the pieces together, but everything was so jumbled.

"You went into the woods," Mrs. Jones said, as if that were enough of an explanation.

Lenora looked down at her lap. She had not touched her food—two pieces of brown toast topped with jam. She did not feel hungry, even though, according to Mrs. Jones, she had been asleep for days.

"I couldn't tell you," Lenora said. "About the woods."

"Why not?"

"Because you wouldn't have let me go." And it would disappear. She couldn't say this part aloud.

Mrs. Jones's eyes traveled the length of Lenora's face. "You're right. I wouldn't have. Look at you."

Lenora looked down at her dress. She knew it was dirty. She had ruined yet another of the gifts from her uncle. He wouldn't be able to buy her dresses indefinitely, would he?

Mrs. Jones cleared her throat. "You think I didn't know." It was not a question.

Lenora's throat burned. Her eyes snagged on Mrs. Jones's face, full of pain and regret.

"Your absence, your excuses, your hair." Mrs. Jones's voice cracked. "But what was I supposed to do? Keep you a prisoner in your own home?" She didn't seem to be talking to Lenora anymore.

"I feel better when I am in the woods." The words were accidental. Lenora had been thinking them one moment, and the next, they spilled out.

Mrs. Jones said nothing.

"I feel less alone," Lenora continued. She had to, now that the secret was out. "I feel like I am home."

"*This* is your home." Mrs. Jones's voice was a sharpened point that carved a trench in Lenora's heart. "You do not belong in the woods."

"I do not belong anywhere," Lenora said.

"Stonewall Manor has been in your family for centuries," Mrs. Jones said. "You belong *here*."

Lenora shook her head. "I never even knew about Stonewall Manor," she said, her voice rising in anger. Or was it sorrow? She could not even tell the difference anymore. "Why did I not know about my home if this is my home?"

The air sizzled between them. Mrs. Jones's eyes flashed with as much anger—or sorrow—as Lenora's. Uncle Richard entered at that moment, his face expressionless. But when he spoke, it was with a voice that seemed to hold all the love in all the world. "Lenora," he said. That was all it took to make her crumble. The tears tasted salty and somewhat disappointing. She wanted to remain strong, defiant, resolute. They could not take the woods from her. Not when she had seen so much that restored her joy. Not when it eased her sorrow.

Uncle Richard sat on the side of her bed. He didn't say anything for a long time. Finally, he cleared his throat and said, "What have you done?"

Lenora said nothing. He knew what she had done; she had ventured into the woods.

"What did you tell the woods, Lenora?" His voice was tight and thin.

Tell the woods? What did he mean?

"Did you tell them your name?"

"They already knew my name. Someone called me."

Uncle Richard ran a hand along his mouth and chin. His voice turned desperate. "And your story? Did the woods ask for your story?"

"Bela did." Lenora clapped a hand over her mouth; she was not supposed to be saying anything about the woods and what she had seen or who she had met.

Uncle Richard's shoulders slumped. "I knew it." The words were a breath, wispy and frail. He stared into space, leaving this world behind.

But Lenora would not let him. She lifted her chin. "The woods are beautiful," she said. "They're not dangerous."

Uncle Richard's eyes snapped back to her face. "There is much you do not know," he said.

"Then tell me!" Lenora's voice was wild and shrill, like the squall forming in her chest. The words tasted bitter. She knew the answer before Uncle Richard even spoke again.

He did not tell her anything except, "The woods are no place for a child."

The fury burned through her words. "I have walked all the way through the woods," she said. "They have never hurt me. Not even once." The silvery waters crept into her mind. She shoved them away.

Uncle Richard's voice turned wild now. "They will take you and keep you and kill you!"

"You are as mad as they say you are!" The words were loose before she could stop them.

"Lenora!" Mrs. Jones's voice rose in a high-pitched reprimand. Lenora dropped her eyes to her lap.

The room was so silent she dared not move.

Finally, Uncle Richard spoke. "Your father knew the truth of those woods. I didn't listen. And my son paid the price."

Lenora shook her head. She wanted to tell him that Bobby was in the woods, that Bobby was safe, that she would bring him home. But she knew he wouldn't believe her. He hadn't seen what she had seen; her father hadn't seen what she had seen. They didn't know the truth of the woods.

"Don't go back to the woods, Lenora." Uncle Richard sounded broken, defeated, and Lenora lifted her eyes. She could see the pain in his, and it squeezed her chest. She was sorry for what she'd said. She wished she could take it back. He dropped his eyes. "They may not let you go next time."

She would prove him wrong.

"Mrs. Jones?" This time Uncle Richard's voice was strong, unbendable.

"I'll make sure she doesn't return," Mrs. Jones said.

Before Lenora could say anything else, Uncle Richard was gone.

Lenora turned her face away from Mrs. Jones. The next time she looked, her room was empty. But she could see the shadow of feet outside her door. A guard.

Now she was a prisoner.

His strength, in death, was tangled up in sorrow, as his power had been in life. The grieving were the easiest victims to deceive; they were all too unquestioning of another's motives, blinded by sorrow and pretty words of understanding. He had used them liberally.

Death shifted his focus to the young—those wealthy in grief, rather than material goods. The young could not always comprehend the shifting nature of sorrow; they often felt like grief and its accompanying pain would last forever. He promised otherwise, and that was enough to lure them into his realm.

Sorrow is a constant in life. One does not truly live without it.

And so the woods continued, and he along with them.

April 29, 1947

I will not let the woods take her. I will not let them have another victim. They—he?—almost lured her into the abyss while I was off traveling, gathering supplies for the final piece—the piece that will return my son to me (if he is still alive; I am not entirely certain he is, but at least I will ensure that no one else will become like him), the piece that will save my niece's life. When Mrs. Jones told me that she had not been able to find Lenora on the grounds of Stonewall Manor or inside the house, though the day had surrendered to dark, the panic flared so fiercely and profoundly in me that I hardly thought I could do anything but retreat to my work, immediately. I almost gave her up for gone.

But courage is often surprising, and mine moved my feet for me, with hardly a second thought. I did not hesitate to breach the woods, calling her name, carrying the brass bell I constructed myself to ensure that I could escape whatever spell is woven around those who enter the trees. This bell is comprised of the scientific and the spiritual—a blend of metal and spirit that can pierce both. I have used it many times myself. I thought it might work for Lenora, too.

I did not locate her on my search inside the woods, but I found her, hours later, lying right on the border between the woods and the grounds. I caught only a glimpse of a strange creature—pink with golden eyes—before it scrambled away. It was very near Lenora's crumpled form. It had touched her. I am certain of it. Perhaps it even whispered in her ear and caused her to stumble. I do not doubt the possibility of anything anymore.

I do not know what kind of creature it was; I did not have my eyepiece with me, which allows me to see things more clearly and up close. I suspect it is a creature the world has never known. But even that does not convince me the woods are worth saving. Let every sinister species inside die together with it.

It will burn, yes. But burning is not enough. To end the curse of the woods, which could remain indefinitely, I must destroy the presence that resides deep within them, and that will need more than fire. That will need . . . me.

I am not noble; I am merely desperate.

Lenora will return to the woods. I could see it in her eyes. There is a chasm of loneliness and sorrow in my niece, and while I am grateful that I can recognize it in her as I could not in my son, it frightens me. Sorrow and loneliness are strong allies, and I cannot provide solace. The woods, however . . .

I must finish my work as soon as I can. I must destroy the evil that hovers around us. And I must do it while watching Lenora closely and ensuring that she does not run to the woods and its charms again.

I have never faced a more impossible task.

—excerpt from Richard Cole's *Journal of Scientific Progress*

DEEPER INTO THE WOODS

45

The sticky days of April lengthened into the steamy days of May. Lenora spent most of her time now in the garden, clearing away the weeds, watering plants, nursing them back to life. She was delighted at how green everything still was. During the longest part of the summer, the plants would likely dry up, as they did everywhere in Texas, or so her mother had always complained. But they were beautiful for now.

The woods called to her regularly. Once she even saw Bela standing at the opening, summoning her. She would like to return, but every day she spent in the garden or walking the grounds or pretending interest in the trees that arched over the sidewalk in front of Stonewall Manor, Mrs. Jones kept close behind her. Even when she explored Stonewall Manor, Lenora had a shadow.

The tables were growing dusty, since Mrs. Jones could not do her work.

As the days passed and Lenora did as she was told, Mrs. Jones settled herself into the creaking rocking chair on the porch of Stonewall Manor. She fixed her eyes on Lenora and would not look away, not even for a moment. Lenora knew the watching was her uncle's doing. He did not want her to disappear into the woods again. Anger and sadness warred within her. She grew lonelier, less hopeful, angrier every day that passed.

Though he did not take any more trips, Uncle Richard was hardly ever around except at their silent suppers, during which he said next to nothing most days but every now and then, surprisingly, asked her how her work in the garden was coming along or what book she had read for the day. Lenora looked forward to the suppers where he broke his mysterious, contemplative quiet, but they did not come often. Immediately after eating, Uncle Richard usually locked himself away inside his laboratory and worked on his secret inventions until Lenora shuffled up to bed, alone.

Lenora wanted to know what consumed his attention. Her curiosity was untamable. But with her shadow, she could not investigate.

So, instead, she thought.

Bela had said Uncle Richard wanted to destroy the woods. Uncle Richard, then, must be working on something that could do it—but what? Was there anything in existence that could destroy woods that had been around since the beginning of sorrow, which Lenora assumed was the beginning of time?

Lenora often found her gaze drawn to the windows of Stonewall Manor, which seemed to stare back at her, perhaps even glaring. Sometimes she would see Uncle Richard peering out of the window where he worked.

She began to loathe Stonewall Manor. The spacious hallways were filled with shadows and secrets, and Lenora did not think they were all good. There were so many questions: What had happened to Uncle Richard's wife and daughter? Why had his son run away? Should Lenora run away? When would she have a chance? Mrs.

Jones watched her every move. And if not Mrs. Jones, Uncle Richard.

She was a captive in a place that was supposed to be a home.

She had attempted, many nights ago, to escape. She had listened carefully, to make sure the house had settled into sleep. When she was sure of it, she emerged from her bedroom to find Uncle Richard sitting in a chair right beside her door, staring at the room across the hall—Bobby's room. His head had jerked up, and his eyes had stared at her blankly. She had not said a word, had simply fled back into her room and pulled the covers up to her eyes.

She had not fled, however, before she'd noticed the mark on her door. And in the blackness under her covers, she had shivered.

It was the same silvery X that she'd seen on Bobby's door.

What did it mean? Had Uncle Richard marked it? And if not Uncle Richard, then who—or what?

She had searched for the mark the next morning, but she had seen nothing.

The minutes and hours and days and weeks passed, and Lenora began to forget what Mother and Father and John and Charles and Rory looked like. It felt like the worst act of betrayal to forget their faces. She tried to imagine them when she was alone in her bed, in the moments before sleep, but her memory was blurry, almost blank. They had vanished as easily from her mind as they had from her life. She did not want to forget the way Father's eyes pinched up at the corners even when he wasn't smiling, which made him appear perpetually amused. She did not want to forget how beautiful Mother looked in her simple apron, plunging her dirty hands into the soil outside their house. She did not want to forget the music of Rory's magical piano hands, the way John looked with his nose stuck in a book, Charles's voice when he teased her.

How she missed them.

She roamed about the halls of Stonewall Manor, searching for a picture of her father, but she could not find him anywhere. He had left this home entirely. Her mother and sister and brothers had never been here at all.

Every morning that she woke without her family near, a heavy sadness pressed on the back of Lenora's neck. She bowed beneath its weight.

It would not be long before she broke.

She had to find a way back into the woods.

46

Lenora sifted dirt through her hands in a somewhat distracted manner. She breathed the usually soothing smell of grass and plants and freshly turned dirt, but it did not soothe her today. She placed her palms down flat on the ground and closed her eyes, trying to feel the hum of the earth that Mother had felt when she tended her garden. She tried to picture Mother, bent over flowers. She could not see her. She could not smell her mother's rose scent. She touched the pearl necklace, but even it did not conjure her mother's image.

She could not let them die.

Lenora opened her eyes, blinking hard.

A movement on the south wall of the garden caught her eye. A bird hopped along its length and sang a trilling melody. It seemed to be performing for her. Lenora smiled in spite of herself. Perhaps it was one of the birds from the woods.

Perhaps it had come to save her.

She needed to escape, to return. The woods would tell her what had happened to her family, once and for all. The woods would give her company, joy, a place to belong. The woods would ease her pain.

And her uncle's, too, if she could find Bobby. If she could bring him home, before Uncle Richard destroyed the woods.

She would not let him.

Lenora eyed the garden wall on which the bird sat, looking at her as it sang. She squinted back at Mrs. Jones. The bird was just out of Mrs. Jones's line of vision. She was sure of it. She glanced in the woman's direction again and then moved quickly toward the wall. The bird flittered away. Lenora scrambled over the wall and pressed herself flat against the smooth brown stone. She peeked around the edge to see what Mrs. Jones was doing. Mrs. Jones had disappeared, probably to prepare lunch. Lenora looked behind her, just to be sure she had not discovered Lenora's plan. But no one was there.

It was her first time alone in weeks. Perhaps Mrs. Jones trusted her more now. Lenora felt a pang in her chest.

But she would not waste this opportunity. She raced across the grass, breathing hard. The heat today was already thick and suffocating.

Lenora did not run toward the woods, as she had fully expected to do. Her legs carried her, instead, toward the window that looked into Uncle Richard's laboratory. She could not explain this; she could only go where her legs took her. She hid in the shadows beside the window and raised herself on her toes, her hands gripping the sill. The curtains were pulled across the window, concealing most of the view, but there was a crack in their middle, where one side did not quite touch the other, as though someone had been in a hurry to close them. Lenora could see something moving inside. A dark form crossed the window, and she stepped back, pressing herself against the stone of the house. She waited, trying to still her heart and quiet her breath. When she was sure that Uncle Richard would not be looking right back at her, Lenora peered inside again. She saw her uncle, huddling in a corner. The enormous white sheet had been removed, and she saw a giant rhinoceros made of the same materials she'd seen on the robots that lined the hall into his laboratory—copper, metal, gears of a thousand shapes and sizes. It looked as though it wore armor, and its horns, even from here, appeared sharp and lethal.

Lenora drew in a breath.

How on earth would he get something so large out of his laboratory? And why would he want to?

Lenora saw a puff of steam blast out of the rhino's mouth. Her uncle flipped a switch, and the eyes— which were light bulbs—blazed to life. Lenora watched, mesmerized.

Her uncle flipped another switch, and the rhino began to move in slow, lumbering steps. She could hear its thundering through the walls. Uncle Richard hastily flipped another switch, and the rhino shuddered and stilled. Uncle Richard looked toward the door of his lab, his face creased with concern.

Lenora had never seen anything like it. It was remarkable. Extraordinary. Magnificent.

Dangerous.

The word slammed into her chest. What did Uncle Richard plan to do? Lenora could not even guess, but she knew, somehow, that it had something to do with the woods, the destruction he had promised. (Had Uncle Richard promised it, or were those the words of Bela? Her mind was a muddle.)

Lenora's legs were stiff, frozen, unyielding, and there was nothing she could do about it. Not even when Uncle Richard turned and spied her at the window. Not even when he crossed the room with a look that could only be called furious. Not even when he shouted through the glass: "Leave me!"

But when his eyes turned menacing, shooting daggers through the pane, Lenora did leave him. This time she ran in the direction of the woods.

She did not look back.

47

Bela was there to receive her.

"Lenora. I have been waiting for your return."

"I know," she gasped. "I have been a prisoner at Stonewall Manor." She knew it was untrue, but it *felt* true, after days under guard. "They do not want me to return to the woods."

"They know you will heal here." Bela's golden eyes blinked. "They do not wish it."

"But why?" Lenora pressed a hand against her chest, trying to ease the ache there. "Why wouldn't they want my sorrow healed?"

"Miserable people often enjoy spreading their misery," Bela said. "They are threatened by those who learn to heal, to live a fuller life. If one is unable to find peace, it is easier to believe peace does not exist. You will learn this about people."

Bela began walking Lenora deeper into the forest, one hand on her arm. She did not object. She knew Uncle Richard had seen her; the deeper they went, the longer she could stay. And it felt so good to have company again.

But something nagged at the back of her mind. "Why was I so unwell last time I left the forest?"

Bela did not stop walking. "You were unwell?" he said. He seemed surprised.

"I slept for many days."

"That was not the forest's fault, Lenora."

"Then whose?"

"Tell me, Lenora." Every time Bela said her name, Lenora felt herself pulled forward by an invisible thread. "Did your uncle tend you after our last meeting?"

Lenora nodded.

"Did he give you something?"

Lenora hesitated.

"A sleeping tonic, perhaps?"

She could not say for sure. The doubt wedged into the corner of her mind.

Bela said nothing more, but his silence said

everything. He took one of her hands and placed it against the bark of a tree.

Lenora's vision flashed with images she had never before seen. An army of steel, powered by fire. A crumpled car. A boy, running for his life. Her uncle, vines wrapped around him.

Her hand burned. Lenora rubbed it.

Her uncle was a dangerous man. He intended to destroy the woods, with fire. He had been responsible for the deaths of his wife and daughter. His son had fled from the man whose mind was marred by sorrow and sickness.

He had almost died here. He might die here in the end.

No. It couldn't be.

But Lenora had seen it.

She swallowed the burning rock in the back of her throat.

"You are safe as long as you remain in the woods," Bela said.

"Uncle Richard said the woods are dangerous," Lenora said.

"But you have seen."

Yes. She had seen.

Still, the confusion fogged up her mind. She could not think straight, could not settle the warring emotions in her chest.

He was her family. But what did she know of Uncle Richard and his life before her?

"Take me to the Waters of Aevum," she said.

Bela smiled.

48

A glass surface sparkled in front of Lenora and Bela, mirroring the dark tops of trees that seemed to lean in and purposefully cover up the sky. A layer of mist hung above the water, and a thin blue light emanated from beneath it. The clearing was completely silent, except for Lenora's thumping heart. It smelled as clean as the laundry her mother used to hang on the clothesline to dry—like earth and hope all mixed together. Lenora closed her eyes and breathed.

Coming to the Waters of Aevum was the right thing to do, then.

The waters rippled toward her like the keyboard of a piano, played by invisible fingers. And when it reached her, a vine of silver water arranged itself into a question mark.

"What would you like to know?" The voice that

reached her ears was like the collective whisper of a thousand people.

Lenora scrambled back from the bank, remembering the other water that had nearly taken her to its black depths. Bela placed a glowing pink hand on her head.

"Do not be afraid, Lenora," he said. "This water will not hurt you. It will tell you whatever you desire, but you must only ask it one question."

One question. She had so many to ask.

"I cannot ask more?"

Bela shook his head. "The waters will answer only one. If you ask it another, it will drag you to its bottom. And . . ." Bela paused. "I am not entirely sure it has a bottom."

Lenora shuddered. So there was some danger here.

"Are you ready?" Bela said.

Lenora nodded, but she could not speak. It was too much pressure, only one question, when so many plagued her mind. She closed her eyes and breathed.

"Look into the waters, and you will find your answer," the Waters of Aevum said in their multitudinous whisper.

Lenora peered into the waters. She saw her reflection briefly, before it disappeared. She did not see anything for a moment, except for the water's silver glass, and then the surface shimmered and wrinkled and rose and fell. Her face turned into her mother's face and her father's face and her brothers' and her sister's and her mother's again. Her mother said only, "He needs you." And then the vision disappeared.

It could mean so many things.

"But—"

"You must ask nothing else," Bela said sharply, pulling her away from the edge of the pool.

"Another day?" Lenora felt the tears welling up within her. She had no answer at all. *He needs you?* Who? Her father? Bobby? Uncle Richard? The waters had not done their work. They had not kept their promise. She had no clarity at all.

Lenora clenched her fists. "They tricked me," she said.

"What did you see?" Bela said.

"My family. It was not an answer to anything."

"The Waters of Aevum are difficult to decrypt," Bela said. "You must try your best."

Lenora shook her head. "There is so much I don't know." Her voice wavered. "Everywhere. There are questions people refuse to answer, questions that cannot be answered, questions that should be but aren't answered." She glared at the water. "I would like to go home."

"Where is home?" Bela said, and the words choked Lenora.

Where was home? Was it here, in the woods? Was it with Uncle Richard? Was it back in Texas City? She did not even know what had happened in all these days after the disaster. What if Texas City didn't exist anymore? Then what?

"I must find out what happened to my family," she said. "What happened to my home."

"You have no need of your former home," Bela said. "You have a home here. With the creatures of the forest." Eyes pierced the darkness around them, eyes that lifted the endless black curtain and shone into it a golden promise. Connection. Companionship. Belonging.

As if to punctuate the promise, one of the white rabbits that had invited her to tea brushed against her leg. He was warm and comforting. She felt Bela's words tugging at her, pulling her to her feet, drawing her deeper than she had ever been before. But she strained against them, still unready to remain in the woods.

"I must know," Lenora said. "I will never truly enjoy a new home until I know."

Bela stared at her for a moment before dipping his head. The fur around his neck shifted with the movement. "Very well, Lenora," he said. "I will take you back. But you may not return." His eyes were very sad as he turned away.

"I will."

"Your uncle—"

"I promise."

Bela did not answer.

Before crossing the border between Stonewall Manor and Gilgevnah Woods, Lenora hugged Bela tightly. "You are my best friend," she said. "I will always come back to you."

The Scorlaman glowed with a radiant pink light that

Lenora had come to understand, in their days together, was his expression of joy. She smiled as she turned away.

But the smile soon slid from her lips, for there, just outside the border of the woods, stood her uncle, a storm gathering in his eyes.

49

Uncle Richard did not say anything. And that was much worse than the words she expected to hear.

All the way up to the house, all the way across the porch, all the way into the dining room, he remained silent. And Lenora quaked. She knew the storm in his eyes would eventually break.

Lenora was surprised to see that the sun was low in the sky. Had she been gone so long? Time did not pass the same way in the woods as it did outside, it seemed. She glanced back, but only for a moment.

She followed Uncle Richard to the supper table. Mrs. Jones looked at her with eyes that sparked and flared. She set down Lenora's plate with a loud clatter. She did not apologize for the noise that caused Lenora to jump; in fact, she looked as though she thought Lenora deserved it.

And Lenora thought she was probably right.

Lenora turned over in her mind every opening in this room, trying to determine whether she could pull off a stealthy escape between her uncle's exit from supper and Mrs. Jones's entrance to clear the plates. She was afraid of Uncle Richard's wrath, but she was more afraid of Mrs. Jones's.

She stared at her plate and moved her food in slow circles, rearranging it to look like she had done more than simply play with it. The silence wrapped around her neck and squeezed, making it difficult to breathe. The waiting was torture.

Uncle Richard ate his chicken and scraped up a forkful of peas and twisted off a small piece of bread and still said nothing. Lenora glanced at him every so often. His face had smoothed now and did not appear so terrifying, but she could tell his jaw was still clenched tight. When he chewed, there was a small muscle that vibrated. That had never been the case before.

When supper was nearly done, she grew tired of waiting for words. She wanted to get this over with, so she said, "You did not have to wait on me to eat supper." She felt rebellious, contradictory.

Uncle Richard's head snapped up. His dark eyes studied her, as though she were a curious specimen he was examining beneath a microscope in his lab. "One does not eat supper until the entire family is gathered," he said. "Your grandfather taught me that."

A boulder dropped inside the middle of Lenora's chest. Yet another member of her family she had never known. The sorrow of it—the anger of it—emboldened her. "We are not a family," she said.

The words felt true; a family talked to one another, spent time in the presence of one another. A family laughed, cried, played, planned together. Since coming to Stonewall Manor, Lenora had done none of those things with Uncle Richard.

Uncle Richard set down his fork with a loud clang, and Lenora flinched, for the second time since supper began. He patted the corners of his wide mouth with a perfectly white napkin. He looked so proper, so unapproachable in his pressed blue vest and dark gray shirt buttoned up to his neck. A brass timepiece poked from the pocket of his vest like a miniature robot captured within a fold. She took a second glance. No. It was only a timepiece.

"You are my niece," Uncle Richard finally said. "We are a family."

"There is more to a family than blood," Lenora said. She remembered Father saying something similar, when he talked about the men on his volunteer fire team. He loved them like they were brothers, sons, fathers. Did she love Uncle Richard? And, more important, did he love her?

Uncle Richard stared at her for a long while, and though Lenora dropped her gaze to her still-full plate, she could see him out of the corners of her eyes. His head tilted, then straightened. He looked at his plate and back up at her.

What was he trying to find?

When the silence grew too heavy in her throat, Lenora spoke to the table. "I do not expect you to understand. Perhaps your family operated differently than mine did. But in my family, we enjoyed each other's company."

She braved a look at her uncle now. His face was

divided into lines of ancient sorrow. He looked much older in that moment, and she tried to rub the pinch from her chest, but her pressing did little to ease it.

"And you believe I do not enjoy your company," Uncle Richard said.

Lenora bit her bottom lip.

"My son thought the same." The words drew Lenora's gaze back to Uncle Richard's face. "It is why he ran away."

It was the first time Lenora had heard Uncle Richard speak freely about Bobby, and she sat still, hardly breathing, not wanting to break the spell. Perhaps he would tell her now what had happened to his family. Perhaps she would learn that he was not someone to fear but someone to love. She longed to trust Uncle Richard, but trust did not come without knowing another person, and she knew nothing about him, only the pieces she had been accidentally given, the pieces the woods had shown her.

She would like to be given pieces on purpose.

So she waited.

Uncle Richard leaned back in his chair, and his next

words were entirely unexpected. "It is not easy losing the ones we love, is it?"

Lenora sucked in a breath. What was he telling her? His eyes were unreadable, dark pools of shadow and mystery. He seemed very far away from this room.

"I did not know how I could possibly live after I lost Edith and Mary." Uncle Richard's breath shook out into a whisper. "And then Bobby."

Still Lenora waited, a silent statue. But she could not remain invisible; Uncle Richard was an observant man. His eyes moved and fixed on her. They were disturbing eyes now, angry and disappointed. "You were in the woods again." It was an accusation that snatched her heart, spun it around, and let it loose so it galloped and thrashed in every direction. "Why were you in the woods again? Do you wish to die?"

Lenora's legs tensed involuntarily, as if she were preparing to flee. She didn't know what to say, and even if she did, her voice had left her already.

Uncle Richard must have noticed the terrified look on her face, because his eyes softened and glistened. "I want only to protect you, Lenora," he said, his voice gentle. "That is all. I swear it."

Lenora closed her eyes. It could be Father's voice.

She said, "There are no dangers, Uncle." She opened her eyes. "Bobby is there."

Uncle Richard's eyes widened.

"He is alive," Lenora continued.

"No." Uncle Richard shook his head. "No, Lenora."

"He is! I will bring him home to you. Only don't destroy the woods."

"Is that what the woods told you?" Uncle Richard shoved his chair back. It clattered to the floor. "The woods lie for their own purposes."

Lenora shook her head. "No." It came out like a whisper.

Uncle Richard placed two hands on the table and leaned toward her. It was a large table, but she could feel his anger. "From now on, you will be a prisoner at Stonewall Manor." His voice was rough and jagged.

"I will not be a prisoner!" She was surprised by her own fury.

"It is the only way I can keep you safe."

"You are not my father. This is not my home. It will

never be my home. And you will never be my family."

She gasped and smacked her hand to her mouth.

She had not meant it. Not at all.

Uncle Richard straightened. He tugged on the bottom of his vest, rubbed his nose, closed his eyes. He took a deep breath. "Stay away from the woods, Lenora. I will not lose you, too."

He was gone before she could say another word.

If he had remained, she would have said so much, starting with, *You are wrong.* Or maybe, *I will not lose you, either.*

Which would have made the bigger difference?

50

Mrs. Jones entered the room immediately, as though she had been listening at the door. Lenora knew she had been.

"Here, love," Mrs. Jones said. "Come with me."

Mrs. Jones wrapped an arm around her and helped her through the kitchen door and into a chair. Her legs felt so weak. She was so tired.

"Would you like some tea, love? And perhaps a bit of cake?"

Lenora didn't answer, but Mrs. Jones set both in front of her anyway. Her throat throbbed, but she cut off a small chunk of the cake and shoved it in her mouth.

After a time, Mrs. Jones spoke. "You cannot stay away from the woods, can you?" Her voice was soft, gentle, understanding—a warm balm on chapped skin.

She folded her hands in front of her and leaned back in her chair.

Lenora licked icing from her fork and stared at the table.

"Bobby couldn't stay away, either," Mrs. Jones said. She whispered the next words: "It was our little secret."

Lenora's eyes flicked to Mrs. Jones's earnest face. "You let him go?"

Mrs. Jones nodded and smiled sadly. "If your uncle knew . . ." She shook her head. "Bobby would visit the woods while his father worked. I kept an eye on him, and he would tell me the wonders he had seen." Her hands squeezed each other.

But Bela had said the woods would disappear if she told anyone what she had seen. Why hadn't they disappeared when Bobby told their secrets?

"I could not see the wonders, but Bobby described them well." Mrs. Jones wrestled something from her pocket and placed it on the table. It was a small brown book. She tapped the cover. "In fact, he wrote about them in his journal. He was a wonderful artist." She paused. "Maybe he saw what you see."

Mrs. Jones pushed the journal across the table. Lenora looked at the book and back at Mrs. Jones. "Why are you showing me this?" she said.

Mrs. Jones hesitated before saying, "If there is a way to put Bobby to rest and give your uncle peace, well . . ." She let the words trail off. Her eyes took hold of Lenora and seemed to warm her all over. "If his body can be found in the woods, we must find it."

"He's in the woods," Lenora said. "But he's alive."

Mrs. Jones shook her head. When she spoke, her voice had a wistful tone. "I gave up my hope long ago," she said. She nodded toward the journal. "His last entries were . . ." She paused, as though searching for a word. "Disturbing." Her eyes turned to glass. "I should not have let him go that last time."

"But the woods are not evil," Lenora said.

Mrs. Jones shrugged.

Lenora tried again. "They heal our sorrow. We should all go."

"The woods tell you what they want to tell you, Lenora. That does not make it so."

"But why would Bobby have stayed all these years?" Lenora stared at the journal.

"Bobby died in those woods," Mrs. Jones said. "He would not have left the father he loved."

Lenora thought it best not to mention the visions the trees had shown her today.

"Sorrow is a necessary part of life," Mrs. Jones continued. "The only thing that can heal sorrow is time. And even then . . ." She took a long, deep, shuddering breath and let it out. "Even then, it does not always heal straight. It sometimes heals crooked." Mrs. Jones glanced at Lenora, then down at her hands. "That is what happened to your uncle."

"What does he want?" Lenora said. She wasn't sure what she was asking. What her uncle wanted with the woods? With her? With an army of robots? Maybe she was asking all those things.

Mrs. Jones lifted her eyes and looked at the ceiling, as though it could give her answers to all the deepest wonderings. "He wants a family," she finally said. "But he doesn't know how to make one."

"Which is why he needs Bobby," Lenora said.

"Which is why he needs you." There was no doubt in Mrs. Jones's words, only certainty.

The words rang in Lenora's ears, the same words she'd heard from her mother, reflected in the Waters of Aevum: *He needs you.*

"He doesn't need me."

"He needs you more than even he knows." Mrs. Jones leaned back again in her chair. "I want to tell you a story, Lenora. Do you want to hear it?"

Yes. Of course she did.

51

Lenora thought the story might be about her family. And she was right, in a way. Just not the family she expected.

"Your father and your uncle loved one another more than any brothers I had ever known," Mrs. Jones began. "I cared for them. I had cared for many children before them. I should know." She smiled. She must have seen the confusion on Lenora's face. She said, "I only became a cook when your father and your uncle were too old for a nanny. I wanted to stay and watch them grow up."

Lenora leaned forward.

"They were brilliant young men—loving, handsome, promising. It broke my heart when they separated."

"Because of science and faith," Lenora said.

"Yes. But there was something more." She sighed. "Your uncle had fits. He would stare blankly into space sometimes, or he would fling himself on the ground, his eyes rolled back and his tongue hanging out. Sometimes he would bite his tongue so badly it would swell up and he would have trouble breathing. It was frightening for your father." Mrs. Jones wiped at an invisible spot on the table. "The people in this town were always narrow-minded. They whispered about your uncle, said he had been possessed by demons."

"That's ridiculous," Lenora said.

"Yes, well, we know more about the disease—epilepsy—than we did before." Mrs. Jones paused, then began again. "The things people said—they were hard on your father. He wanted to be a preacher."

Lenora had never known this. "He wasn't one."

Mrs. Jones was quiet for so long that Lenora said, "I haven't seen Uncle Richard have any fits."

"Your uncle takes medicine for it now. He began medication soon after your father left."

"Then why didn't Father come back?"

Mrs. Jones shook her head. "It had something to do with the woods. Your uncle has hinted that much. On the day your father left, I heard him say he would not remain to raise his family in a house where children disappeared." Mrs. Jones's eyes glazed over. "I still remember the day your father came out of the woods with white streaks in his hair. They were the same streaks I saw in Bobby's, years later."

Cold dripped down Lenora's spine. She thought of her own hair, white in places. She thought of the children in the pictures lining Uncle Richard's hallway. They'd all had white hair, too.

What could it mean?

"How many children have disappeared?" Lenora was afraid to ask, but she did it anyway.

"Every generation of the Cole family has lost a child," Mrs. Jones said. "Stonewall Manor was built on sorrow."

Lenora touched Bobby's journal.

"Your father left after a big row," Mrs. Jones said. "He shouted his piece, and your uncle called him foolish, superstitious. Your father didn't take kindly to that." Mrs. Jones smiled to herself. "They were both strong-willed boys. Stubborn as mules."

"Father never returned," Lenora said. "And he never told any of us about this place."

"Yes. I don't understand that part." Mrs. Jones tilted her head. "Your uncle tried to send your father letters. Your father never answered."

"That doesn't sound like Father," Lenora said.

"I didn't think so, either. But your uncle could not be convinced. He thought your father had cut his brother out of his life. He never tried to visit or call or write again."

"How sad."

Mrs. Jones nodded.

Since Mrs. Jones had shared so much about the past, Lenora could not help but ask, "What happened to Aunt Edith and Mary?"

Mrs. Jones's eyes were pools of grief. "If your uncle has not told you, love, then I do not think it is my place."

"I only want to know," Lenora said. She needed to know. She needed to know if their deaths were the fault of her uncle, as the woods had suggested.

Mrs. Jones stared at her hands for a long time. Finally, she said, "There has been enough suffering in this family because of silence," and Lenora knew she would tell her.

"Your uncle was driving your aunt and cousins to town one day. It was Mary's birthday. They were going for ice cream." Her eyes glazed over again. "Your uncle had forgotten to take his medicine that day. There is a curve on the way to town—a dangerous one that wraps around trees." Lenora remembered that curve. She had felt almost like the trees were reaching for her when Lloyd maneuvered it so slowly she could have walked faster.

Mrs. Jones continued. "And just when his car came upon the curve, he had a fit." Mrs. Jones pressed her lips together. "The entire right half of the car was crushed so badly you couldn't tell what kind of car it had been. Edith and Mary died instantly, but your uncle and Bobby climbed out a window before the car exploded. They watched it burn. The only thing left was your uncle's pocket watch, stuck on the time. 3:07."

The lump in Lenora's throat swelled. Her uncle had watched his family burn. Just like she had seen Texas

City burn. She felt a sob rise up, twist, and tear out of her mouth. She could smell the smoke and see the flames.

Mrs. Jones rushed to her side and folded her into her arms.

She murmured soothing words. "It's all right, Lenora. Everything will work out in the end. It always does."

She said it so many times that Lenora found she halfway believed it.

52

The next morning, Lenora woke feeling refreshed, as though she had been given a measure of strength during the night. She had read Bobby's entire journal and learned that they had seen the same things—the trees with faces, the field of thistle people, the Waters of Aevum. But his last entries were as disturbing as Mrs. Jones had warned. She found a list of names, scrawled in messy handwriting that looked hurried and unlike his other, neater entries: *Benedict, 1839; Stephen, 1874; Gladys, 1912.* She found incomplete questions that had no answers: *How does the woods . . .; Where do they take . . .; How do they choose . . .* She found fear, and that made her wonder.

Was Bobby as free to come and go as Bela had suggested?

Why did he continue visiting the woods, then? That

was the question Lenora had taken to sleep with her.

And this morning she intended to find out—not just find out, but bring Bobby home.

She padded down the stairs and into the kitchen, where a cold breakfast of ham and boiled eggs and a small glass of orange juice waited for her. She did not see Mrs. Jones, but that was just as well. She would rather not share her plans today; Uncle Richard had made her a prisoner yesterday, but perhaps Mrs. Jones had decided it was unnecessary. She had, after all, given Lenora Bobby's journal. They were on the same side now, weren't they?

Lenora emerged into a bright and shining day, the air heavy but not suffocating. Her feet took her to the garden. It was not what she wanted it to be, not yet, but if Bobby came home . . .

Lenora felt giddy with the thought. She would have company, too.

Sweat trickled down Lenora's back. She had almost turned away from the garden when something glinted in the grass. It was pressed up against a far wall. She strode over to it. A small toy. A robot, one that looked almost exactly like what Lenora had seen in her uncle's hallway. Lenora stared. She held the toy up to the burning sun, like an offering, and sunbeams flashed off the copper. She turned it over and on its side and upside down so she could examine every tiny little part. It was exactly what she had seen, under the white sheets, except in miniature. She was sure of it. She stood and turned toward the window of her uncle's lab. It was the only window that today did not have its drapes shielding it.

Strange. It was unusual for him to open the drapes.

Lenora looked back at the robot in her hands. Her uncle had transformed a little toy into a life-sized toy. It was remarkable—so remarkable it nearly made Lenora smile. Then she thought about what her uncle intended to do with the life-sized robots he had created.

Did he intend to destroy the woods? To bring his son home? Or something else entirely?

He was a difficult man to know. Lenora wished she had tried harder. But there was no time for that now.

She had something important to do. And it might be dangerous. It might even be . . .

The urgency of her mission propelled Lenora's legs

forward. She moved toward her uncle's window. She saw him, bending over a table, a large eyepiece strapped to his right eye that magnified it in a comical way. He was entirely consumed with whatever he was building. He did not even notice the movement at the window. She pressed her nose to the pane, which smelled of rain and dust, and then, thinking that he might want to see the toy robot again, she placed it, standing, on the windowsill and slid to the side so he wouldn't see her but she could still see him, barely.

It took Uncle Richard quite some time to move to the window, but at last he did. Lenora saw him drop down until he was eye level with the robot. She could see his whole face open into a shining look of surprise and wonder and hope, and then, just as suddenly, crumple into a mask of sorrow and despair. Tears cascaded down his cheeks, and Lenora's vision blurred—but not before she saw him place one hand flat on the window, as though touching the robot or whoever might have held it once upon a time.

And Lenora could not bear the grief that matched her own in both power and intensity—could not bear the thought that she might have caused it. Her legs made the decision for her: They ran.

Into the woods, away from pain, toward a future of magical proportions.

Did it matter if that magic was dark or light?

53

Bela was not waiting, so Lenora folded into a ball on one of the sitting trees and rocked herself as she wept. Her stomach clenched and twisted. She let herself cry until she could not cry anymore, until she was emptied of everything, and when she was finished, when the agony had finally lessened enough for her to open her eyes, Bela was there.

"You are very sad today, Lenora," he said. The trees rustled.

Lenora nodded. She could not speak.

"I know why you are sad," Bela said. "You are thinking of Bobby."

Her worries didn't seem so troublesome here, in the woods. Lenora dropped her feet to the ground and could feel the vibration of something. Was it the magic?

"My uncle misses him very much," Lenora said.

Bela folded his hands together. "He chose to remain here. Why?"

Lenora could not answer that question; the whys were impossible to imagine.

But Bobby could answer it. So she said, "Could I see him?"

Bela did not answer. He merely said, "He came to us because of his sorrow. Because he could not find a place to belong." Lenora's insides shook and twisted. "And we gave him peace. We gave him a home." Bela's eyes glowed brighter. "Would you like that as well, Lenora?" The trees hissed again.

Lenora tilted her head. Did the trees hiss every time Bela said her name? What had her uncle meant when he asked if the woods knew her name?

It must matter.

"Where is Bobby now?" Lenora said. Her tongue felt thick and inefficient. Her vision shook a little. She blinked, and the world righted. It must have been her imagination.

Bela gestured to the trees. "He is all around us."

Lenora's heart raced. What did Bela mean? Was Bobby dead, then?

"You said I could see him," she said. She tried to remember what Bobby had written, the things she had seen. A clearing. A tree. A man.

Was that the last thing he had seen?

She said, "Take me to the man."

Bela smiled. "You know about the Master of the woods, then."

"He has Bobby, doesn't he." Lenora was sure of it now.

"No one has Bobby." Bela lifted his reptilian chin. "Bobby is here because he wants to be here."

Lenora wasn't sure of anything anymore. Were the woods good or bad? She had seen such wonders, but wonders could be evil, too, could they not? If they stole life—time, presence—from the living.

She thought of Uncle Richard, with his robot army. He would destroy the woods. She could feel it. Stonewall Manor was charged with a new air this morn-ing: hope mixed with determination. She had thought it was her own, but she knew now that it belonged to Uncle Richard.

He had finished his work.

Lenora said, "If you give me Bobby, if you let me take him home, these woods can remain."

Bela shook his head. "These woods will always remain."

"My uncle will destroy them."

"You think your uncle can destroy us?" Bela laughed. It was a melodic sound, entirely unexpected from a creature so reptilian. "He is only a man."

"Man is capable—"

"Man is no match for the spirit world." Bela's voice was now large and terrifying. Lenora cowered. She looked behind her, searching for an exit from these woods, but the trees had closed around her.

How had it happened? She'd been just inside the woods, and now she was deep—too deep to find her way out.

At least alone. But Bobby knew these woods.

She would finish her quest. She would find Bobby and bring him home, whatever the cost.

Uncle Richard deserved that, didn't he? For Father's silence, for Lenora's impertinence, for the losses that had lined up in his life like unwanted potions on a shelf?

Lenora stood from her place on the sitting tree, and immediately her vision cleared. She could see the way out. But she had already decided.

She said, "Take me to the Master." Bela studied her for a moment. Could he see it in her, the resolution? Could he tell she meant to betray him?

And then he smiled.

54

The deeper they went, the more Lenora could feel the magnetic magic of the woods and the less she could see. The light dimmed and faded in degrees. She felt an immense terror at the darkness, the depth, the imagined dangers she had read between the lines of Bobby's words. What had he seen? What had he known? And why had he gone back in spite of his gathering fear?

For the same reason she went? To save someone she loved?

Lenora looked for the familiar things—the white rabbits and the waist-high flowers and the trees with faces. But she had never been this deep in the woods, and there was nothing familiar about it. The air hung thick and cold. The light had vanished; only Bela's golden eyes guided them. He held her arm, and she was, at least, grateful for that.

"Step carefully," Bela said. "There are poisonous frogs all around you. They mean you no harm, so long as you do not touch them." He glowed brighter, and Lenora looked around. There were, indeed, frogs. She could just make out their colors—orange and yellow and blue and green—and the black spots on their backs. They watched Lenora and Bela weave through them.

"What happens if you touch one?" Lenora said.

"You will die," Bela said. "And it is a painful death that takes hours. It will make you feel as though you are burning alive."

Lenora shuddered. "What if they touch me?" Frogs could jump, after all.

"These frogs don't harm those who come in peace," Bela said.

Had she come in peace? And could the frogs tell?

"The woodland creatures respect the children who come to us," Bela said. "We know you do not mean us harm."

"Have there been other children?" Lenora thought of the names written in Bobby's journal, and she remembered now where she'd seen those names. The pictures in her uncle's hallway. The pictures showing children whose hair had turned white and whose faces had been crossed out.

Because the woods took them?

Lenora's fear swelled. But she could not turn back now, not without Bobby. The woods would not keep her here against her will; Bela had told her that at the beginning.

But what about the other children? What about Bobby?

Lenora shook her head, trying to shake away the thoughts.

Bela continued walking, gently pulling Lenora along with him. "A child is very valuable to these woods," he said.

"Why?" Lenora was almost afraid to hear the answer.

"Because children can see our magic. A child's life must be preserved, because if no one sees these woods, do they exist?"

It was not a question he needed her to answer. He continued. "There are those who seek to destroy us. Because they don't understand us." The words had a mesmerizing effect on Lenora. She felt the confusion winding around her wonderings, felt the doubts grow hazier, felt the certainties strengthen.

She could stay here. She could be happy.

"We must have our protections," Bela said.

"Like the frogs?" It made sense.

"Yes."

"And the silvery black waters?"

"Precisely." He squeezed Lenora's arm. A reassuring warmth spread through her.

They were silent until some time later, when Bela said, "Careful of the vines here," and Lenora looked at the thick vines lining a small path, forming a maze of sorts through the wood. Their leaves were shaped into hearts. They reached for her.

"We must run," Bela said, his voice urgent. "They do not seem to be in good humor today."

Because she did not come in peace? Lenora's heart staggered.

"Ready?" Bela looked back at Lenora.

She could only nod, and Bela cut a path with the hand that was not on her arm. The vines wrapped around Lenora's ankles and tripped her every other step, but Bela pulled her ever on. One reached for her waist; Bela severed it with his foot. Another twisted around her braid; Bela snapped it with his teeth.

The vines kept coming.

Bela chopped and pulled and shouted, "Let us pass!" and at last the vines retreated, as though chastened.

Lenora stared in both wonder and horror. Her breath came in gasps. When she could finally speak, she said, "What were those?"

"Choking vines," Bela said. "They protect the Master. They do not always take kindly to invaders, for whatever reason they come." He gave her a significant look. Lenora looked at the ground.

Did he know?

"How much farther?" Lenora said. She didn't want to go any farther, if it contained dangers like that.

"We are here," Bela said, and he turned and gestured to the scene before him. "Welcome to the home of the Master."

55

It was a spectacular sight. The grass in the clearing glimmered, painted with tiny invisible dewdrops. The air looked as though it held diamonds; they twinkled everywhere Lenora looked. The light had a silvery glow that seemed altogether divine.

It was not an evil place; it couldn't be.

Lenora's eyes fixed on the center of the clearing, where the largest tree she had ever seen stood tall and wide and majestic enough to have been one of the original trees of humanity—the Tree of Knowledge or the Tree of Life. Its trunk was so thick it would take twenty men—or more—holding hands to encircle it. Its limbs snaked out from the middle, some going up, some bowing down. It was a perfect climbing tree—one John and Charles and Rory would have loved to spend a day exploring.

And then she saw the limb. The notches. The initials. It was exactly as Bobby had drawn it.

Lenora pressed her hands to her sides, to still the trembling.

A hole gaped from the bottom of the trunk, carved like a fairy-tale door, though there was no door, only a black cavity that led—where?

Lenora squinted. Is that where Bobby was?

And then she had a sudden, horrifying thought. "Is Bobby the Master of these woods?" she said.

Bela laughed. "No. He is merely the Master's assistant."

What did that mean? Who would receive her? The Master or Bobby?

And how could she run away with the Master's assistant?

Lenora began to doubt the wisdom of coming here, alone. Uncle Richard was right; the woods were dangerous. She could feel it now, in this hollow.

She glanced behind her. The choking vines blocked the way; how would she escape?

Bobby. She had to find Bobby. She said, "I want to see Bobby."

"In time," Bela said.

"Where is he?"

"Perhaps he is sleeping." He gestured toward the tree. "Would you like to go inside?"

No. No, she would not like to go inside. Never, ever, ever.

"Yes," she said. She would have to go inside; it was the only way.

Bela took her arm and pulled her forward. They stopped several feet away from the tree's gaping hole. It was even blacker up close.

"The Master must approve your entry," Bela said.

Lenora waited for Bela to call. When he didn't, she said, "How will he know we are here?"

"The Master knows everything in these woods, Lenora." The tree in front of them gusted with a violent wind. Lenora shivered.

"You have nothing to fear, Lenora." Bela's hand on her arm was warm and comforting. The wind settled and twirled around them. A leaf landed on her foot. She kicked it off, but not before she saw the shimmering X that marked her black shoe.

She swallowed hard.

"Many have come to visit over the years," Bela said.

"And where are they now?" She tried to stop her voice from shaking, but it was impossible.

"They are in the tree," Bela said. "Living happily ever after, without sorrow."

Was happily ever after real? Mrs. Jones had said sorrow was a necessary part of life.

"The Master has been waiting for a long time to meet you," Bela said.

"Why?" Lenora's words were nearly drowned out by the trees' hissing.

"You are brave and kind and . . ." Bela paused. "Young."

Something cold knotted inside Lenora's chest. She suddenly wanted very badly to flee. Right now.

"I would like to return to Stonewall Manor now," Lenora announced, her voice high and shrill. She glanced back toward the choking vines. Would they let her back through?

"But you have not met the Master yet," Bela said. His hand warmed her arm again. Was that magic he was using? "You are not afraid, are you?"

Yes. Very much so. But all Lenora could do was shake her head.

"You have come so far, and you will meet Bobby soon." Bela's eyes shone into hers.

"I want to go home." It was weak, insubstantial. Did she even believe it?

Bela clearly didn't. He smiled. He leaned forward. He said, "He is here."

Something emerged from the tree.

Lenora quaked.

56

He was not at all what she had pictured, this Master of the woods. He was much more terrifying, much more ancient. He looked as though he were made of mud—a mud-mummy. He wore a hood around his head, but Lenora could clearly see the black hole for a mouth and the bottomless black eyes that seemed to reach out and grab her by the throat. A shadow cloaked his body—real, or imaginary? Lenora couldn't be sure. A rope dangled from his crooked neck and unraveled at the end that dragged along the ground.

Lenora had seen something like him, in the history books, in the faces and figures of those who were hanged as witches or pirates.

The man held up a bony hand, covered in mud, and pointed one finger at Lenora. His head had a permanent tilt.

Lenora looked at the tree, at the limbs that twisted and turned. A hanging tree? Is that what it was? Had this man lost his life on it?

It was much worse than she had imagined.

The man began to move toward her with leisurely, measured steps. Lenora tried to run—he was so slow, outrunning him would be easy, except that she could not move.

Bela wrapped a pink arm around her, exuding warmth and comfort. But no amount of warmth and comfort could still Lenora's thrashing heart or her shaking shoulders.

And then the man stopped and spoke.

"Lenora," he said. "I have missed you."

Lenora faltered. "Father?"

He had the voice of Father. Could it be? Was this a trick of the imagination, or was it real? Had Father finally returned?

Lenora took a step closer, and Bela's arm fell away from her shoulders.

The man did not answer. He did not smile, since he had no mouth with which to smile. He simply stared at her with that strangely tilted head and crept closer and closer and closer. His steps were so slow she almost couldn't tell he was moving. He stopped several feet from her. All the air sucked out of the clearing.

"Lenora," the man said, exactly the way her father had always said it—tender, loving, as though she were his favorite person in the world.

Tears streaked down Lenora's cheeks. She knew how improbable it was, but these woods were magical. What if?

The man limped two steps closer. She could smell the wet mud that covered him.

Run! her heart said. But she remained.

"Father." All her pain wrapped around the one word.

"Come with me, Lenora," the man with her father's voice said.

But she could smell it now. The death, the decay, the danger. This was not her father. This was not her home.

The man reached out to touch her, but Lenora cringed away.

"Lenora."

"You are not my father."

"I am many things." And the voice changed. It *was* the voice of many—men, women, children. How could it contain so many?

Lenora stared at the man—living or dead?—for a moment longer, and then she ran.

She did not pay attention to where she was going. She heard Bela behind her, but she did not stop. She rain straight into the vines, which wrapped rapidly around her wrists and ankles and neck. She screamed and struggled and tried her best to break free, but they only tightened around her, cutting off her breath. "I want to go home!" she choked. "I don't want to be here!"

The ground shook, and the vines released her. Lenora gasped and stumbled away from them. She ran as fast as she could. She did not know if she could outrun what chased her.

Without Bela, Lenora had no sense of direction and not enough light. Everything looked the same—the trees, the flowers, the butterflies. She tried to ask some flowers for directions, but they had all closed up like fists. She tried to beg the trees to point the way, but they had all shut their eyes. She tried to find the Waters of Aevum and ask them for help, regardless of the consequences, but she found only blackened, dried-up trenches.

Had the woods lost its magic?

"Bela!" she cried. She would not be able to make it out of these woods without Bela.

A light glowed ahead—a fantastically golden light—and she nearly cried out with relief. But when she came to the clearing from which the light seemed to emanate, the glow disappeared. There was another, farther away, and she chased it as well, all the while calling out for him. He never showed himself, but soon she found herself in the familiar grove of sitting trees.

She sat on one of them, waiting, her hands shaking. She could not be sure whose side he was on, but she was close enough to the boundary. She would escape if he was not her friend.

Bela emerged some minutes later, his pink paler now.

"You left me in the woods," she said. Her chest blazed with a fire she had not felt in a long time. It almost felt good.

"I did not leave you," Bela said. "I gave you my light."

She could not argue; the golden light is what led her here, to safety.

"Tell me," Bela said. His voice was colder, angrier than it had ever been. "Why do you wish to return home, when Bobby was waiting in the tree?"

"Was he waiting?" Lenora glared at Bela.

"You doubt my word."

Lenora shook her head, but, yes, she did. She doubted these woods. Bobby had, too. And Bobby had disappeared.

Was it his choice, or was it someone else's? And how would she know?

Lenora paced.

"He spoke with the voice of my father," she said.

"To comfort you. He knows he does not have a pleasant face or form."

"He is not a man at all, is he?"

Bela tilted his head. "Does it matter what he is?"

Did it?

Bela gestured around him. "He created these woods." He paused, his eyes taking in the trees, the grass, the sky that could hardly be seen through the leaf cover. "Do you really think someone who created something so beautiful would harm you?"

She didn't know. She was so confused. Here, away from the man with bottomless eyes, the woods didn't seem so harmful. Why was she afraid?

Lenora looked down at her feet. "He frightened me. That is all."

"Bobby was frightened at first, too," Bela said. "It is nothing to be ashamed of. The bravest often have the most fears."

Lenora said nothing.

"Bobby trusted the Master." Bela's voice seemed to weave around her, threading through her doubts and turning them to golden ashes. Lenora shook her head, trying to clear away the confusion. "You could, too."

Lenora swiped at her eyes.

"Lenora." The trees rustled. "You will come back, won't you?"

Lenora nodded.

What else could she do?

Lenora strode toward the boundary to the woods,

still unsure about everything she had seen and heard and felt.

"Beware of your uncle," Bela called. "We will need your help to survive."

Lenora turned back, her throat tight. But she nodded; let him think what he wanted to think, until she figured out what was true and what was false.

She was almost out of the woods when Bela said, "I will always find you, Lenora. You will never be alone."

The words were a magical salve.

Lenora looked up at the sky. Clouds gathered in gray puffs, as if the sun were forbidden to shine today on the weary walls of Stonewall Manor. She only glanced back once at the woods.

It was glowing golden, like a promise.

57

Mrs. Jones sat in the rocking chair on the front porch of Stonewall Manor. Upon seeing Lenora, she gasped.

"Oh, love." Her words twisted in Lenora's stomach. "Come with me, Lenora."

Lenora did as she was told. She followed Mrs. Jones through the front door and into the kitchen. "You must be hungry," Mrs. Jones said, busying herself with a plate, on which she placed a sandwich and some red grapes. When she turned, her face had creased in worry.

"What is it?" Lenora said. Perhaps news about her family had finally come.

Mrs. Jones stared at Lenora for a moment, her eyes sparkling. "It's your hair, love," she finally said. "It's turned completely white."

Lenora touched her hair, which was pulled tight into

a long braid. She swung the tail of it over her shoulder. It was, indeed, completely white. Not a trace of the brown remained.

She felt a tug in her belly.

"Why?" Lenora said.

Mrs. Jones shook her head.

"It is the woods," Lenora said. "They have marked me."

Mrs. Jones raised her eyebrows. "Now you are talking like your uncle, love." The words cradled a gentle reproach. But her eyes looked troubled, as though she, too, knew.

Had she seen what Lenora had seen? The names in Bobby's book. The children in the pictures. The white hair.

"My father had white hair," she said. "You said he went into the woods."

"Perhaps the white is passed down through the generations," Mrs. Jones said. She bit her lip. She did not even believe her words; Lenora could tell.

"I was looking for Bobby," Lenora said. "I went

deeper than I have ever been. I met . . ." She wondered if she should say.

Mrs. Jones said, "Bobby is gone."

"But you said—"

"I did not mean for you to endanger yourself."

And there they were, the words of admission. Mrs. Jones *did* believe her.

Mrs. Jones covered her face with her hands. "Bobby's hair looked like that the day before he disappeared."

"I won't disappear." She put a hand on Mrs. Jones's shoulder. Mrs. Jones folded her hand around Lenora's.

"Your uncle would not survive another lost child," Mrs. Jones said. "Don't make him have to try."

"But I don't mean anything to him," Lenora said. The words felt sharp and stiff, like bits of splintered wood. Had they come from the tree? Did she really believe them?

And why wouldn't she?

"Is that what you think?" Mrs. Jones said. "Even still?"

Lenora looked at the table.

"Then you are more foolish than I thought." Mrs. Jones let out a heavy breath that could have been mistaken for a choke. After a minute she said, "You mean everything to him."

"But he's never around," Lenora said. "He doesn't even know me. He never talks to me, never looks at me, never seems to care what's—"

"You look with the wrong eyes." Mrs. Jones's voice was loud, harsh, brittle. Lenora's throat tightened.

Silence shifted around them. Lenora said, "I know where Bobby is."

Mrs. Jones's eyes snapped to her face so fast Lenora could almost hear them. Her mouth dropped open.

"He's in the tree, in the woods," Lenora said.

Mrs. Jones shook her head. "No." The whisper wrapped around Lenora's chest and squeezed.

"He is. I'm going to find him. I'm going to bring him home."

Mrs. Jones closed her eyes. "No, Lenora." Louder now.

"He's still alive."

"Stop!" Lenora had never heard Mrs. Jones raise her

voice like this. She looked into Mrs. Jones's eyes. They flashed and glinted. "You talk the same foolishness Bobby did."

"Because it's true."

"He spoke of a child, too. Gladys. A child who disappeared many years ago, a child who had lived in this house, a child he never knew, a child who . . ." Mrs. Jones's shoulders shook. Lenora could do nothing else but take her hand.

She had seen the name in Bobby's journal, along with the date. 1912. She almost opened her mouth, but Mrs. Jones looked up and said, "I watched Gladys's hair turn white. I watched her walk into the woods. Just like I did with Bobby." Her hand pressed around Lenora's, her eyes clearer now than they had been before. "I will not let you do the same."

"What if she didn't die?" Lenora said, so quiet she could almost imagine she had not said the words aloud at all.

But Mrs. Jones hissed. She said, "I didn't believe them about the woods. Spirits and demons and invisible things. It's not logical." She seemed to be talking to herself, working it out. "But now . . ." She didn't finish, only changed her direction. "Death is a part of life, Lenora. We all see it at one time or another. It does no good to dwell on what might have been. Bobby couldn't understand that. But you must." Her eyes softened, along with her voice. "You must."

Lenora dropped her eyes to their entwined hands. Mrs. Jones stood up and shuffled to the other side of the kitchen. She came back with a newspaper.

She slid it toward Lenora.

Lenora looked at the date: June 1, 1947. Today's paper. The front-page picture showed a line of sheets, raised in places as though something lay beneath them.

"It's time you saw this," Mrs. Jones said. "Your uncle wanted to spare you, but I fear you will never move on if you don't know."

Lenora skimmed the article, which told of the multitude of bodies found in Texas City that were missing body parts or so mangled they could not be identified. Lenora stared at the line of sheets, under which she now knew were the dead bodies to which the article referred. She swallowed something large and jagged and shoved away the paper. "This doesn't mean anything," she managed to say, though she could not feel her lips moving.

Mrs. Jones's voice was low when she said, "It means you may never know. Will you wait for them forever, since you do not know for sure?"

Lenora could not answer. She did not want to think about it—not at all. Why had no word come by now if they were alive?

Would she keep waiting forever?

For what?

"It's a process of elimination," Mrs. Jones said. "Those who are alive have already notified their families."

Lenora shook her head. She wanted to say, *They will come*, as she always did, but the words tangled in her throat.

She did not believe them anymore.

58

Mrs. Jones didn't say anything for a very long time. And when she did, the words were not what Lenora wanted to hear, but perhaps they were what she most needed to hear. "Four hundred and five people died and were identified," she said. "Sixty-three bodies have not been identified. As hard as it is to consider, I believe your parents and your sister and brothers are among the unidentified. It is why no word has come in all these months."

"No." Lenora's throat pinched. Her nose burned. Her arms shook.

No.

"This is your home now," Mrs. Jones said. "We are your family."

Tears streamed down Lenora's face. "This will never be my home." The words had no conviction. They were shards in her mouth.

If not, then where?

"It's not an easy place, I know," Mrs. Jones said. "But we'll make it a home again. We'll start a new life."

Lenora's eyes burned. "I don't want to start a new life!" Her breath heaved, wobbled, shattered. "I want my old life! I want to go home!"

"There is nothing left in Texas City, love," Mrs. Jones said. "And the sooner you understand that, the sooner you can move on." She lowered her voice. "It is what your father would have wanted. I know this, because I knew your father."

Lenora lifted her eyes to the shining blue ones of Mrs. Jones. She could see everything there: sorrow, understanding, love. Lenora leaned into her.

"My husband's body was never found," Mrs. Jones said. Lenora blinked, her cheek smashed into Mrs. Jones's chest. Her voice vibrated in Lenora's head. "He was missing in action during World War II. I got the letter. I never saw his body." Mrs. Jones took a deep, shuddering breath. "I held on as long as I could. And then, after a few years, I let him go." She sniffed. "It was all I could do. I had to move on."

Lenora wanted to say something, but her throat was much too raw.

"Death touches us all," Mrs. Jones said. "But it doesn't have to break us."

They remained like that—Lenora pressed to Mrs. Jones, Mrs. Jones curved around her—for quite some time, until Mrs. Jones said, "I must prepare supper now. Would you like to help?"

Lenora shook her head. What she would like to do was sleep.

But her bedroom was so lonely.

Her vision blurred. She stumbled toward the door and was nearly through it when Mrs. Jones called to her. "I found this," Mrs. Jones said. She held up Mother's pearl necklace. "In the garden. I thought it might be yours."

Lenora had not even noticed it was gone.

Mrs. Jones knelt, her eyes wide and searching. She said, "The dead are always with us. You contain pieces of your mother and father, pieces of your sister and brothers. They will always be with you, wherever you go. When you need them, just listen to what your heart says." Mrs. Jones wrapped Lenora in a tight hug, and for a moment Lenora closed her eyes and breathed deeply the cinnamon and orange of Mrs. Jones's hair. It was over before Lenora was ready, and she raced from the room, from the stifling house, aware that she would not make it far without crumbling.

She made it as far as the garden, where she plunged her hands into the soil, uprooting weeds in a furious rhythm that matched the emotions warring in her chest. She wanted to get away from here, away from the sorrow that seemed to eat her from the inside out. She wanted to retreat to the woods, but fear held her back. She did not want to see the Master again, and she feared that Bela would take her there by force this time.

Was nowhere safe?

She'd thought she had found companionship in the woods, but was that true? What did they really want of her? Would she disappear like Bobby and Gladys and all the other white-haired children?

Or was that just coincidence?

She glared at Stonewall Manor. It represented the possibility—the certainty—of death and how it had altered her life forever.

She missed them all so much. She missed their life together. She'd never had her day off from school, had never properly celebrated her birthday, had never told Rory she was sorry for being mad. She'd never shown Mother the stains on her brand-new dress. She hadn't told Father she loved him that day; did he know?

Lenora sobbed as she worked. She closed her eyes and let the wind dry her cheeks. She tried to clear her mind, but it was impossible. The pearls in her left hand burned, pressed against the earth.

Lenora turned the pearl necklace over in her hands. She pressed the pearls to her lips, pressed them to her nose, pressed them to her chest. She put them on.

A beam of brilliant light caught her attention. It came from the window that was Uncle Richard's laboratory. Lenora scrambled through the iron gate, careful not to let it swing shut or cause any noise. She crept toward her uncle's window, which she saw was completely exposed.

Had he been careless, or was this on purpose?

Lenora's mouth dropped open. Staring back at her from the window was the mechanical rhinoceros. It was even larger than she'd, at first, thought. As she watched, the light bulbs of its eyes glowed to life in two pointed beams. More lights flickered on. She saw a line of robots, their eyes lit with the same bulbs.

So this was why Uncle Richard needed light bulbs.

The rhinoceros moved a thundering step forward, its head nearly crashing through the window. Lenora ducked away, but the rhinoceros stopped abruptly.

It was much too tall to get through the window. Uncle Richard had created a massive mechanical rhinoceros that would live forever inside his laboratory.

Lenora watched her uncle guide the rhinoceros into an empty space between the line of robots. Uncle Richard faced his army, not Lenora. There was a drawing in his hands, held behind his back. Lenora squinted.

The drawing showed the Master of the woods.

Uncle Richard turned then, and Lenora ducked into the shadows, but not before she could see the mad gleam in his eye.

The supper bell clanged.

59

At supper, Uncle Richard was quiet, as usual, but the quiet felt heavier. Lenora could feel it pressing on the back of her neck, the sides of her head, the middle of her chest. She stole glances at him periodically, trying to make sense of what she had seen but unable to do anything of the sort. He had built robots, but what was the purpose of robots with light bulbs for eyes and a mass of buttons on their backs?

"So you have been in the woods again." The words were so unexpected that Lenora dropped her fork. It clattered to her plate.

She tried to think of something to say, but there was nothing.

"Your hair has turned white," Uncle Richard said. "Just like my son's. Just like my sister's."

"Your sister's?" Father had never mentioned a sister.

"Gladys," Uncle Richard said, and Lenora's chest turned cold.

Without thinking, she said, "I know where Bobby is." She wanted him to understand. "I think he needs us."

Uncle Richard's fork hovered in midair. "My son is dead," he said, and his eyes dropped to his plate.

She could tell, though, that he didn't fully believe it. So she said, "I think he's alive. He's in the woods. I think we can save him."

Uncle Richard shook his head. "That's foolishness. The woods must be destroyed." He leveled his eyes at her, and they were dark and unreadable. "They will take you, too."

She could tell, by the set of his jaw, by the blaze of his eyes, by the way he held his fork—the same way he held the door in the car—that he would not listen. She said, "And you intend to destroy the woods?"

Uncle Richard did not say anything.

She would have to stop him, then, or at least accompany him, until she could be sure that Bobby was not alive and trapped.

Uncle Richard put down his napkin and lifted his chin. "Do you know why you go into the woods and come out with white hair?"

She wasn't sure she wanted to know, but she shook her head anyway.

"The woods steal your vitality, your color. They exist only if they can trap a captive." Uncle Richard picked up his fork again, as though he intended to continue eating, but he did not move. "My son has been a captive for eight years now. He is likely drained of life, and it is very nearly finished."

"What is finished?" Lenora could not help but ask.

"The end of the Cole family." Uncle Richard did not falter on the words. He was sure, unwavering.

"How do you know this?" she said.

"There are stories. Your father tried to show me, but I did not listen." Uncle Richard put down his fork again and leaned back in his chair. "I have read them all now."

She would like to read the stories. And perhaps that was clear on her face; Uncle Richard said, "The stories are scrawled in journals. In my lab."

"Your journals?" Lenora felt the cold spreading; perhaps her uncle really was mad.

"The journals of others in our family."

Our family. The words sounded like a promise.

"They kept good records," Uncle Richard said. "They were called mad for their claims. I thought the same. But they were the sanest people alive." His shoulders hunched.

Lenora saw what he carried—sorrow, disappointment, regret. Mostly it was regret.

"I wish I had listened," he said.

"It's not your fault," she said. She wanted him to understand this, needed him to. It wasn't his fault that his sister had disappeared in the woods, that Bobby had as well, that Lenora had explored what he'd forbidden her to explore. "You didn't know."

Uncle Richard's face cleared. "You must not return, Lenora. Promise me. Until I have finished what must be done." His eyes pleaded with her, and she felt the warmth of his attention, his care, spread into her chest.

She could not promise, though. She loved him too

much—she knew this now—to let him lose his son, if his son could be saved. So she merely nodded her head.

A promise could not be bound without words.

Could it?

60

When Mrs. Jones entered the dining room, she carried a large birthday cake, with a glowing candle. She walked over to Uncle Richard, set it down in front of him, and began singing in a low and melodic voice.

Lenora joined in the singing.

Uncle Richard smiled politely and said, "You always did remember, didn't you."

Mrs. Jones cut a generous piece for Uncle Richard and a smaller piece—but still a generous one—for Lenora. The cake was chocolate all the way through.

For a while, the only sound in the dining room, after Mrs. Jones left, was that of forks scraping against plates. The cake consumed their attention. It was rich and delicious.

"Stonewall Manor is a lonely place," Uncle Richard said around his napkin, which he used to wipe the corners of his mouth. "You have found solace in the woods. A friend, perhaps?"

Lenora stiffened.

"Bobby found a friend as well," Uncle Richard said, without waiting for her answer. "That's why he returned."

Silence again. Lenora could think of absolutely nothing to say. Uncle Richard was trying; why could she not?

She had almost opened her mouth when Uncle Richard said, "Thank you for clearing the garden." Lenora's eyes met his. She could see that he meant the words, and they felt warm and . . . safe.

Perhaps there was somewhere safe for her after all.

He said, "When summer is finished we can plant some new flowers. Make it beautiful again." He spoke in the same halting way he always did, but it did not seem as strange as it used to. He thought before he spoke. He chose each word with care. Words meant something to him. He was very much like her father.

"I would like that," Lenora said, her throat tight.

Uncle Richard looked at her for a moment longer,

and then he said, "I have something to show you. Will you come?"

At first she thought that Uncle Richard might show her his lab, and her heart fluttered with expectation, but he took her not toward the east wing, where he worked, but toward the entrance to Stonewall Manor. Mrs. Jones was waiting out front, smiling.

Lenora didn't know why until she saw what leaned against the house. There were two bikes—one a sleek black and the other a rosy red. The wheels were thin and large, and the handlebars curved out, up, and back toward the seat. Lenora gasped.

"I used to ride with Bobby," Uncle Richard said, his voice thick. "I thought it might give us something to do together."

Lenora shook her head. "I don't know how to ride a bike," she said. "I've never had one."

Uncle Richard seemed taken aback. "My brother loved riding," he said.

Lenora looked at her feet. "My parents didn't have much money," she said, and then she glanced back up at Uncle Richard.

His face was pained, his eyes dim. He shook his head and bit his lip, lifting his eyes to the sky. "I wrote to him," he said. "I thought for sure he would answer at least one of my letters. I wanted him to come home." He leveled his gaze at Lenora. "I wanted to know you and your brothers and sister. I wanted . . ." His voice broke, and he shook his head, his hand wiping at his cheeks.

Mrs. Jones slipped inside the house. Lenora and Uncle Richard were quiet for a while, before Lenora said, "I don't understand why he didn't write back. My father was a good man. A kind man. A forgiving man. He must have loved you. I'm sure of it."

Uncle Richard nodded, swallowing hard. "Yes," he said. "But we both said many unforgivable things. We were foolish." He gazed up at the front of Stonewall Manor. "He didn't want anything to do with this house. He wanted to protect his children."

Lenora's vision blurred. He hadn't been able to protect his children after all.

"I wish I had another chance to tell him how much he meant to me," Uncle Richard said.

"Me too." The words were out before Lenora could stop them. She felt a hand in hers. Uncle Richard had moved close.

He said, "I think he knew."

And maybe that was enough.

They both turned their attention to the sky, which blazed with a glorious golden glow, day curving into night.

"Should we teach you to ride before the day is gone completely?" Uncle Richard said. "You're old enough to have the balance. You just need to get the rhythm. It shouldn't take you long."

Lenora nodded; she couldn't trust herself to speak.

Uncle Richard held the bike while Lenora climbed onto it. He limped behind her, his hand on the back of the seat, but Lenora was a fast learner, and she was soon riding on her own. Uncle Richard had been right about the balance; she felt like she had always known how to ride a bike.

At some point, Uncle Richard climbed on his bike and pedaled beside her. Lenora could see that riding pained him; he winced every time his left leg bent. The trees curved overhead as though protecting them from the wide expanse of sorrow and holding them in only this moment.

After riding for half an hour or so, Lenora lost control of the handlebars and sprawled out on the ground, causing Uncle Richard, who pedaled behind her, to swerve. He ended up on the ground as well. They both dissolved into laughter before picking up the bikes and walking them back to the porch of Stonewall Manor.

As she walked, Lenora glanced toward the woods. There stood Bela, glowing with a brilliant pink, a look of such fury on his face that she shivered and dropped her eyes to the ground. When she looked back, he was gone, and it was easy for her to convince herself that she had not seen anything at all.

61

Before retreating upstairs, Lenora stopped by the library. She scanned the shelves, looking for stories about the woods. Uncle Richard had said they existed–but where?

She heard the voices of Mrs. Jones and Uncle Richard, floating in from down the hall.

"I hope you had a good birthday." Mrs. Jones.

"Thank you. For the cake." Uncle Richard.

"Thank you for teaching Lenora how to ride a bike."

"It was enjoyable." She could hear a smile in his voice.

"She will need you now."

"I know."

Silence.

Then: "I miss him so much." Uncle Richard. His voice was higher, strained. Lenora heard a muffled sob, and she turned toward the door.

"Everything will work out." Mrs. Jones. She'd said

the same thing to Lenora.

"I wish I had been a better father."

"You'll get another chance now."

"I wish I had been a better man."

"Regrets don't change anything, love. They just hinder us from moving on. Life doesn't end for those of us who remain. We must keep living, as well as we can."

Lenora felt the words as though they belonged to her, as though Mrs. Jones intended her to hear them.

Uncle Richard made another sound that squeezed Lenora's chest. "I wish I could tell him I love him one more time."

Mrs. Jones didn't answer.

Lenora swallowed hard.

When she heard Uncle Richard close himself behind the door in the east wing and Mrs. Jones pad down the hall, Lenora slipped from the library and raced up the stairs to her room. (The darkness was still the worst monster.) She sat up in her bed for a long time. Then she crossed the hall and moved into Bobby's room.

Only one lamp worked, the one that sat beside his bed. She flicked it on and studied the shadows it made near the doorway. She moved about the room much like she had done the first time she had entered. She studied the drawings in his bathroom and noticed now that many were creatures she had seen in the woods. She touched the flowers that opened up and sang. She touched the trees that danced. She touched the strange spiked fish she had seen jumping from one of the pools.

She sat on his swing.

What would he want her to do? Could she feel him, alive? Did he want her to rescue him?

Could she?

A voice reached her. *Lenora,* it said. *Come to me.*

It was only a whisper, but it sounded like her mother. She shook her head. The window was open. She crossed the room in a hurry and shut it. The voice did not return.

Before climbing into her bed, Lenora looked out her window, toward the woods. They were still and dark. Endless, it seemed. She thought of Bobby, hidden deep within them. She thought of Uncle Richard, still mourning his son, though it had been eight years. She thought about the Master and the tree and the lost

393

children hidden within it.

She would enter the woods as soon as she woke tomorrow. She would bring Bobby home. And together they would stitch what remained of their family back together.

Love, she understood now, was the only antidote for loneliness and loss.

He lured in only children belonging to one family: the Coles, who had been responsible for his death all those years ago.

As he had swung from the tree—the tree that was now his home—he had watched them disappear into the forest. They had not stayed to gawk at him as the townspeople would have done for a public execution in those days. Still, he had seethed. He had vowed to fight for his life, if only to orchestrate his revenge.

But the life had seeped out of him before he could escape from his bonds.

It did not matter after all. He was permitted his revenge. He was given another opportunity to eliminate the Cole family from existence—as they had eliminated him. No more scientific men, analyzing his suspicious behavior. No more sheriffs following his every move. No more pretty ladies falling for his flattering words.

At this, his heart squeezed, and a gentle face with piercing blue eyes hovered before him.

He shoved it away; he did not have time for love, only hate. Love did not belong with revenge; hate was its partner. She had been his downfall. She had been his weakness. She had been . . .

He groaned, wailed, keened, the trees bending and twisting in the wind of his grief. Then he turned his attention on what must be done.

It was time.

June 1, 1947

How fitting that I should finish the most important work of my life, an army of steam-powered creations, on my fortieth birthday.

It is time. Tomorrow, in the early-morning hours, I will march my army into the woods, and I will defeat the spirit torturing this home and its people. I entertain no illusions that by my victory I will save my son. I believe he has been in the woods far too long. But I can, at least, save Lenora. And I will.

The future is what matters now, not the past.

My steel and copper men will follow me into the woods in a structure of my own making, pulled by the glory of my scientific career: a robotic rhinoceros (it looks more like a dinosaur, to be accurate) that runs on fire, water, and steam. I will bring, too, my cane, which I have modified in the last months to contain and spit fire—a supernatural kind, a blend of the spiritual and the scientific, unexplainable in its power.

My army and my weapon contain within them enough steam and fire to burn the entire woods—and, most important, the hanging tree, where I believe the spirit resides. It is the tree where he died; the connection must be severed. I hypothesize that its destruction will spit him out so that I can eliminate him with the supernatural fire confined in my cane. I have not tested this; I go in faith: Good always triumphs over evil.

I have planned my escape, but if I cannot make it out . . . well, my sacrifice will be worth it. My affairs are in order, placed in the top left drawer of my desk, in case someone finds this record first. Lloyd and his wife, Nadine, will care for Stonewall Manor, along with Mrs. Jones, until Lenora is of age. Lloyd and Nadine are welcome to live at Stonewall Manor. They always wanted a daughter. I think they will be delighted to have Lenora, and she will be delighted to have them.

Now there is only the cog-wheel clock to watch as it ticks toward the end.

—excerpt from Richard Cole's *Journal of Scientific Progress*

THE OPEN DOOR

62

A crash startled Lenora from a deep and dreamless sleep. She sat up in bed, her eyes still filmy. She blinked and looked around. What had she heard? She was sure the walls had shaken. But everything was silent and still. The sun had not even come up yet. Perhaps she was dreaming.

And then the sound came again and shook the foundations of Stonewall Manor. Lenora scrambled from bed and moved to the window. She stared out, but the grounds were mostly dark. The moon was low and large in the sky, its bottom punched out by the treetops. Lenora could see nothing in the woods. They were completely cloaked in black.

Something glinted beneath her, and she pressed her face to the windowpane, straining to see. Something else glinted. She squinted and could just make out the shadows. Something was moving out on the lawn.

She padded out of her room and raced down the stairs. (More accurately, she rode the banister; it was much faster and she didn't have time to think about what might be chasing her from the darkness of the hall.) She tried to exit the front door, but it was locked tight. She pulled and pushed and jiggled the knob with her hand. She looked under the rug just inside the door. There was no key. She searched the tables that lined the entryway. She picked up all the candelabras, but a key was nowhere to be found.

Had someone locked her inside? She looked back the way she'd come. The house was still sleeping.

A creak sounded in one of the hallways, and Lenora ducked into a corner. Someone was coming. She heard the footsteps thumping in a rapid rhythm, but she could see nothing, it was so dark. Then a pale, ghostly face appeared. Lenora pressed her hand against her mouth as the face drew nearer and nearer. She turned her own face to the wall when the figure reached the entryway. She did not want to see the specter that had come for her.

But the figure passed right by her and put a hand on the door. For a moment, Lenora thought whoever it was might open the door, and she could race out and past it before she was even noticed. But then she saw the long, somewhat crooked fingers tug on the door and fall back.

"I thought I'd locked it." It was the voice of Mrs. Jones. She sighed. "No one's getting out or in tonight. Just let them try."

Lenora stepped from the shadows just as Mrs. Jones turned around. Mrs. Jones let out a startled yelp and pressed her hand to her chest. "Lenora!" She breathed. "You startled me, love. What are you doing down here?"

"I heard something. A crash."

Mrs. Jones's face puckered. "Yes, well, I don't think it's anything to worry about." She seemed dismissive, evasive perhaps.

"It sounded like the house exploded," Lenora said. She could not keep the worry from her voice. Her uncle was a science man; what if an experiment had gone wrong?

"Your uncle is very particular about who visits the

east wing," Mrs. Jones said, as though Lenora didn't already know that.

"But shouldn't we check on him?"

Mrs. Jones looked toward the front door and back at Lenora's face. Finally, she nodded.

When they reached the door to the east wing, it was locked. Mrs. Jones pulled a collection of keys from the pocket of her dress. She searched for one, then held her hand aloft near the keyhole. "It's so early," she said. "He will not be in good humor if we wake him. He was never an early-morning person."

"I heard a crash," Lenora said. "I want to make sure he's okay."

Mrs. Jones nodded and unlocked the door.

Lenora ran down the hallway. It was empty, no white-sheeted robots lining it. She burst through the door of Uncle Richard's laboratory. A giant hole gaped at her from the far wall. Lenora gasped.

"What is it?" Mrs. Jones cried, rounding into the room. She stopped when she saw the hole in the wall. "What on earth has he done now?"

Lenora did not stay to answer. She launched herself

through the opening, hurdling over glass and steel and stone, barely hearing Mrs. Jones calling her back.

She raced toward the woods.

63

Lenora stopped near the border, just inside the woods. She listened, but everything was still and eerily silent. "Uncle Richard!" she called into the hush.

She had to find him. She had to protect him from the dangers of these woods. She had to save Bobby.

She thought about what Bela had said—the creatures and marvels of the forest are dangerous to those with ill intent. Uncle Richard intended to destroy them; what would they do to him?

Lenora felt sick to her stomach, but she had no time to waste.

The birds did not sing. Neither did the flowers nor the trees, so Lenora could not follow their song deeper into the forest. There was no golden or pink light to guide her. She moved from tree to tree, slowly, carefully, unsure what hostilities she might find now that her uncle was inside with his army of robotic men.

Bela seemed to appear from nowhere, in his human-sized form. His pink skin was the darkest she'd ever seen it, a shade that could almost be mistaken for red. "Lenora," he said. "You should not be here. We are about to engage in a war."

"Please," Lenora said. "You cannot."

"Your uncle has brought danger to our woods," Bela said. "He has brought fire."

"Take me to him. I can stop him."

Would Bela believe the words?

"You know where he has gone." Bela's eyes probed hers. She held steady, but she could feel her courage slipping.

"To the tree," she said.

"You cannot stop him, Lenora. You cannot stop the woods."

"Tell me what I can do!" She felt desperate to do something. She couldn't let her uncle die in these woods. She couldn't be alone again.

Bela considered the trees. "There is something you can do."

"What?"

"It would make us stronger."

"And my uncle would be safe?"

"If he agreed to leave us as we are. As we will be."

Lenora did not fully understand the words, but she said, "I will do anything." Anything to protect him.

Bela stared hard at Lenora. He gestured. "Come with me, then." He moved quickly, and Lenora struggled to keep up.

"Please slow down," Lenora said. She had forgotten her shoes. She thought the grass might be feathery inside the woods, but it was surprisingly prickly.

Bela stopped between two trees and held out his arms. "Would you like me to carry you?" Lenora stared at him for a moment, considering, before she nodded. He picked her up, cradling her the same way Uncle Richard had done when he'd found her outside the woods, and the two of them moved so rapidly the woods blurred around her.

"You have made the right decision," Bela said. "Your sorrow will no longer plague you. The Master will take it all away."

The Master. She hadn't agreed to go to the Master, had she?

She had said she'd do anything.

How would the Master take away her sorrow? Would he make her forget her family, forget the tragedy in Texas City, forget that she'd ever had anything to lose?

"He will reunite you with your family," Bela said, as though he could hear her thoughts. Had she spoken aloud? Bela laughed. "I can feel your thoughts." His eyes glowed brighter. "I can feel the deep well of your sadness." A tear dropped from his eye and landed on the underside of Lenora's left arm. It burned a pink heart on her skin.

Lenora stared at it.

"I apologize," Bela said. "I did not mean to burn you."

Lenora said nothing. She tightened her hold on the back of Bela's neck. She'd thought he might feel slimy, but his skin was as rough as the bark of a pine tree. She tried not to lean her head on his chest, but she felt so weary.

After some minutes of travel, Bela said, "We are nearly there."

"What will happen to my uncle?" Lenora said.

"There is not much you can do for your uncle, except urge him to leave us."

"He has brought a mechanical army."

"The vines, I believe, are taking care of that." And, indeed, as they passed the vines that protected the Master's domain, Lenora saw several robot heads and robot arms. She felt sick to her stomach. She had seen this before, only with real people. She closed her eyes. She could not bear to see Uncle Richard harmed.

"And now," Bela said, "we are here." He set Lenora on her feet and moved forward.

"Wait," Lenora said, placing her hand on his arm. "I must see—"

"There is no time to waste if you want to save your uncle. And Bobby."

Bobby? The name slammed into her chest.

If she could give Uncle Richard his life and his son, would that not be worth everything?

Lenora stepped forward.

64

The Master was waiting.

"Lenora," he said, his hand outstretched. This time his voice was higher, like the voice of a young boy.

"John?" she said. It didn't sound exactly like John's voice, but it did sound similar.

"Will you come?" the Master said.

"Charles?" she said. But no, it wasn't exactly Charles's voice, either. It was a boy's, but she could not place it. Maybe . . .

"Save me." The Master beckoned. She felt the haze clouding her mind. Confusion wrapped around her.

"Bobby." The name had barely passed her lips when the Master looked at her with his bottomless black eyes.

"Come."

She could take his hand. It would be easy. She could trade places, step in for Bobby, give him back his life.

What did she have to lose?

Still she hesitated. She said, "Your father is here, Bobby. Will you come out?" She glanced toward the dark opening of the tree. She did not want to go in.

"You must come inside," said the Master in that same childlike voice. "Come inside the tree."

"What's inside the tree?" Lenora said.

"I am," the Master—Bobby?—said.

"What else?" Lenora could not trust the voice completely. It shifted and rearranged according to what it wanted.

The Master was silent.

"What else is inside the tree, Bobby?"

"Nothing to fear," Bela said in the Master's place. "I thought you were courageous, Lenora. I thought . . ." He let the words trail off. He nudged her forward, but Lenora wasn't ready. She stumbled.

"The only way to save me is to enter the tree," the Master said. He held out his bony hand. It looked like white stone caked with mud in places. "Come."

Lenora hesitated.

"Take my hand."

Lenora took a step forward.

"I will take away all your pain and sorrow."

Lenora stared at the dirty bones that reached for her. She felt Bela's hand on her back, but she shook it off. If the Master erased her pain and sorrow, would he also erase all the joy and laughter of life? What if she could not hold on to the good memories without the bad ones? Would it be better to erase all her memories of her parents and her brothers and sister, because she could not bear the horrific ones? How could a person bear a life without love, without family, without the memories that wrapped the two together?

Bela said she would be reunited with her family. But how could that be? They were dead.

The realization felt like a fist smashing into her stomach.

She couldn't go into the tree. She had to remember the way Charles had grinned at her the time she'd told him the answer to his seventh-grade math problem, because she had a mind for mental math. She had to remember the way Rory had banged away on the piano, the same songs over and over and over again until the

413

whole family agreed that it was time for a change. She had to remember John rocking on the porch swing, oblivious to the wondrous painting of another sunset on water because he was more interested in the book he held in his hands. She had to remember the countless kisses and hugs Mother and Father had given her during their thousands of moments together.

She would not erase those memories so that she could escape sorrow.

"I can't," Lenora whispered.

"You must, Lenora," the Master said. "It is already too late." And this time his voice joined a great gust of air that blasted toward her face. Lenora took a step back. The Master took a step forward. His black eyes practically consumed her. She could not look away, and she found that she could not move another step back. She was pulled steadily forward, a prisoner in the clutches of something dark and dangerous.

65

Something crashed off to her left, and Lenora finally tore her gaze from the Master and saw the most spectacular sight. A massive rhinoceros stood with glowing eyes. Lenora nearly laughed with relief. But then she saw, out of the corner of her eye, the Master moving swifter than she thought possible. He was heading straight for her.

Lenora leaped toward the rhinoceros, and more crashes felled trees and ripped leaves and shook the ground. A thick vine flew through the air and landed at her feet. It writhed like a snake, and she hopped over it, racing toward the rhinoceros.

Toward her uncle.

"Lenora!" Two voices called her, from opposite sides of the clearing. One belonged to Bela. His eyes were fixed on her, two perfect beams of gold lighting the way for the bog man. And the other belonged to Uncle Richard, who wore a look of horror. He was dressed in a full suit of armor—armor unlike anything she'd ever seen before. He looked just like one of his robots, all gears and copper pieces.

"What are you doing here?" Uncle Richard shouted. He moved his hands frantically. "Get out! Get out of here now!"

"No! I won't leave you!" She thrust the words in his direction.

"Run, Lenora!" Uncle Richard shouted. "You must get out of here! It's not safe!"

"Bobby is in there!" She pointed. "He's in the tree!"

And for a moment, she thought Uncle Richard might reconsider what he was about to do. His eyes softened, and he looked toward the tree, his gaze filled with so much longing that Lenora couldn't breathe. And then he shook his head. "It's too late for Bobby," he said. "It's too late for me. But it's not too late for you."

What did he mean when he said it was too late for him?

"You can't leave me," she said. Her voice was small.

She couldn't bear the thought of losing another person she loved.

They were only feet away from each other, but Lenora felt exposed, unsafe. She could feel the stillness behind her, could sense the Master waiting for the right moment. The back of her neck tingled. She had to get out of the way. She had to let her uncle do this.

But she couldn't. Not if there was a chance.

Something ripped at Lenora's hair. A voice pierced her ear. "I have you now," it said. She swung around, wincing at the pain in her head.

"Bela!" Lenora struggled to free herself. "Let me go! Please!"

"I cannot, Lenora," Bela said, and the trees roared. Her name echoed through the air. She felt her mind cloud.

"I thought you were my friend!" She shoved the haze away, but it always came back.

"It's for the good of the woods," Bela said. He pulled her roughly toward the Master. Lenora struck him and twisted and planted her feet in the dirt, but he was much stronger than she was. She felt fire burst past her ear, and Bela exploded into flame, his hand slipping from her tangled hair.

"Let her go!" Uncle Richard bellowed, his voice strong and commanding. It did not halt or trip or crack. Lenora looked back at him. He had his cane. It was pointed directly at Bela as though it were some kind of gun. He leaned heavily on his right leg. "I have enough fire in my army to set all the woods aflame."

"Ah," Bela said, flames licking at his face. "But you have already lost." And in one movement, he flung Lenora toward the Master, who lunged toward her at the same time. But Lenora, by accident, stumbled on the severed vine over which she had earlier jumped, and fell hard to the ground. Without a moment's hesitation, she continued with the forward roll, like she and Rory had often done in their yard—a game to see who could roll the farthest. She rolled and rolled, continuously, until she was out of the way, caring nothing for the nightdress she still wore. She heard the Master scream behind her, and she launched herself to her feet and took off running toward Uncle Richard and his army. She ducked behind a tree and peered out. Bela was still on fire, and Uncle Richard aimed a continuous stream of fire at the Master. She felt a thickness settle in her throat. She tilted her head. A silver X—the same one she'd seen on Bobby's door and her own—gleamed on the ground in front of the tree.

"Don't hit the tree, Uncle!" Lenora said. She hurled herself out of hiding and raced toward the tree, toward the Master, toward the place where Bobby rested.

She had to see. She had to make sure.

"Lenora!" Uncle Richard shouted, and that's when the clearing shook. Lenora looked back, and then she wished she hadn't, because there on a large rolling platform with the wheels of a locomotive was her house.

Her house. From Texas City. Home.

She shook her head, trying to clear it. Surely this was only her imagination. But she did not have time to think more about it. The Master seized his opportunity and wrapped a bony hand around her arm. She tried to peel off his fingers, but they were like stone manacles.

He dragged her toward the tree.

"We will save the woods," he said in a raspy voice she had never heard before.

Lenora tried to shake him off, tried to run back toward her uncle and the rolling home—her home—but she could not free herself from the iron grip of a man long dead and buried in mud.

This was all impossible.

Lenora screamed.

The limb above her burst into flames, raining sparks down on both her and the Master. The Master doubled over. Lenora saw her chance. She ducked inside the tree, where the ground was soft and wet. The mud nearly reached her knees, but she continued slogging through the sludge. The bog was larger than she'd thought—much larger. It must be some trick of the mind. It went on forever.

How would she ever find her cousin? She had almost decided on the futility of this foolish quest when she heard a whimper near her. Someone was there. She waded through more mud, trying not to notice the bits of bone that her movements uncovered.

The mud pulled at her thighs now, but she didn't care. She reached the shadowed form in five more steps.

"Bobby?" she said.

It was a boy. He looked up at her with the same large, round, shining eyes she had seen on the boy in the portrait that hung in the hallway leading to Uncle Richard's lab. This was Bobby. She was sure of it.

She pulled his arm. The mud pulled at her. She was sinking.

Lenora tried to remember what John had told her when he went through his obsession with quicksand. It had been annoying at the time, but now?

It would help. She remembered.

She laid flat on top of the mud, her legs squelching into the depths, and wriggled toward the tree's opening, dragging Bobby gently along behind her. She still sank, but much slower than she had before. It was a painfully protracted escape, and she almost didn't think she would make it. But at last she reached the entrance to the tree. She shifted, pushed Bobby out first, and crawled out after him.

"Almost there," she whispered in his ear. A hand locked on her ankle. She looked back and saw the leering, toothless grin of the Master. The deep pits of his eyes made her dizzy.

"You think you can defeat me?" he said. "I am the Master here."

The words vibrated through the trees, through the ground, through the whole world. Lenora shrank back from him. She glanced in the direction she had last seen Uncle Richard, but she could not find him anywhere. Twenty or so of his robots lay strewn about, destroyed. What had they done to him?

The Master yanked her back toward the tree. But Lenora would not have it. She would not become someone's slave—dead or alive. She was overcome by an anger so fierce that one well-placed kick loosened his grip on her ankle. It was all she needed. She scrambled to her feet and pulled Bobby farther into the clearing. He weighed almost nothing at all, only skin and hollow bones, it seemed.

"Uncle Richard!" she shouted just before the Master was upon her again. She screamed and fought, but she could not overpower him. He pushed her down, and this time he grabbed both her ankles.

"You cannot win!" he shouted into the chaos. He wrenched her back toward the tree. The mud seemed to come alive, reaching for her limbs and curling black tendrils around them.

She scratched at the earth, and it worked temporarily; for a split second, she remained outside the dark hole long enough to see Uncle Richard launch another fireball at the center of the tree. His entire army burst into flames.

It was the last thing she remembered: fire.

66

Lenora woke minutes or hours later; she could not be
sure. Her head ached. The entire clearing was on fire, and
she was surprised that she could see it. She gasped, suck-
ing hard for air, but it was too smoky. Her vision flashed
with scenes from Texas City, and her courage faltered.

She could not do it again. She could not.

But she crawled on the ground, moving toward
where she had seen Uncle Richard stand with his line
of burning copper men.

Where was he?

The rhinoceros was the only thing left standing.
It was breathing fire in a continuous stream from its
wide-open mouth. Bobby was gone. Lenora wondered if
Uncle Richard had saved him the moment he'd seen his
son again. She had not even gotten a good look at him.

Would Uncle Richard come back for her? She

doubted it. She would die here, in a fire, the way her family had done. She would be reunited with them after all.

Lenora's arms buckled. She could crawl no farther. She gazed at the trees. They were all in flames. Crawling would do no good.

She could feel the heat from the house that had been her home, which stood burning beside her, and her insides burned right along with it. She closed her eyes.

Someone picked her up. "Lenora."

It was her uncle. He had come back for her after all. He held her tightly and kissed the top of her head. "I'm sorry," he was saying, over and over again. And if she'd had words, she would have asked why. But her head lolled to the side, bouncing against his chest as he picked her up and tried to run as best he could. One of the copper men met him, and, in a haze, Lenora saw the robot flip back its headpiece. It was not a robot at all. It was Lloyd.

"Take her," Uncle Richard said, and he shoved Lenora into Lloyd's armored arms and ran back toward the burning clearing.

"Where are you going?" Lloyd called.

"To make sure it's done," Uncle Richard flung behind him.

"But you'll die in there!" Lloyd shouted.

"Get her out of the woods!" was all Uncle Richard said, and Lenora felt her chest rip open with the knowledge that this might be the last time she saw her uncle. She forced her eyes open, though they were so hot and dry, and she watched his form growing smaller, the dark peppered hair on the top of his head standing straight up.

Lenora moaned.

"He'll be fine," Lloyd said. "You'll see."

He didn't sound entirely convinced. Lenora closed her eyes.

When next she opened them, she was lying on the lawn of Stonewall Manor, close to the stone steps. The woods shook and crumbled, engulfed in flame.

She sat up. "No!" She could hardly breathe, even here, outside the burning woods.

Mrs. Jones took Lenora in her arms, and they both sat, watching the trees snap and pop. Lenora looked toward Lloyd, a few feet away. He had Bobby in his arms. Both were silently staring at the woods. A woman knelt beside them, leaning against a cane that looked very much like the one Uncle Richard carried. She had golden-brown eyes that reminded Lenora of Bela, and when she saw Lenora staring at the cane, she held it up and pointed it toward the woods. "This one comes equipped with water." She patted a large barrel on the ground beside her, from which a black hose attached it to the cane. The way she said it made Lenora wonder if this was all prearranged, if this woman had known about Uncle Richard's early-morning plans. The woman nodded toward the woods. "We can't let that fire spread." She and Lloyd exchanged a look.

Another hose extended across the lawn; to where, Lenora did not know.

"Where's Uncle Richard?" Lenora said.

"Still inside the woods," Mrs. Jones said. She stroked Lenora's hair.

Lenora eyed her cousin. He was smaller than she expected. He had been gone eight years, but he didn't look older than twelve.

Mrs. Jones glanced at Bobby, too. Tears streamed down her cheeks. She pressed her lips together and shook her head.

"Do you think he was frozen in time?" Lenora said.

"I know nothing about that," Mrs. Jones said. "Your uncle . . ." Her voice split down the middle.

They stared at the blazing woods for what seemed like a very long time. The air smelled acrid and sulfurous, just like the air in Texas City the day of the disaster. Lenora shuddered. When she closed her eyes, all she could see was fire.

"Perhaps we should take them inside," Lloyd said softly.

Lenora's throat tightened. He couldn't be gone. He couldn't.

Lloyd motioned to the woman. "I'll take the hose, Nadine. You take the boy." Nadine looked at Lloyd sadly, touched his cheek, and nodded.

Mrs. Jones pulled Lenora to her feet.

"Can you walk, love?" Mrs. Jones said.

"I think so," Lenora said.

Nadine was a small woman, but she carried Bobby

with little effort. He looked like a doll in her arms, bony and limp.

"Will he live?" Lenora said as she watched Nadine climb the steps to the porch.

"I've sent for the doctor," Mrs. Jones said. It didn't answer Lenora's question, but it told her there was hope.

Mrs. Jones glanced back toward the woods. Lenora followed her gaze.

At that moment, the entire woods exploded with such a violent crack that no one who stood even remotely near it could hear for some minutes. Lloyd was knocked off his feet by the blast. Mrs. Jones, Nadine, and Lenora were shoved from behind. Lenora turned in what felt like slow motion. Wood and leaves rained down around her.

It was too much.

The sorrow in her heart exploded like the woods, and she ran straight for the trees, her mind a blur of thought.

Uncle Richard.

No one could stop her.

67

The heat stung Lenora's face when she entered. The smoke made it hard to breathe. Everywhere she looked was the same: gray and hazy.

Where was he?

The woods were vast; how would she ever find him?

Deeper and deeper she ran, ignoring the warning voices in her mind. She would not go back. She would not leave him. She would not let him die.

She would do everything she could—even if it meant sacrificing herself.

He had a life now. He had Bobby.

When Lenora saw Uncle Richard, she thought it was a dream. Her lungs ached, clawing for air that did not exist.

He was facedown. She dropped to his side. "Uncle Richard!" She wanted to shake him, but she didn't know if that would make everything worse.

The eye she could see blinked open, and he struggled to roll over onto his back, moaning. The left side of his face was badly burned. "Lenora," he whispered. "You shouldn't be here."

"Come on," she said. She tried to pull him up.

"No," he said. "Leave me. My leg. It's twisted."

Lenora looked at his legs, and she saw that he was talking about his right leg. His good leg. She searched around for his cane. "Where's your cane, Uncle?" she said.

"Go, Lenora," he said. "Please." His head dropped back to the earth. The woods crackled around them.

"No. I won't leave you." She slid an arm under his neck and heaved with all her might.

"You must live."

"Not if you die!"

"You have Bobby now. He'll need you."

"No, Uncle!"

Uncle Richard closed his eyes again. "Go," he said. His voice seemed to be growing fainter. They were running out of time. Lenora could feel it in her chest, too.

"Get up!" she screamed. A tree branch above them split and crashed to the ground near Lenora's left foot.

"Save yourself, Lenora," Uncle Richard said. He didn't even open his eyes. "Everything I did, I did for you."

"I'll never leave you!" The woods seemed to vibrate in time with Lenora's words. Another flaming branch landed beside her hand.

The woods would fall on top of them, but she would not leave. She would not leave like she had done in Texas City.

"Get up, Uncle!" The pitch of Lenora's voice had become a shriek. "Get up! Get out of the woods! Don't leave me! I don't want to be alone again! Please!"

She sank to her knees, sobs shaking her.

"Lenora."

Lenora looked up. "Lloyd."

Hope bloomed in her chest.

"Get out of here, Lenora." Lloyd's face was covered with copper armor, so his voice was muffled. Lenora didn't hesitate this time. She ran, the bottoms of her feet burning on sparks that danced across the grass and the fallen tree limbs.

Lloyd nearly beat her out of the woods, though he was carrying Uncle Richard.

"Is the doctor here?" Lloyd shouted toward the manor's porch. He gently set down Uncle Richard in the grass and turned his attention to the woods, which snapped and sizzled behind them. He had picked up the water gun, ready to stop the fire as soon as it touched the grounds of Stonewall Manor.

But it never did. It burned and raged inside the woods, but it never crossed the boundary line.

And before the fire was done with its burning, the trees unbent and untwisted and straightened their backs. They became like any other ordinary pine trees—tall, thin, majestic.

Alive.

Three silver birds—at least Lenora thought they were birds—fluttered into the sky and disappeared.

68

The doctor spent most of his time with Bobby.

He couldn't find a scratch on him. He prescribed rest and nourishment—the lack of which he attributed to Bobby's stunted growth. His lips pressed into a thin line at the declaration.

But Lenora knew it wasn't lack of nourishment or stunted growth; it was the Master and the woods. They had preserved Bobby in time, kept him exactly as he had been the day he'd disappeared. He had not aged a day in the eight years he'd been gone. He was twelve when he'd walked into the woods for the last time, and he was twelve when he'd walked back out. Somehow. Science couldn't explain it, but many wonders of the world could not be entirely explained with science. Some called that magic, and maybe it was.

Uncle Richard had three broken ribs, a broken leg

(the right one this time), and a battery of bruises. The left side of his face was treated for third-degree burns, and he would need more treatment as well. He refused the hospital.

Dr. Kane examined Lenora last.

"A bit of rest will do her good," Dr. Kane said to Mrs. Jones, who hovered beside her. He was a tall, wiry, white-haired man with steely gray eyes that missed nothing. "She's inhaled a lot of smoke, but I don't see anything else wrong." He lifted her arm and pointed. "The bottoms of her feet are blistered a little, and there's a small burn here, but it's nothing rest won't heal." Lenora had forgotten all about the mark of Bela's tear. Her heart thudded. Dr. Kane looked at her with keen, intelligent eyes. "You'll make a full recovery, I think." He straightened and twined his hands together, rocking on the balls of his feet. "It seems as though it's a happy ending for all." His voice teetered at the edges, and malevolence crossed his face, but he smoothed it away easily. Lenora watched him closely. She did not trust him entirely, now that she'd seen that flicker of darkness.

She hoped he would leave.

Instead, he lingered. He said, "Your uncle found a boy he can call his son."

"Bobby," Lenora said. "We found him."

"He's been gone a very long time. Eight years." Dr. Kane examined a fingernail.

Lenora balled up her fists. "He was trapped in the woods and—"

"Thank you, Doctor," Mrs. Jones said, steering Dr. Kane toward Lenora's door. "That will be all."

The doctor hesitated at the door. "I'll come by again tomorrow, to check up on everyone."

Mrs. Jones nodded and said, "Thank you." She closed the door softly and returned to Lenora's side.

"He doesn't believe us," Lenora said.

"Yes, well." Mrs. Jones smoothed the cover on Lenora's bed. "You know how men of science are."

"My uncle is a man of science."

"Your uncle is . . ." Mrs. Jones seemed to search for a word. "Unusual."

"How can Dr. Kane deny that it's Bobby?" Lenora shook her head. It was incomprehensible to her. The likeness was obvious.

"Some men don't believe in miracles." Mrs. Jones smiled grimly. "Dr. Kane was once a friend of your uncle's. Now he's his most outspoken opponent."

"Is there no other doctor?"

"Not in Nacogdoches, I'm afraid." Mrs. Jones sat down again.

"You should be with Uncle Richard or Bobby," Lenora said. "I'm not ill or wounded."

Mrs. Jones patted her hand. "They have each other. And, besides, Nadine is seeing to Bobby's needs and Lloyd to your uncle's." She looked wistful for a moment. "It's good to have help around here."

"Why doesn't Lloyd live here like you do?" Lenora said.

"That's a very long story," Mrs. Jones said.

Lenora loved stories. She said so.

Mrs. Jones laughed. "I know you do, love. But you need your rest." She stood. "I'll leave you to it, but I'll be just outside your door."

And Bobby and Nadine were right across the hall.

When Mrs. Jones reached her doorway, Lenora said, "Do you think it's gone?"

"What, love?" Mrs. Jones's eyes grew soft. "The woods?"

Lenora nodded. "And the Master."

"I think the woods have been restored," Mrs. Jones said. "To what they once were. Something . . . good." She tapped the doorframe. "You were very brave. Bobby wouldn't be here without you."

Lenora's voice was soft when she said, "But I couldn't save . . . them." Her breath knotted in her throat.

Mrs. Jones crossed the room again and knelt by Lenora's side. "No one expected you to save them, Lenora." She pressed Lenora's hands. "It was a terrible thing, what happened in Texas City. So many died. But you didn't."

"I was supposed to stay home from school that day," Lenora said. "It was my birthday. Mother and Father always let me stay home from school on my birthday. I should have been with them. But instead I was the only one who left home and watched the explosion from the windows of my school."

She didn't even try to brush the tears away; there were too many.

"And you are alive, Lenora." Mrs. Jones's eyes were glassy, too. "And look what your living has done."

Lenora thought about Uncle Richard and Bobby and the mechanical army her uncle had built to destroy the woods. Bobby would not have survived without her. And this, at least, made her feel warm inside.

When Mrs. Jones reached the doorway again, Lenora said, "Would you leave it open, please?"

Lenora could see all the way to the other side of the hall. Bobby's door was open, too.

This made her smile.

69

Some days later, Lenora felt strong enough to walk up and down the stairs. Every time she passed Bobby's room, she peeked inside. He was always sleeping.

On one particular morning, a week or so after the burning of the woods, the newspaper waited on the kitchen table when Lenora entered. A headline caught her eye, and she turned the paper around to face her. In a little more than two weeks, Texas City would be holding a memorial service for all the unidentified bodies that had been recovered in the disaster.

Lenora shoved the newspaper away and rubbed her eyes.

Was she ready to let go of the hope that she would one day see them again? Did she have to? Father had always said death was not an end, but a beginning. It sounded like a beautiful idea.

This was a new beginning. It was time to embrace it. Mother and Father wouldn't want her to continue grieving over their absence, would they? John would have called her unbearably melancholy and handed her a book. Rory would have done anything in the world to make her laugh. Charles would have gathered a bouquet of bright flowers.

Lenora smiled.

"I left the paper out today." Mrs. Jones had entered silently, and Lenora startled. "Sorry, love. I didn't mean to disturb you." She gestured toward the paper. "I thought you might want to see the news."

Lenora couldn't trust herself to speak, so she only nodded.

Mrs. Jones looked at her for a while, and then she said, "Yes, well, would you like some breakfast, love?"

"I'd like to go." Lenora's voice wavered and cracked. Her throat thickened. "I'd like a chance to say goodbye." The words felt heavy, but she lifted her chin. She meant them.

Mrs. Jones crossed the kitchen and knelt at Lenora's side, her knees giving their customary pop. "I'm sure we could arrange that. And you wouldn't have to go alone." Mrs. Jones wrapped her arms around Lenora, and they were so soft, so warm, so encompassing, that Lenora closed her eyes. Her nose burned.

Some thumps and curses sounded behind them. Uncle Richard burst in with a brass chair that rolled on oversized carriage wheels. "I made myself something," he said, gesturing to the chair. His left cheek was still bandaged. He'd have a burn scar, the doctor said. It would make him look even more scientific, Lenora thought.

Mrs. Jones and Lenora stared at Uncle Richard's chair with gaping mouths.

Uncle Richard shrugged. "I had some spare parts." He was in a jovial mood. "The stairs give me some trouble, though." He waved a hand. "But that's only temporary. Lloyd's working on an elevator."

"Wow," Lenora said. A home with an elevator!

Uncle Richard grinned. "What's for breakfast?"

He was altogether changed. He radiated a light that could not be dimmed. It made Lenora smile. Uncle

Richard winked at her. "Bobby's coming down this morning."

"Really?" Lenora said.

"Really," said a voice behind her, and Bobby wheeled in with the same kind of chair Uncle Richard had, except slightly smaller. His face was still sharp angles and pale skin. His clothes still hung from his stick-figure limbs. But he was alive.

Bobby's eyes met Lenora's. "That was the wildest ride down the stairs I've ever experienced." Laughter gleamed from his dusk-blue eyes. Lenora couldn't help but grin back. "You'll have to try it."

The words, the invitation, fluttered on the air, angled toward her chest, and curled up inside. It was almost like having a brother again.

Lloyd and Nadine stood in the doorway, Lloyd's arm curved around Nadine's back. They smiled at Lenora.

"How about we eat breakfast together?" Uncle Richard said. "Bobby and I don't need chairs."

Everyone laughed.

Uncle Richard and Bobby rolled their chairs to the

kitchen table. Mrs. Jones and Nadine rearranged the chairs so they'd all have a place. Mrs. Jones served them biscuits and gravy and sizzling bacon and pancakes—all for Bobby, who could not decide what kind of breakfast he wanted.

"I've missed this," Bobby said.

And Lenora knew his presence would change everything.

70

It was such a festive meal that Lenora debated whether or not to mention the memorial service. But she knew it was necessary. So when the laughter died down and it appeared as though breakfast would soon be ending, she said, in a voice small and apologetic, "There will be a memorial service in Texas City." She stared at the floor. "For all the unidentified people." She couldn't say "bodies." She cleared her throat. "For the ones who are still missing."

No one said anything.

"I would like to go."

When Lenora looked up, Nadine and Lloyd and Mrs. Jones had slipped silently out of the room. It was only Lenora, Uncle Richard, and Bobby.

Uncle Richard said, "I would like to go, too."

"I want to honor them," Lenora said. "I want to

remember and then . . ." She couldn't finish, but her words hung between them anyway. *I want to move on.*

Bobby sniffed, but Lenora didn't dare look at him.

"We will," Uncle Richard said. He reached across the table and took Lenora's hand. His was warm and calloused, like her father's. "We'll go together. He was my brother, and I loved him." Uncle Richard's voice splintered. Lenora's breath caught, and a sob climbed out.

Uncle Richard patted her hand for a moment before reaching into his suit jacket. He pulled out an envelope. "Lloyd found something near the woods the other day." He took a piece of paper from the envelope and unfolded a letter. He cleared his throat. "'Dear Brother,'" he read. "'My heart is heavy over your loss. I would like nothing more than to come see you at Stonewall Manor. Please let me know when it might be convenient for my family to visit. I have two sons and two daughters, and I know they would love to meet their uncle Richard. I named one of my daughters Lenora, after Mother. Write soon. Your loving brother, Johnny.'" Uncle Richard let the letter fall to the table. His eyes took on a faraway look. "Johnny. That's what I used to call him when we were kids."

Lenora's eyes blurred.

Uncle Richard said, "There were several letters. Some addressed to you, too. From . . ." He examined one of the letters. "Emma Green." He placed two envelopes on the table, but Lenora didn't want to see them; they reminded her only of sorrowful things. She kept her eyes on Uncle Richard's face. "They must have been caught in the woods."

"But why?" Lenora said. "How?"

"The woods were strengthened by sorrow," Uncle Richard said. "They made sure we remained trapped in it."

"I don't understand," Lenora said.

Uncle Richard glanced at Bobby. Bobby said, "A long time ago, the Cole family was responsible for the sentencing of a criminal."

"How do you know this?" Lenora said.

"The Master," Bobby said, and Lenora shivered. Just thinking about the Master of the woods made her feel breathless. Bobby continued. "He'd stolen a significant fortune from the Cole family after pretending to love one of the daughters. Abigail. At least, the family thought he was pretending. He wasn't." Bobby paused. "They hung him anyway. On the tree."

"So he died," Lenora said.

Bobby nodded. "His spirit remained, and it wrapped around bones and mud and became the Master. He created the woods, and with it, he took revenge on the Cole family. He existed on the sorrow of children he could convince didn't have a place to belong. Who couldn't bear their own pain. Who believed that erasing it would make them happy."

Bobby stared at the table. He knew, because he had been one of them.

Lenora knew; she had been one of them, too.

"And by taking children, the Master ensured that sorrow would continue—a curse on Stonewall Manor," Uncle Richard said. "Parents lost children. Brothers lost sisters. Children grew up and lost their own children." His voice faded into a murmur. "Some saw the pattern. Some refused to look."

The scientific and the spiritual, at odds with each

other. Lenora nodded. But there was still something that didn't make sense. She looked at Bobby. "But why did you go into the woods?"

"I thought I could stop him," Bobby said. He looked at Uncle Richard. "I thought I could break the curse. Stop children from disappearing and sorrow from . . ." He shook his head. "But he was more powerful than I thought, and before I knew it, I was a prisoner." He shuddered.

"And why did he want *me*?" Lenora asked. This troubled her, too. Bobby had been the only stolen child who'd come back out alive. That had to mean something.

"The Master needed five children to live again," Bobby said.

Lenora shook her head. "How can the dead live again?"

"It wouldn't have been forever," Bobby said. "Only long enough to destroy the rest of the Coles. To eliminate the family line. Half human, half . . ." Bobby paused, as though he wasn't quite sure what to say.

"What an awful purpose," Lenora said.

"Revenge is a curse," Uncle Richard said. "It has made many men stumble."

Bobby looked at Lenora. "You saved us."

Lenora shook her head. "Uncle saved us."

Uncle Richard took Bobby's hand and Lenora's, too. "But now we are all together," Uncle Richard said. "And the woods are only woods."

Lenora's chest warmed.

She didn't have to be alone after all.

Before they went to bed that night, Lenora watched Uncle Richard stop in front of the brass clocks hanging above the table at Stonewall Manor's entrance. He took them down, one by one, and changed their time to 7:39.

The proper time.

It was her face, her form. The woman he loved: Abigail Cole. He was sure of it. She wore a look of love and forgiveness, and the warmth of it stilled him. She smiled, beckoned, and turned.

He hesitated, then followed. The rope around his neck melted, his pardon granted in full.

The whole earth was alive, and their ethereal forms dissipated into a golden dawn.

June 21, 1947

Tomorrow I will return, once again, to Texas City. This time I will not pick up a niece or search for lost ones or rummage for spare parts. This time I will return to say goodbye to my brother. I will say goodbye to a niece and nephews and a sister-in-law I never knew. I will say goodbye to regret and whatever sense of guilt I have been harboring all these years. Mrs. Jones said it best: Brothers love one another. That's all there ever is, and I know Johnny felt the same way. I don't need his words, his lost letters, to confirm it.

Lenora asked me yesterday evening about the house she saw in the woods—her house. I told her I wanted to give her home one more chance to do something great. In Texas City, it miraculously (Johnny would chuckle to hear me use that word) survived a horrendous explosion. It preserved memories of the people she loved. But it also reminded her of all she'd lost. It represented death and sorrow and loneliness.

In the woods, the house was given one purpose: to

452

carry the robots that would destroy the curse that had hung over Stonewall Manor and all its people for centuries. And it did, efficiently. It also exploded beautifully, hastening the fire that saved us all.

I worried about her response to this, but she surprised me. She smiled. She said, "My home saved us." I did not agree or disagree, but I must confess that my heart is no longer as heavy as it was.

Lloyd has recovered pieces of my robots and has daily been piling them up in my laboratory, which still remains open to the elements. I will call a contractor soon to repair it, though I think I would like to put a door on the hole, rather than seal it up with more stone; my rhinoceros, when I rebuild it, will have need of going out now and then, stretching its legs.

Lloyd, much to my surprise, knows quite a lot about the science of invention. I have been in need of an assistant for years. Perhaps I will ask him. He has, after all, been a loyal driver all these years. And there is plenty of room here at Stonewall Manor for him and Nadine and any children they might one day have. He and I could do great work together, I believe.

And Lenora, too. She is a bright pupil.

I feel invigorated, rehabilitated, as though I have been brought back to life.

It is good to have a son and a daughter again.

I will care for her well, brother. I promise.

—excerpt from Richard Cole's *Journal of Scientific Progress*

GOODBYE

71

Sixty-three bodies remained unidentified more than two months after the Texas City disaster. Lenora's parents and brothers and sister might be among them. Lenora had heard nothing from those who notified the living relations of the dead. She had heard nothing, either, from those who notified the living relations of the still living.

Texas City did not look at all like the beautiful town she remembered. Cleanup crews were still working, sweeping up tons of wreckage, clearing out streets, rebuilding. City hall had new front windows that shone in the sun as they passed.

Lloyd drove Uncle Richard's strange car through the city and on toward the northern edge of town, where Loop 197 intersects with Twenty-Ninth Street. He parked it on the side of the highway. A line of cars stretched in front of theirs. "We should have been here earlier," Uncle Richard murmured. He climbed from the car and gazed in front of them, where a stream of people were walking toward what appeared, from here, to be a walled garden. He looked at Lenora, and his eyes seemed to say, "Are you ready?" She nodded and climbed out, too.

Lenora wore a long black dress that was more beautiful than anything she had owned when she lived in Texas City. It was old-fashioned—the kind of dress women wore during the Industrial Revolution, layered and extravagant. She felt somewhat silly—and a little overheated—but her uncle stood next to her in a black top hat and a slick black suit with a spot of orange peeking from his coat pocket. He had reassembled his cane, which still looked to her like a flame-throwing gun, but to the outside observer who didn't know about the woods, it would only appear to be an eccentric walking apparatus.

Bobby walked beside her and looked quite dashing in a suit that was identical to Uncle Richard's, except for a spot of green poking out of his pocket. Lloyd, dressed in a simpler black suit, walked next to Bobby. Mrs. Jones and Nadine had come in Lloyd's car.

The six of them made their way slowly to the large grassy plot surrounded by a stone wall. An iron gate was open, and the stone pillars that held it were inscribed with the words MEMORIAL CEMETERY TEXAS CITY 1947. Inside the walls was a rectangular field with an oval pathway. People gathered at the edges, near the walls. Lenora, Uncle Richard, and Bobby joined them. Lloyd, Nadine, and Mrs. Jones stayed back.

Sixty-three caskets, each topped with a spray of colorful flowers, trickled in, carried by a legion of men. Lenora cast her eyes down so she did not have to see someone she recognized. She could not bear it.

She stood numbly through the service, listening to the mayor and others speak about the tragedy that had befallen Texas City. At some point, she realized that Uncle Richard had taken her hand. His hand radiated warmth and hope, even in the midst of such debilitating sorrow. She let her tears fall. She let them wet the ground where her family might soon be buried. She let them nourish the green that would return to this field when its dirt was packed around the caskets.

She did not recognize the last man who spoke to the crowd of thousands. But she remembered his words long after the service was finished. "Our people have lost their families and their homes," he said. "But we will carry on. It is what humanity does."

Uncle Richard squeezed her hand and offered her a sad smile.

When the pallbearers lowered the caskets into three neat rows inside the oval pathway, Lenora gazed up at the sky. It was magnificently blue. The sun was magnificently hot. A bird swooped and twirled in the endless expanse.

They would carry on.

Before they left the cemetery, Lenora tossed her mother's pearl necklace into one of the graves. It thumped against a casket.

As they passed back through Texas City, Lenora looked toward the docks. They were damaged and scarred. She arranged them in her mind, imagined Mother standing against the rail, looking for Father coming off the ships from his frequent visits to check mechanical issues. He was always aware of anything that might cause a dangerous fire in Texas City. How had he not known about this one?

She imagined John and Charles and Rory leaning beside Mother on the dock, the three of them pointing to the golden-orange plume of smoke that had colored the sky that day.

Lloyd pulled the car past the dock, or what was left of it, and the image faded away. Lenora did not look back.

Some story ideas come to authors while we're reading an obscure book that mentions something in passing that is seemingly unrelated to anything on our horizon of Worthwhile Project Pursuits. Some arise from a striking picture of the natural world that kindles a memory—the way the light fell just so on the ground inside that forest and made the grass and flowers dance. Some find us in the middle of the night, when we hope what we've dreamed isn't real.

My introduction to *The Woods* came by way of all three: It began with a photo of the piney woods of Huntsville State Park in Huntsville, Texas, where my husband and I spent a few Octobers years ago, biking paths strewn with tree roots that grew above the earth like twisting, arthritic fingers, making the way treacherous (if you were my husband trying to bike too fast). In this photo, I imagined a young girl lying under the trees, thinking of all the people she had lost in a fire: her mother and father, two brothers, a sister named Rory.

All I had was a character and a vague premise, pushed

way back on my priority shelf, until I read in a book I can't even recall today a passing mention of the Texas City Disaster.

Being a lifelong Texan, except for a year spent in Ohio when I was nine, this mention hooked onto my brain. It interested me because (1) I took several years of Texas history, required for most elementary and middle school students here in the Lone Star State, and (2) I had never heard of the Texas City Disaster.

This disaster was a tragedy of significant proportions. Two explosions, originating in two ships docked at the Port of Texas City, practically leveled the town. The SS *Grandcamp* exploded at 9:12 a.m. on April 16, 1947, and fifteen hours later, the SS *High Flyer* exploded. Both ships carried large amounts of ammonium nitrate, a highly volatile chemical compound used for making bombs (World War II had recently concluded and the Cold War was a new threat) and in 1947, a fertilizer to replenish soils leached of nutrition during wartime. The explosions wiped out nearly an entire city of working-class Texans, many of them minorities who lived in the overcrowded housing, known as El Barrio and The Bottom, that hugged the coastline and the string of chemical facilities lining it.

Official estimates say 405 people died, 113 went missing, and 63 bodies were unidentified. Investigators say the death count was likely much higher, since there were no recent census records, and Texas City was one of the fastest growing cities in Texas. Every member of the city's volunteer fire department was killed in the blasts, save for one man who was fortuitously out of town the day of the disaster.

Why had I never heard of this tragedy? Was I just not paying close attention all those years ago? I asked my oldest sons—one in sixth grade, another in fourth, if they had ever heard of the Texas City Disaster. They hadn't.

Part of my responsibility as an author is to tell the truth. That sounds like two diametrically opposed things: truth and fiction. But as an author I am also a recorder of human history. If we forget such a devastating historical event, which many consider the worst industrial accident in American history, what happens to all those lives lost?

They are worth remembering.

Looking at that picture of the Huntsville woods, remembering my dream of a mysterious presence in those woods, compiling my research of the Texas City Disaster, I knew I had my story: Lenora Cole, her family lost in a true-life tragedy, a redemptive opportunity to show how humanity carries on even amidst great setbacks.

The Texas City Disaster was the starting point and the foundation for *The Woods*. Lenora must come to terms with the effects of that disaster—lives lost too soon—as so many had to do in 1947. And while she has the slight benefit of an eccentric uncle, a safe home, and fantastical woods to help her heal, so many were left with nothing. They lost their families, their homes, their livelihoods.

And yet they persisted—because it is what humans do.

Texas City was rebuilt, its people endured, lessons were learned—but it took the entire community working together to do it.

In his book, *City on Fire*, Bill Minutaglio says, "Some

said only an 'act of God' could bring a divided Texas City together." On June 22, 1947, members of different denominations and different races—both thoroughly segregated in this Southern town—gathered to bury their sixty-three unknown dead in one mass grave. Catholics and Baptists, Methodists and Episcopalians, Jews and Gentiles, black people and white people and brown people, all resting in peace, together.

When we feel most alone, when our lives have practically fallen apart, when the world explodes and it does not seem like we have what it takes to repair what has been broken, it is in our leaning on one another that we learn just how strong we can be.

So don't be afraid to lean hard.

In love,
R.L.